一次戰勝新制多益

TOEIC
必考聽力

攻略 ➕ 解析
➕ 模擬試題

SINAGONG 多益專門小組、趙康壽、金廷根（Julia Kim）／著

林芳如／譯

要學就學必考的！

NEW TOEIC LISTENING

保證高分、實戰取向的工具書！

學習現學現用的「實戰」理論。

　　應考多益測驗時，要先確認自己的程度，設定好想達到的分數後，在短期內專心攻讀。實力不足的考生經常不曉得該從何處著手，便從理論開始慢慢學習。但盲目背誦不知該如何應用於解題的理論，是無法培養實戰經驗的。為了改善這一點，本書透過解題讓考生學習理論，將重點放在結合理論和實戰。此外，本書也提供了比任何入門理論書都還豐富的實戰題目。

這是一本為了「自學」考生量身打造的書。

　　本書完全針對沒有參加補習班或線上課程，打算自學的考生而量身打造。其中包含最適合自學的學習步驟，以及易於理解的簡潔說明和解答。

短期內就能讓分數急速上昇。

　　雖然無法考取高分的原因，有一部分是因為英文能力不足，但也有可能是因為考生尚未完全掌握多益的出題模式。多益測驗具有一定的出題模式，只要熟悉此模式，就能輕鬆考取高分。本書完整分析十幾年來的官方多益出題趨勢，集結能夠考取高分的「理論＋實戰」精華。

善用提高基本實力的「聽寫訓練」。

　　本書著重於培養考生的實戰經驗，並提供所有實戰題的「聽寫訓練」，以利考生培養基本聽力技巧。「聽寫」是累積基礎聽力能力的最佳訓練方式，解題技巧和聽寫訓練同時並行的話，不僅可以更快速地提高分數，也對累積多益以外的英文能力大有幫助。

SINAGONG 多益專門小組

獲得解題的自信！

全書內容架構依照出題類型完整分析，我覺得很好，既可充實基礎，內容也非常豐富。書中不僅提及文法，也同時說明如何應用在解題上。對於像我一樣的多益新手們，能一邊順利解題，一邊提升自信心。強烈推薦給考生們！

金武元（上班族）

可以快速應用在實際考試上！

在攻略解題法的單元中，我學到如何掌握解題線索，並實際運用到考試中快速解題。像我這樣需要快速提升多益分數的初學者，也能夠把握解題要領，這點讓我很滿意。另外，單字整理的部分，就算沒有另外列出單字表，透過例題的解說，也能讓我學到裡面的單字，對我的幫助非常大。

裴慧妍（大學生）

可以被稱作「多益法典」的一本書！

如果準備多益考試有所謂的「法典」，那麼我認為多益的學習法典就是這本書。因為這本書即時反映了多益出題趨勢，並將出題類型細分，收錄精華部分，是一本適合在短時間內衝高分數的工具書。

黃仁德（大學生）

適合自學的一本書！

對於第一次考多益、多益基礎能力不足，或是想輕鬆自學的人來說，是一本非常適合的工具書。本書將出題類型做出細分，同時系統性地整理出應試時所需的解題重點、基本字彙、基礎文法，以及出題模式等。

李碩昊（大學生）

適合不懂解題技巧的人的工具書！

我因為沒有時間去補習班，所以選擇自學，但卻無法將學過的文法理論實際應用在解題上，因此成績不見好轉。而這本書，對於像我這樣不懂解題技巧的人來說，是本非常適合的工具書。跟一般市面上的工具書不同，本書最大的優點是以解題說明為主，可以讓人立即運用到實際考試之中。此外，不拖泥帶水的重點解析，以及不生硬的設計，讓人讀了不乏味。拿到本書，讓我非常期待之後的分數能夠提升到什麼程度呢！

趙雅蘭（大學生）

同時學習「基本觀念＋解題要領」！

本書是以「基本觀念＋解題要領」為主的一本工具書。一個章節結束後，解析同類型模擬試題的同時，讓人能夠重新複習剛剛學到的內容，這點非常好。讓人有種在閱讀一本整理得很完善的筆記的感覺，可以瞬間領會到重點。如果已經厭倦了市面上強調文法的工具書，那麼請翻翻看這本書。

李沼庭（上班族）

獲得解題的自信！

透過題型來掌握解題重點，再帶入文法概念的教學方式很不錯。因此自己一個人也能輕鬆地準備多益。這是一本處處皆有體貼自學者之處的工具書，雖然市面上也有不少針對初學者的書籍，但沒有一本能像這本書一樣讓人輕鬆上手。

趙雅拉（大學生）

自學中，卻仍像是上了一堂猜題精準的名師課程！

透過本書，讓第一次準備多益的人可以很快掌握考試中需要注意的部分。另外，本書也系統性地整理出解題的步驟，對於像我這種初次面對多益的人，也能很快學到解題方法。如果老是在某題型出錯的人，也非常適合透過本書學習。明明是自學，卻讓人如同在上補教名師的課，無論是針對各題型需注意之處的叮嚀，或是拆解問題方法的教導，對於考試時快速進入狀態非常有幫助。內容囊括了單字、基本文法、模擬試題，讓我對之後的多益考試無後顧之憂。

金允熙（上班族）

可以同時學習到文法與解題技巧！

如同書名的「攻略」二字，為了讓入門者能夠把握重點，針對問題的解析非常詳盡。同一題型會反覆練習，因此對於自學者來說，學習時不費吹灰之力。相較於市面上的多益工具書，本書收錄了更多例題，並且，讀者除了可以學習到文法外，同時也能學到解題技巧，我非常喜歡。

金夏蓮（研究生）

不只是多益分數，我的英文能力似乎也跟著提升了！

在倉促的準備時間下，光是讀了這本書，在我考試時就已經有很大的助益了。當我閱讀完本書後，不僅加強了我的多益解題功力，英文實力也似乎跟著提升。這是一本整理出所需重點，讓初次應考生也能快速上手的工具書。希望大家也能透過此書，增加對自己英文能力的自信心。

朴南洙（公務員）

共同完成書籍的各位：林卞碩、姜成模、蔡秀妍、李燦宇、徐宇振、裴智賢、鄭秀鎮、姜泯、徐宥拉、金小爾、林恩熙、鄭恩周、金聖祿、李仁善、金秀庭、李瑟琪、朴智賢、崔賢浩、延正模

不僅可以加強理論觀念，
還能培養解題能力的工具書！

撰寫本書時，我們採訪了一百多位多益考生。大部分考生的煩惱都是整天背誦別人說「有用」的參考書，但實際上卻不會解題。把沒辦法運用到題目中的理論背得滾瓜爛熟有什麼意義呢？雖然學習理論也很重要，但是「能順利解題」才是學習理論最重要的原因吧。

因此，本書將重點放在學習能應用到實戰上的理論。本書架構為一邊解題，一邊將理論應用於解題過程中，並專攻必要的解題理論。我們剔除了不常見的理論，只收錄多益測驗中會出現的重要理論。照著步驟學習的話，多益考生也能體驗到解題的樂趣，有望在短時間內大幅提高分數。

1. 先解題，再學習理論的結構！

本書著重於培養考生的解題能力，而非一味地學習理論。因此，學習過程依序為：先作答題目，透過建議的解題方法掌握解題的靈敏度，接著再去了解答題時必備的理論。之後再練習實戰題，將學到的理論和解題方法學以致用。

Step 1　　　▶　　　**Step 2**　　　▶　　　**Step 3**

查看攻略解題法　　　學習重要理論　　　應用理論並練習實戰題

2. 藉由解題來學習重要理論的精華！

本書並不會為了累積考生的基礎實力，就讓考生死背大量的理論。因為多益考生不需要記那麼多理論，而且背了卻不懂得應用的話也沒用。本書只以一頁左右的篇幅，精簡收錄考生為了考取高分的必備重要理論。

3. 多元且高命中率的模擬試題＋深究錯誤答案的詳盡說明＋免費下載
　 多益模擬試題

本書的宗旨是要讓考生「體驗到解題的樂趣」，所以涵蓋的題目比其他多益書豐富許多。所有題目皆如實反映出最新的多益出題趨勢。除了書中的試題，考生還可以免費下載一份多益聽力模擬試題。請掃描QR碼直接下載試題與解答。

為了讓考生獨自解題後，也能充分理解，本書還分析了正確答案和錯誤答案，並提供詳細的說明。

＋

📖 第一冊：攻略本　　　　　　　　📖 第二冊：解析本

4. 培養基本聽力實力的聽寫訓練！

本書集結實戰題，另外規劃了聽寫訓練。聽寫訓練是培養基本聽力實力的最佳學習方法，在解題過程中同步訓練的話，可望更快速提高分數。

此外，本書的實戰題全數改編自多益考古題。藉由聽寫訓練來熟悉出題模式，也能在應考多益測驗時預測題目內容。建議考生可多加利用聽寫訓練來增強自己的聽力實力。

多益是什麼呢？

TOEIC是Test of English for International Communication的縮寫，為針對英語非母語人士的測驗，以語言中最主要的「溝通」為重點，評價出工作或是日常生活上所需的英文能力。考題主要為商業用，或是日常生活中的用法。

考題的出題領域與特徵

一般商務	契約、談判、行銷、銷售、商業企劃、會議
製造業	工廠管理、生產線、品管
金融／預算	銀行業務、投資、稅務、會計、帳單
企業發展	研究、產品研發
辦公室	董事會、委員會、信件、備忘錄、電話、傳真、電子郵件、辦公室器材與傢俱、辦公室流程、文字簡訊、即時通訊、多人互動線上聊天
人事	招考、雇用、退休、薪資、升遷、應徵與廣告
採購	比價、訂貨、送貨、發票
技術層面	電子、科技、電腦、實驗室與相關器材、技術規格
房屋／公司地產	建築、規格、購買租賃、電力瓦斯服務
旅遊	火車、飛機、計程車、巴士、船隻、渡輪、票務、時刻表、車站、機場廣播、租車、飯店、預訂、脫班與取消
外食	商務／非正式午餐、宴會、招待會、餐廳訂位
娛樂	電影、劇場、音樂、藝術、媒體
保健	醫藥保險、看醫生、牙醫、診所、醫院

多益中會避免出現適用於特定文化的考題，而同時，各個國家的名稱、地名都有可能出現在考題中。另外，美國、英國、加拿大、澳洲、紐西蘭的口音，也都有可能出現在聽力考題中。

多益題型架構

類型	Part	內容		題目數量	時間	配分
聽力測驗	1	照片描述		6		
	2	應答問題		25	100題	約45分鐘	495分
	3	簡短對話		39		
	4	簡短獨白		30		
閱讀測驗	5	句子填空（文法／字彙）		30		
	6	段落填空		16	100題	75分鐘	495分
	7	閱讀	單篇	29		
			多篇	25		
Total	7 Parts			200	約120分鐘	990分

考試時程

時間	行程內容
9：30～9：45	分發答案用紙並進行考試說明
9：45～9：50	休息時間
9：50～10：05	第一次身分證檢查
10：05～10：10	分發考題紙並確認是否有破損或缺頁
10：10～10：55	進行聽力測驗
10：55～12：10	進行閱讀測驗（第二次身分證檢查）

＊上表僅供參考，實際時程依多益考場規則而定。

多益報名方式

報名期間與報名方式：多益官方網站（www.toeic.com.tw）／**報名費用：**1600元

網路報名、通訊報名、臨櫃報名、APP報名／須附上照片

＊追加報名 　　開放追加報名期間，只能透過網路報名，報名費用為1900元。

考試準備注意事項

■合格身分證件 　本國籍年滿16歲（含）以上之考生，僅限「中華民國國民身分證」正本或有效期限內之「護照」正本。未滿16歲之考生則可攜帶「健保IC卡」正本。若無身分證明則無法應試，請務必攜帶入場。

■文具 　　　　2B鉛筆（推薦考生將筆尖削粗，比較方便使用。一般鉛筆或自動筆也可以，但原子筆是不能使用的）、橡皮擦都必須攜帶入場。

成績查詢與成績單寄送

在成績查詢開放期間可透過多益官方網站，或是使用APP來查詢多益成績。紙本成績單則會於測驗結束後16個工作日（不含假日）以平信方式寄出。若未收到成績單，可於測驗日起兩個月內致電多益測驗中心詢問，洽詢專線：(02)2701-7333。

Part 1 照片描述（6題）

從四個選項中選出最符合照片描述的選項。

題目範例

題本	音檔
1. 	**NO 1.** Look at the picture marked number 1 in your test book. (A) A man is putting on glasses. (B) A man is working at a computer. (C) A man is listening to music. (D) A man is using his cellphone.

Part 2 應答問題（25題）

聽完題目後，從三個選項中選出應答得最好的選項。

題目範例

題本	音檔
7. Mark your answer on your answer sheet.	**NO 7.** How long did your job interview take? (A) An open position. (B) A new employee (C) Only half an hour.

Part 3 簡短對話（39題）

聆聽兩名或三名男女之間的對話後，從四個選項中選出與題目相關的正確答案。每則對話各有三道題目，總共十三則對話（39題）。最後兩到三則對話會出現包含視覺資料的題目。

題本	音檔
32. Why was the woman late for the meeting?	**Questions 32-34 refer to the following conversation.**
(A) She was using public transportation.	
(B) She just came back from his vacation.	W : Hi, Mr. Anderson. I'm sorry. I was late for the meeting this morning because of the traffic jam. What did I miss?
(C) She was stuck in traffic.	M : Oh, on Thursday, we are going to install a new program for all of the computers in the Sales Department.
(D) She lives far from the company.	W : So is there anything we have to do to prepare for it?
33. When will the speakers install the new program?	M : No, but I suggest that you come early on that day. We will have a lot of work to do.
(A) On Monday	
(B) On Tuesday	
(C) On Wednesday	
(D) On Thursday	
34. According to the conversation, what does the man suggest?	
(A) To come early on Thursday	
(B) To visit the Sales Department	
(C) To buy an airplane ticket	
(D) To leave for a business trip	

Part 4 簡短獨白（30題）

聽完男子或女子的獨白後，從四個選項中選出與題目相關的正確答案。每則對話各有三道題目，總共十則對話（30題）。最後兩到三則對話會出現包含視覺資料的題目。

題目範例

題本	音檔
71. Where most likely are the listeners?	**Questions 71-73 refer to the following instruction.**
(A) At an airport	
(B) At a train station	Good morning, everyone. Welcome to our seminar on the international fashion industry. I'm very pleased to introduce our guest speaker today. I'm sure all of you know that Ms. Melissa Rin is one of the most famous fashion designers in the global fashion industry. She has worked in the fashion industry for 30 years ever since she became a fashion designer. Ms. Rin's speech today is entitled "International Fashion Design." She will be sharing some of her experiences with us. Everyone, let's give a big hand for Ms. Melissa Rin.
(C) At a bus stop	
(D) At a port	
72. What has caused the delay?	
(A) Aircraft maintenance	
(B) Repair work on the runway	
(C) An accident	
(D) Bad weather	
73. What will the listeners do next?	
(A) Present their boarding passes	
(B) Board the plane	
(C) Go to Gate 13	
(D) Fasten their seatbelts	

目錄

PART 3　簡短對話

PART 4　簡短獨白

8週進度表（一週5天，總共40天）

此進度表推薦給初次準備多益，或是已經考過多益，分數在300分上下，想要仔細地、認真準備的考生們。這是針對那些不熟悉多益考題常見用法，以及幾乎無法了解題目意思的人所設計的進度表。此外，如果覺得本書難易度偏高，請按照下列進度表學習，兩個月內便可讀完本書，並且累積多益的基礎能力。

	Day 1	Day 2	Day 3	Day 4	Day 5
第1週	Unit 01 出現單人的照片	Unit 02 出現雙人以上的照片	Unit 03 事物、風景照片	Unit 04 人物、背景照片	Unit 05 Who問句
	Day 6	Day 7	Day 8	Day 9	Day 10
第2週	Unit 06 When、Where問句	Unit 07 What、Which問句	Unit 08 How、Why問句	Unit 09 一般問句	Unit 10 選擇疑問句
	Day 11	Day 12	Day 13	Day 14	Day 15
第3週	Unit 11 建議（請求）句	Unit 12 陳述句	Unit 13 詢問主題、目的的題目	Unit 14 詢問職業／對話地點的題目	Unit 15 詢問說話者的建議的題目
	Day 16	Day 17	Day 18	Day 19	Day 20
第4週	Unit 16 詢問接下來會做什麼事的題目	Unit 17 詢問細節的題目	Unit 18 掌握句子意圖的題目	Unit 19 結合視覺資料的題目	Unit 20 餐廳
	Day 21	Day 22	Day 23	Day 24	Day 25
第5週	Unit 21 飯店	Unit 22 購物	Unit 23 購票	Unit 24 徵人、辭職	Unit 25 教育、宣傳
	Day 26	Day 27	Day 28	Day 29	Day 30
第6週	Unit 26 設施、網絡管理	Unit 27 會計、預算	Unit 28 事業規劃	Unit 29 公司內部公告	Unit 30 公共場所公告
	Day 31	Day 32	Day 33	Day 34	Day 35
第7週	Unit 31 語音訊息	Unit 32 自動回覆系統	Unit 33 天氣預報	Unit 34 交通廣播	Unit 35 新聞
	Day 36	Day 37	Day 38	Day 39	Day 40
第8週	Unit 36 人物介紹	Unit 37 導覽	Unit 38 產品廣告	Unit 39 折扣廣告	Final Test

4週進度表（一週5天，總共20天）

推薦給曾準備過多益卻中途放棄的人，或是多益分數在400～500分之間的考生。這是針對那些稍微熟悉多益考題常見用法的人所設計的進度表。此外，如果覺得本書難易度與自身能力相差不遠，請按照下列進度表學習，可於四週內讀完本書，並培養解題能力。

	Day 1	Day 2	Day 3	Day 4	Day 5
第1週	Unit 01 出現單人的照片 Unit 02 出現雙人以上的照片	Unit 03 事物、風景照片 Unit 04 人物、背景照片	Unit 05 Who問句 Unit 06 When、Where問句	Unit 07 What、Which問句 Unit 08 How、Why問句	Unit 09 一般問句 Unit 10 選擇疑問句
	Day 6	**Day 7**	**Day 8**	**Day 9**	**Day 10**
第2週	Unit 11 建議（請求）句 Unit 12 陳述句	Unit 13 詢問主題、目的的題目 Unit 14 詢問職業／對話地點的題目	Unit 15 詢問說話者的建議的題目 Unit 16 詢問接下來會做什麼事的題目	Unit 17 詢問細節的題目 Unit 18 掌握句子意圖的題目	Unit 19 結合視覺資料的題目 Unit 20 餐廳
	Day 11	**Day 12**	**Day 13**	**Day 14**	**Day 15**
第3週	Unit 21 飯店 Unit 22 購物	Unit 23 購票 Unit 24 徵人、辭職	Unit 25 教育、宣傳 Unit 26 設施、網絡管理	Unit 27 會計、預算 Unit 28 事業規劃	Unit 29 公司內部公告 Unit 30 公共場所公告
	Day 16	**Day 17**	**Day 18**	**Day 19**	**Day 20**
第4週	Unit 31 語音訊息 Unit 32 自動回覆系統	Unit 33 天氣預報 Unit 34 交通廣播	Unit 35 新聞 Unit 36 人物介紹	Unit 37 導覽 Unit 38 產品廣告	Unit 39 折扣廣告 Final Test

Listening
Preparation

- 了解發音基礎！
- 美式 vs. 英式發音
- Check up Quiz

1) 辨別聽起來類似的發音

[p] vs [f] 發音

[p] 發音是嘴巴緊閉後憋住氣流再像爆破般發出的聲音，[f] 發音則是下嘴唇輕輕碰到上齒後吐氣發出的聲音。

fill [fɪl] 填滿	**pill** [pɪl] 藥丸	**full** [fʊl] 充滿的	**pool** [pul] 水池
file [faɪl] 檔案	**pile** [paɪl] 堆疊	**fair** [fɛr] 公平的	**pair** [pɛr] 一對
face [fes] 臉	**pace** [pes] 速度	**suffer** [`sʌfɚ] 經歷	**supper** [`sʌpɚ] 晚餐
staff [stæf] 員工	**step** [stɛp] 步伐，階段	**often** [`ɔfən] 經常	**open** [`opən] 開啟

Check up 01 聽完音檔後請依序排列。

1. (1) cheap   **2.** (1) cuff   **3.** (1) coffee
   (2) chief   (2) cup   (2) copy

[l] vs [r] 發音

[l] 是舌尖碰到上齒時發出的聲音，[r] 則是舌頭往後捲的同時發出的聲音。

light [laɪt] 光	**right** [raɪt] 正確的，右邊的	**load** [lod] 行李，裝載量	**road** [rod] 路
low [lo] 低的	**row** [ro] 列	**glass** [glæs] 玻璃	**grass** [græs] 草地
flame [flem] 火焰	**frame** [frem] 架構，框架	**fly** [flaɪ] 飛翔	**fry** [fraɪ] 油炸
law [lɔ] 法律	**raw** [rɔ] 生的	**lead** [lid] 帶領	**read** [rid] 閱讀
late [let] 晚的	**rate** [ret] 比例	**loyal** [`lɔɪəl] 忠誠的	**royal** [`rɔɪəl] 皇家的

Check up 02 聽完音檔後請依序排列。

1. (1) lane   **2.** (1) free   **3.** (1) file
   (2) rain   (2) flea   (2) fire

| 正解 | Check up 01 **1.** (2) chief (1) cheap   **2.** (1) cuff (2) cup   **3.** (2) copy (1) coffee
Check up 02 **1.** (1) lane (2) rain   **2.** (2) flea (1) free   **3.** (1) file (2) fire

[b] vs [v] 發音

[b] 發音跟 [p] 一樣要在嘴巴內憋住氣流，不同的是要一邊震動聲帶一邊發出聲音。[v] 發音則是跟 [f] 一樣要下嘴唇碰到上齒，不同的是要一邊震動聲帶一邊發出聲音。

boys [bɔɪz] 男孩們	**voice** [vɔɪs] 聲音	**berry** [ˋbɛrɪ] 莓果	**very** [ˋvɛrɪ] 非常，很
vase [ves] 花瓶	**base** [bes] 基礎	**vote** [vot] 投票	**boat** [bot] 船
van [væn] 小型貨車	**ban** [bæn] 禁止	**vend** [vɛnd] 販賣	**bend** [bɛnd] 彎曲
best [bɛst] 最棒的	**vest** [vɛst] 背心	**curve** [kɝv] 曲線	**curb** [kɝb] 路邊

Check up 03　聽完音檔後請依序排列。

1. (1) bind
   (2) vine

2. (1) bow
   (2) vow

3. (1) bet
   (2) vet

[d] vs [t] 發音

[d] 和 [t] 都是舌頭碰到上顎前面所發出的聲音，差別在於 [t] 是將舌尖彈出去後發出的聲音，[d] 近似於注音符號的ㄉ，[t] 則近似於注音符號的ㄊ。

do [du] 做	**to** [tu] 往～	**sad** [sæd] 傷心的	**sat** [sæt] 坐下（過去式）
bid [bɪd] 投標	**bit** [bɪt] 小塊	**dance** [dæns] 跳舞	**tense** [tɛns] 緊張感
desk [dɛsk] 桌子	**task** [tæsk] 任務	**bud** [bʌd] 花苞	**but** [bʌt] 但是

Check up 04　聽完音檔後請依序排列。

1. (1) feet
   (2) feed

2. (1) try
   (2) dry

3. (1) letter
   (2) ladder

| 正解 | Check up 03　**1.** (2) vine (1) bind　**2.** (1) bow (2) vow　**3.** (2) vet (1) bet
Check up 04　**1.** (2) feed (1) feet　**2.** (2) dry (1) try　**3.** (1) letter (2) ladder

19

[ð] vs [θ] 發音

這兩個發音都是在上下牙齒縫隙間稍微咬住舌頭後用力發出的聲音。不過，[ð] 是會振動聲帶的有聲音，[θ] 則是不會振動聲帶的無聲音。

bath [bæθ] 洗澡　　　　　　　　**bathe** [beð] 洗澡
worthy [ˋwɝðɪ] 值得的　　　　　**worth** [wɝθ] 有～價值的

Check up 05　　聽完音檔後請依序排列。

1. world population _____

2. winning a _____ competition

[ɔ] vs [o] 發音

若不仔細聽，會覺得這兩個發音很類似，須特別留意 [o] 的發音。

want [wɔnt] 想要　　　　　　　　**won't** [wont] will not 的縮寫
saw [sɔ] 看見（過去式）　　　　　**sew** [so] 縫補
caught [kɔt] 捕捉（過去式）　　　**coat** [kot] 大衣
law [lɔ] 法律　　　　　　　　　　**low** [lo] 低的
cost [kɔst] 費用　　　　　　　　　**coast** [kost] 海岸
flaw [flɔ] 缺點，缺陷　　　　　　**flow** [flo] 流動
bought [bɔt] 購買（過去式）　　　**boat** [bot] 船

Check up 06　　聽完音檔後請依序排列。

1. (1) hole　　　　　　**2.** (1) cold　　　　　　**3.** (1) raw
　　(2) hall　　　　　　　　(2) called　　　　　　　(2) row

| 正解 | Check up 05 **1.** growth　**2.** math
　　　　 Check up 06 **1.** (2) hall (1) hole　**2.** (2) called (1) cold　**3.** (1) raw (2) row

20

[ɛ] vs [æ] 發音

[ɛ] 發音類似注音符號的「ㄟㄧ」，而 [æ] 是嘴巴兩端更用力發出的聲音。

mess [mɛs] 混亂   **mass** [mæs] 大量，多數的

bet [bɛt] 打賭   **bat** [bæt] 蝙蝠，球棒

bed [bɛd] 床   **bad** [bæd] 壞的，不好的

letter [ˋlɛtɚ] 信件   **ladder** [ˋlædɚ] 梯子

| Check up 07 | 聽完音檔後請依序排列。

1. (1) set   **2.** (1) band   **3.** (1) men

   (2) sat   (2) bend   (2) man

[i] vs [ɪ] 發音

發音上沒有差異，不同之處在於哪個發音較長或短。

leave [liv] 離開   **live** [lɪv] 生活   **reach** [ritʃ] 達到   **rich** [rɪtʃ] 富裕的

heat [hit] 熱氣   **hit** [hɪt] 擊中   **beat** [bit] 打   **bit** [bɪt] 有一點

seat [sit] 座位   **sit** [sɪt] 坐   **feel** [fil] 感覺   **fill** [fɪl] 填滿

list [lɪst] 清單   **least** [list] 至少的   **beach** [bitʃ] 海灘   **bitch** [bɪtʃ] 母狗

| Check up 08 | 聽完音檔後請依序排列。

1. (1) pill   **2.** (1) knit   **3.** (1) meat

   (2) peel   (2) neat   (2) meet

| 正解 | Check up 07 **1.** (1) set (2) sat   **2.** (2) bend (1) band   **3.** (1) men (2) man
   Check up 08 **1.** (1) pill (2) peel   **2.** (1) knit (2) neat   **3.** (2) meet (1) meat

發音相同或相似，但拼字不同的單字

break [brek] 打破

fare [fɛr] 費用，乘客

ate [et] 吃（過去式）

our [`aʊr] 我們的

right [raɪt] 右邊

sale [sel] 販賣

flu [flu] 流感

steak [stek] 牛排

working [`wɝkɪŋ] 工作的

weak [wik] 虛弱的

contact [`kɑntækt] 聯絡

wait [wet] 等候

department [dɪ`pɑrtmənt] 部門

whether [`hwɛðɚ] 是否～

new [nju] 新的

attend [ə`tɛnd] 參加

address [ə`drɛs] 演說，地址

brake [brek] 煞車

fair [fɛr] 公正的，展覽會

eight [et] 八

hour [aʊr] 小時

write [raɪt] 寫

sail [sel] 帆

flew [flu] 飛（過去式）

stake [stek] 打賭，椿

walking [`wɔkɪŋ] 走路的

week [wik] 一週

contract [kən`trækt] 合約書

weigh [we] 秤重

apartment [ə`pɑrtmənt] 公寓

weather [`wɛðɚ] 天氣

knew [nju] 知道（過去式）

tend [tɛnd] 傾向

dress [drɛs] 洋裝，使穿著

多益測驗中出現的發音可以分成美國、加拿大、英國和澳洲口音，主要可將其分成美式和英式這兩大類的發音。雖然我們很熟悉美式發音，但全世界使用英式發音的國家更多。接著就來了解這兩種發音的差異和發音方式吧。

1) 子音 [t] 發音

下列單字的美式與英式發音，有所差異的就是字尾的 [t] 發音。母音之間有 [t] 或 [d] 的時候，美式發音類似於注音的「ㄉ」或「ㄌ」。但是英式發音會強烈地把 [t] 發成「ㄊ」的聲音。

sitting 美 [ˋsɪtɪŋ] 英 [ˋsɪtɪŋ] 坐著
better 美 [ˋbɛtɚ] 英 [ˋbɛtə] 比～更好的
matter 美 [ˋmætɚ] 英 [ˋmætə] 事情
meeting 美 [ˋmitɪŋ] 英 [ˋmitɪŋ] 會議
total 美 [ˋtotl̩] 英 [ˋtotl̩] 全部的

later 美 [ˋletɚ] 英 [ˋletə] 之後
bottom 美 [ˋbɑtəm] 英 [ˋbɑtəm] 底部的
waiter 美 [ˋwetɚ] 英 [ˋwetə] 服務生
setting 美 [ˋsɛtɪŋ] 英 [ˋsɛtɪŋ] 設定
letter 美 [ˋlɛtɚ] 英 [ˋlɛtə] 信件

2) 子音 [r] 發音

我們能強烈感覺到美式與英式發音差異的就是 [r] 發音。美式的 [r] 發音會發出捲舌音，但是 [r] 在母音後面出現的話，英式發音不會發出 [r] 的聲音，而是延長前面的母音發音。也就是說，英式發音省略了 [r] 發音。可明顯分辨出美式與英式口音的就是這個 [r] 發音。

car 美 [kɑr] 英 [kɑ:] 汽車
dark 美 [dɑrk] 英 [dɑ:k] 黑暗的
part 美 [pɑrt] 英 [pɑ:t] 部分
store 美 [stor] 英 [stɔ:] 商店
repair 美 [rɪˋpɛr] 英 [rɪˋpɛə] 修理

carpet 美 [ˋkɑrpɪt] 英 [ˋkɑ:pit] 地毯
parking 美 [pɑrkɪŋ] 英 [pɑ:kɪŋ] 停車
cart 美 [kɑrt] 英 [kɑ:t] 推車
stair 美 [stɛr] 英 [stɛə] 階梯
turn 美 [tɝn] 英 [tə:n] 旋轉，使轉動

3) 子音 [tn] 的發音

美式的 [tn] 發音類似「壓抑」住鼻音，而英式則是完整地發出聲音。

mountain 美 [`maʊntn] 英 [`mauntin] 山
curtain 美 [`kɜ-tn] 英 [`kə:tn] 窗簾
certainly 美 [`sɜ-tənlɪ] 英 [`sə:tənli] 無疑地
important 美 [im`pɔrtnt] 英 [im`pɔ:tənt] 重要的

button 美 [`bʌtn] 英 [`bʌtn] 鈕扣
carton 美 [`kɑrtn] 英 [`kɑ:tən] 紙板箱
shorten 美 [`ʃɔrtn] 英 [`ʃɔ:tn] 使變短
fountain 美 [`faʊntɪn] 英 [`fauntin] 噴泉

4) 母音 [a] 發音

有時候美式發音類似注音「ㄟ」，而英式發音類似注音「ㄚ」。舉例來說，英式發音的 answer 會發成「阿恩瑟」，而不是「安瑟」。

ask 美 [æsk] 英 [ɑ:sk] 詢問
bath 美 [bæθ] 英 [bɑ:θ] 洗澡
half 美 [hæf] 英 [hɑ:f] 一半的
manager 美 [`mænɪdʒɚ] 英 [`mænɪdʒə] 經理
pass 美 [pæs] 英 [pɑ:s] 通過

after 美 [`æftɚ] 英 [`ɑ:ftə] 在～之後
chance 美 [tʃæns] 英 [tʃɑ:ns] 機會
fast 美 [fæst] 英 [fɑ:st] 快速的
answer 美 [`ænsɚ] 英 [`ɑ:nsə] 回答
can't 美 [kænt] 英 [kɑ:nt] 無法～

5) 母音[o]發音

[o] 的美式發音通常會是類似注音「ㄚ」的發音，英式則是「ㄛ」。舉例來說，box 的美式發音是「巴克斯」，而英式是「播克斯」。

stop 美 [stɑp] 英 [stɔp] 暫停

doctor 美 [`dɑktɚ] 英 [`dɔktə] 醫生

got 美 [gɑt] 英 [gɔt] 得到（過去式）

job 美 [dʒɑb] 英 [dʒɔb] 工作

body 美 [`bɑdɪ] 英 [`bɔdi] 身體

copy 美 [`kɑpɪ] 英 [`kɔpi] 複製

not 美 [nɑt] 英 [nɔt] 不

lot 美 [lɑt] 英 [lɔt] 一塊地

rock 美 [rɑk] 英 [rɔk] 岩石

contact 美 [`kɑntækt] 英 [`kɔntækt] 聯絡，接觸

6) 其他須留意的單字

也有些單字的美式、英式發音與上述的子音和母音規則截然不同。代表性單字是 schedule。美式發音類似「斯給久」，英式發音則是相似於「薛久」。

advertisement 美 [ædvɚ`taɪzmənt] 英 [əd`vɚ:tismənt] 廣告

data 美 [`detə] 英 [`deitə] 資料

often 美 [`ɔfən] 英 [`ɔ:fən] 時常

schedule 美 [`skɛdʒʊl] 英 [`skedʒul] 行程

vase 美 [ves] 英 [veis] 花瓶

laboratory 美 [`læbrə͵torɪ] 英 [lə`bɔrətəri] 實驗室

garage 美 [gə`rɑʒ] 英 [`gærɑ:ʒ] 車庫

water 美 [`wɔtɚ] 英 [`wɔ:tə] 水

Check up Quiz　聆聽音檔後填空。

01　I hope you take the _____ to relax.

02　You will need a heavy _____ .

03　According to the _____ , how can someone purchase the product?

04　The cars are _____ at a traffic light.

05　We _____ exciting tour packages during your stay.

06　Some trees are being _____ .

07　Our _____ stop on the city tour is Eco World.

08　Why has the man _____ the woman?

09　The lamp has been _____ on.

10　_____ all our experts have spoken, we will collect the cards.

11　A ship is _____ under the bridge.

12　Have you _____ the manager about it?

13　What kind of shoes did you _____ ?

14　They are _____ the plants.

15　What is being _____ ?

16　I'd like to _____ a reservation of the room I booked yesterday.

17　To _____ an appointment, please press '1' now.

18　The _____ staff will participate in the conference.

19　The truck is _____ next to containers.

20　The _____ has been signed.

| 正解 |　**1.** opportunity **2.** coat **3.** advertisement **4.** stopped **5.** offer **6.** planted **7.** last **8.** contacted **9.** turned **10.** After
11. passing **12.** asked **13.** purchase **14.** watering **15.** rescheduled **16.** confirm **17.** schedule **18.** entire
19. parked **20.** contract

PART

1

照片描述

第一大題須聽完描述照片的四個選項，選出最符合照片描述的選項。
（共6題）

Voca Preview

請勾選不認識的單字，學習完類型分析後再重新確認勾選的單字。

- ☐ **carry** 搬運，扛
- ☐ **remove** 消除
- ☐ **plug in** 插入～
- ☐ **take a note** 做筆記
- ☐ **water bottle** 水瓶
- ☐ **prepare a meal** 準備餐點
- ☐ **examine** 檢查
- ☐ **apply A to B** 將 A 貼到 B 上
- ☐ **shop at** 在～購物
- ☐ **have a meeting** 開會
- ☐ **sewing project** 縫紉作品
- ☐ **work on** 從事～
- ☐ **clear a street** 打掃街道
- ☐ **install** 安裝
- ☐ **cross the street** 過馬路
- ☐ **order** 訂購
- ☐ **choose merchandise** 選擇商品
- ☐ **outdoor market** 露天市集
- ☐ **reach for** 伸手拿～
- ☐ **seal envelope** 封住信封

- ☐ **draw a picture** 畫畫
- ☐ **lean against** 靠在～上
- ☐ **railing** 欄杆
- ☐ **pull** 拉，拖
- ☐ **rest on a beach** 在海灘上休息
- ☐ **chain** 用鎖鏈拴住
- ☐ **next to** 在～旁邊
- ☐ **brick wall** 磚牆
- ☐ **enter** 進入，輸入
- ☐ **construction project** 建設工程
- ☐ **lift a ladder** 抬起梯子
- ☐ **assist** 協助
- ☐ **hand** 傳遞
- ☐ **turn off** 關掉～
- ☐ **type on** 在～上打字
- ☐ **serve a meal** 上菜
- ☐ **sweep the floor** 掃地
- ☐ **point at** 指著～
- ☐ **laboratory** 實驗室
- ☐ **unload** 卸下

類型分析

1

以人為主的照片

WARMING UP

診斷評估　聽完 mp3 後，若照片描述正確請打○，不正確請打 ✕。　🎧 01.mp3

1.

Ⓐ (　　)　　　　Ⓑ (　　)

2.

Ⓐ (　　)　　　　Ⓑ (　　)

填空　　再聽一次 mp3 並填空。　　🎧 01.mp3

1. Ⓐ A man ＿＿＿＿＿＿＿＿ some vegetables.

   Ⓑ A man ＿＿＿＿＿＿＿＿ a mirror.

2. Ⓐ A man ＿＿＿＿＿＿＿＿ a car's tire.

   Ⓑ A man ＿＿＿＿＿＿＿＿ in a car.

一邊填空，一邊尋找描述照片時使用的表達方式共同點。

確認解答 & 要點　　確認正確答案，了解以人為主的照片的特徵。

1. Ⓐ A man is carrying some vegetables.　男子正在搬蔬菜。　⭕

   Ⓑ A man is holding a mirror.　男子拿著鏡子。　❌

2. Ⓐ A man is washing a car's tire.　男子正在洗車子的輪胎。　⭕

   Ⓑ A man is sitting in a car.　男子坐在車裡面。　❌

以人為主的照片的題目答案80%取決於動詞和名詞，
動詞通常是現在進行式。比起主詞，請將注意力放在
與照片中的人物動作相關的動詞或名詞上。

Unit 01 出現單人的照片

聆聽音檔前　按照「手部動作→確認外表→確認周遭情況」的順序確認照片中人物的動作，並事先猜測可能
會在選項中出現的動詞。

聆聽音檔時　選擇最終答案時須專心聆聽動詞和名詞的部分。

 代表題型　聽完音檔後請選出合適的正確答案。 02.mp3

(A)　　　　(B)　　　　(C)　　　　(D)

 攻略解題法　了解該如何作答出現單人照片的題目。

　在聽音檔之前確認人物的動作和穿著後，事先預想幾個可能會出現的答案。

She is using the equipment.　她正在使用設備。

She is speaking into a microphone.　她正在透過麥克風說話。

She is wearing a headset.　她戴著耳罩式耳機。

She is wearing a jacket.　她穿著夾克。

　聽到錯誤的音檔內容時，立刻刪除包含照片中沒有的動詞或名詞的選項。

(A) She is removing her headphones.　她正在拿下耳罩式耳機。　✗
▶ 照片中的人物手部動作跟選項的描述不一樣。

(B) She is speaking into a microphone.　她正在透過麥克風說話。　○
▶ 照片中的人物正在透過麥克風說話，所以是正確答案。

(C) She is typing on a keyboard.　她正在用鍵盤打字。　✗
▶ 照片中的人物手部動作跟選項描述的不一樣。出現照片中沒有的名詞（keyboard）的錯誤答案。

(D) She is plugging in a cord.　她正在插絕緣電線。　✗
▶ 照片中的人物手部動作跟選項的描述不一樣。出現照片中沒有的名詞（cord）的錯誤答案。

Step 2 核心理論&基礎形式

若出現單人的照片中,又只露出人物的上半身,該題四個選項的主詞都會一樣,所以要專心聆聽主詞的動作。
不過,出現全身的照片,除了人物之外,也可能會出現關於周遭事物的提問,所以主詞的行為和事物描述都要
專心聆聽。這兩種情況的關鍵都在於動詞和名詞,所以要專心聆聽動詞和名詞。動詞通常以現在進行式描述。

 ### 各種情況的描述

辦公室&戶外

She is taking some notes by hand.

The man is talking on the phone.

The woman is drinking from a water bottle.

The man is walking along the beach.

工作場合

A man is working on a ladder.

A man is checking a tire.

He is carrying some boxes.

A man is repairing a door.

廚房&餐廳&商店

She is preparing a meal.

The woman is studying the menu.

A woman is examining a product.

She is pushing a cart.

Voca Check-up! **take notes** 做筆記 **talk on the phone** 講電話 **walk along the beach** 沿著海灘走 **carry ＋物品** 搬物品 **repair** 修理 **prepare a meal** 準備餐點 **study the menu** 看菜單 **push a cart** 推推車

Step 3 實戰演練 🔊03.mp3

1.

2.

(A)　　(B)　　(C)　　(D)

(A)　　(B)　　(C)　　(D)

▶ 答案與解析請參考解析本第4頁

Unit 02 出現雙人以上的照片

Step 1 | **實戰重點**

 聆聽音檔前 按照「共同的動作→各自的動作→周遭情況或事物的描述」的順序確認出現兩人以上的照片中人物的動作。

聆聽音檔時 選擇最終答案時須專心聆聽動詞和名詞的部分。

🎓 **代表題型** 聽完音檔後請選出合適的正確答案。 🎧 04.mp3

(A)　　　(B)　　　(C)　　　(D)

✏️ **攻略解題法** 了解該如何作答出現雙人以上的照片的題目。

 聆聽音檔前 依序確認照片中的人物的共同動作→各自的動作→周遭情況或事物的描述。觀察照片中的人物，試著預想可能會出現的答案。

They are reading the same book.　他們正在看同一本書。

They are sitting on a sofa.　他們坐在沙發上。

The man is holding a book.　男子拿著一本書。

The man is sitting on the chair with one leg crossed.　男子翹腳坐在椅子上。

 聆聽音檔時 主詞以複數（They、The women、The men）開始的話，要將重點放在共同的動作上。主詞以單數（He、She、A man、A woman）開始的話，要將重點放在該人物的動作上。出現照片中沒有的動詞或名詞的選項應立刻刪去。

(A) They are applying labels to some books.　他們正在一些書上貼標籤。　✗

▶ 主詞是複數（They），所以要專心聽人物的共同動作。照片中沒有名詞（labels），而且兩人沒有做相同的動作，所以是錯誤答案。

(B) The woman is making photocopies of some pages.　女子正在影印其中的幾頁。　✗

▶ 主詞是單數（The woman），所以要專心聽女子的動作。女子並未做出影印的動作，所以是錯誤答案。

(C) They are reading the same book.　他們正在看同一本書。　○

▶ 照片中的兩個人物正在看同一本書，所以是正確答案。

(D) The man is listening to music on his headphones.　男子正在用耳罩式耳機聽音樂。　✗

▶ 主詞是單數（The man），所以要專心聽男子的動作。動詞（listen）和名詞（headphones）都未在照片中出現，而且男子沒有聽音樂，所以是錯誤答案。

Step 2 | 核心理論&基礎形式

出現雙人以上的照片的題目，著重於照片中的人物目前正在做的共同動作，以及各自的動作。因此，主詞以複數（They、The women、The men）開始的話，要專心聽共同的動作；主詞以單數（He、She、A man、A woman）開始的話，要專心聽各自的動作。

各種情況的描述

室內工作

They are looking at some papers.

They are having a meeting at the table.

They are working on sewing projects.

They are sitting at the table.

戶外工作

The men are repairing the roof.

They are cleaning a street.

Workers are installing equipment.

They are crossing the street.

餐廳&商店

Customers are ordering some food from a menu.

People are eating in a dining area.

She is shopping at an outdoor market.

She is choosing some merchandise.

Voca Check-up! **look at** 看著～ **have a meeting** 開會 **sewing project** 縫紉作品 **repair the roof** 修理屋頂 **install equipment** 安裝設備 **dining area** 用餐區 **outdoor market** 露天市集 **shop at** 在～購物 **choose merchandise** 選擇商品

Step 3 | 實戰演練　　🎧 05.mp3

1.

(A)　　(B)　　(C)　　(D)

2.

(A)　　(B)　　(C)　　(D)

▶ 答案與解析請參考解析本第4頁

REVIEW TEST

1.

   (A)   (B)   (C)   (D)

2.

   (A)   (B)   (C)   (D)

3.

(A)   (B)   (C)   (D)

4.

(A)   (B)   (C)   (D)

▶ 答案與解析請參考解析本第5頁

聽寫訓練

Unit 01　出現單人的照片　│　**Step 3** 實戰演練　　　　🔊 dictation-01.mp3

1. (A) He is _____ for a _____.

(B) He is _____ a _____.

(C) He is _____ an _____.

(D) He is _____ a picture.

2. (A) The bicycle is _____ the _____.

(B) The bicycle is _____ by the woman.

(C) A woman is _____ a beach.

(D) A woman is _____ a bicycle to _____.

Unit 02　出現雙人以上的照片　│　**Step 3** 實戰演練　　　　🔊 dictation-02.mp3

1. (A) They are _____ a _____ wall.

(B) They are _____ a _____.

(C) They are _____ a _____ project.

(D) They are _____ a _____.

2. (A) A man is _____ on his _____.

(B) Customers _____ books.

(C) A salesperson is _____ a _____.

(D) A woman is _____ a _____ to the man.

Review Test

🎧 dictaion-03.mp3

1. (A) She is _____ _____ a notepad.

(B) She is _____ a _____ _____.

(C) She is _____ _____ a light.

(D) She is _____ _____ a _____.

2. (A) She is _____ her hands.

(B) She is _____ a _____.

(C) She is _____ the _____.

(D) She is _____ the _____.

3. (A) They are _____ a _____.

(B) They are _____ _____ the board.

(C) They are _____ _____ a _____ _____.

(D) They are _____ _____ the table.

4. (A) Some people are _____ a _____.

(B) Technicians are _____ _____ a _____.

(C) _____ are _____ _____ _____ from the room.

(D) Supplies are _____ _____ from a _____.

Voca Preview

請勾選不認識的單字，學習完類型分析後再重新確認勾選的單字。

- [ ] **lighthouse** 燈塔
- [ ] **construct** 建設，蓋
- [ ] **pile** 堆疊
- [ ] **gather** 聚集
- [ ] **floral arrangement** 插花
- [ ] **unoccupied** 空的
- [ ] **overlook** 俯瞰
- [ ] **under construction** 建造中
- [ ] **grow** 成長
- [ ] **water fountain** 噴泉
- [ ] **be in operation** 運轉中
- [ ] **pass** 經過
- [ ] **hang** 掛
- [ ] **vase** 花瓶
- [ ] **spray water** 灑水
- [ ] **display** 展示，陳列
- [ ] **waterfall** 瀑布
- [ ] **make the bed** 整理床鋪
- [ ] **light bulb** 電燈泡
- [ ] **sweep the floor** 掃地

- [ ] **mow the lawn** 修剪草皮
- [ ] **climb the ladder** 爬梯子
- [ ] **along the shore** 沿著海岸
- [ ] **spend time** 消磨時間
- [ ] **left open** 讓～開著
- [ ] **entrance** 入口
- [ ] **be covered with** 以～覆蓋
- [ ] **extend across** 延伸至～
- [ ] **height** 高度
- [ ] **raise** 提高
- [ ] **wave a flag** 揮旗
- [ ] **splash** 濺，潑
- [ ] **roll up** 捲起
- [ ] **artwork** 藝術作品
- [ ] **arrange** 安排
- [ ] **light fixture** 燈具
- [ ] **suspend** 懸掛
- [ ] **ceiling** 天花板
- [ ] **in the middle of** 在～的中間
- [ ] **draw** 拉～

類型分析 **2**

以事物、風景與
人物、背景為主的照片

診斷評估 聽完 mp3 後，若照片描述正確請打○，不正確請打 ✗。 🎧 07.mp3

1.

Ⓐ (　　　)　　　　Ⓑ (　　　)

2.

Ⓐ (　　　)　　　　Ⓑ (　　　)

填空　　再聽一次mp3並填空。　　🎧 07.mp3

1. Ⓐ A ＿＿＿＿＿＿＿＿ is situated near a ＿＿＿＿＿＿.

   Ⓑ A tower ＿＿＿＿＿＿＿＿＿＿＿＿＿ by the shore.

2. Ⓐ Fish ＿＿＿＿＿＿＿ on top of a box.

   Ⓑ The man ＿＿＿＿＿＿＿＿＿ fish ＿＿＿＿＿＿＿＿＿.

一邊填空，一邊尋找描述事物、風景或背景時使用的
表達方式共同點。

確認解答＆要點　　確認正確答案，了解以事物、風景為主的照片特徵。

1. Ⓐ A lighthouse is situated near a shoreline.　燈塔位於海岸線附近。　○

   Ⓑ A tower is being constructed by the shore.　海岸邊正在蓋大樓。　✗

事物、風景照片會呈現出事物的位置或狀態，There
句型或被動句通常是正確答案。

2. Ⓐ Fish are piled on top of a box.　魚被疊在盒子上面。　○

   Ⓑ The man is gathering fish in a net.　男子正在將魚聚集到網子裡。　✗

若人物和背景照片中只有一個人物，須專心聆聽人物的動作和行為。描述
事物或背景的句子在這種時候也經常會寫成被動句。

Unit 03　事物、風景照片

 Step 1　**實戰重點**

 聆聽音檔前　從照片的中間開始確認事物的位置後，再確認周遭事物的位置。

聆聽音檔時　須注意聆聽表示地點或位置的介系詞。

 代表題型　聽完音檔後請選出合適的正確答案。　 08.mp3

　　　　　　　　　　　　　　(A)　　　　　(B)　　　　　(C)　　　　　(D)

 攻略解題法　了解該如何回答事物、風景照片的題目。

🗣 聆聽音檔前　在聆聽題目前想想看可能會出現的答案。

A floral arrangement decorates each table.　插花妝點了每張桌子。

The tables are unoccupied at the moment.　桌子目前沒人使用。

Glasses have been placed on the table.　玻璃杯被放在桌子上。

The tables have been set.　桌子已經布置好了。

🎧 聆聽音檔時　**聆聽題目時**

(A) A floral arrangement decorates each table.　插花妝點了每張桌子。　⭕

▶ 從照片的中間開始確認，之後再確認周遭情況。每張桌子都用花瓶裝飾，所以是正確答案。

(B) Chairs are full of napkins.　椅子上都是餐巾。　❌

▶ 沒有椅子放了餐巾的畫面，所以是錯誤答案。

(C) The tables are being occupied.　桌子坐滿人了。　❌

▶ 這是沒有人物的照片，而且都是空位，所以是錯誤答案。occupied意即「位置已被占用的」，經常在多益測驗中出現。

(D) Menus are being handed out.　正在發菜單。　❌

▶ 這是沒有人物的照片，動詞（hand out）跟照片沒有關聯，所以是錯誤答案。

回答出現事物或風景的照片題目時，須掌握好事物的名稱、位置或狀態等等，並留心觀察出現了什麼設施。

各種情況的描述

建築物

Buildings overlook the water.

The building is under construction.

Each house has its own balcony.

The building has an arched opening.

植物&公園

Trees are growing on the sides of the road.

There are trees around the pond.

The water fountain is in operation.

The fountain is in a park.

湖水、河川&海邊

The ship is passing under the bridge.

The chairs are unoccupied.

There are buildings near the beach.

There is a bridge over the water.

室內空間

There are lamps on the bed tables.

Pictures are hanging on the walls.

Vases are on the table.

The sofa is unoccupied.

Voca Check-up! **overlook** 俯瞰 **under construction** 建造中 **arched opening** 拱形入口的 **around the pond** 池塘周圍 **fountain** 噴泉 **in operation** 運作中 **unoccupied** 無人占用的 **occupied** 被占用的 **hang on** 掛 **vase** 花瓶

Step **3** 實戰演練
🎧 09.mp3

1.

(A)　　(B)　　(C)　　(D)

2.

(A)　　(B)　　(C)　　(D)

▶ 答案與解析請參考解析本第6頁

Unit 04　人物、背景照片

Step 1　實戰重點

 聆聽音檔前　若出現有人物或背景的照片，比起描述人物動作的選項，描述事物或設施的選項常常會是正確答案。

聆聽音檔時　聆聽時須同時確認與人物相關的動作、外表和周遭事物。

 代表題型　聽完音檔後請選出合適的正確答案。　 10.mp3

　　　　　　　　　　　(A)　　　　(B)　　　　(C)　　　　(D)

 攻略解題法　了解該如何作答人物、背景照片的題目。

 聆聽音檔前　聆聽題目前想想看可能會出現的答案。

A man is spraying water on a field.　男子正在田裡灑水。

Several crops are growing in the field.　好幾個農作物在田裡生長。

Some pots are displayed on the top of the green house.　某些盆栽被放在溫室上面。

聆聽音檔時　聆聽題目時

(A) A waterfall is next to a park.　瀑布在公園旁邊。　✗

▶ 出現和照片中的單字（water）發音類似的（waterfall）詞彙的選項，或是照片中沒有的名詞（park）的選項都是錯誤答案。

(B) Potted plants are being placed on a ledge.　盆栽植物被放在窗架上。　✗

▶ 出現照片中沒有的名詞（ledge）的選項是錯誤答案。

(C) A man is cutting the grass.　男子正在割草。　✗

▶ 關於男子的動作描述有誤。

(D) Some plants are being sprayed with water.　某些植物正在被澆水。　〇

▶ 這是以人物、背景為主的照片，所以要專心聆聽人物的動作和周遭事物的相關詞彙。男子正在幫植物澆水，所以是正確答案。

作答以人物、背景為主的照片時，要專心聆聽人物是怎麼使用周遭物品的。

 各種情況的描述

屋內空間

She is making the bed.

They are moving the furniture.

The man is changing a light bulb.

The woman is sweeping the floor.

戶外空間

He is mowing the lawn.

He is working in the garden.

He is painting the wall.

The man is climbing the ladder.

戶外活動

People are relaxing on the grass.

People are walking along the shore.

People are spending time in the park.

He is fishing at the sea.

Voca Check-up! **make the bed** 整理床鋪 **light bulb** 電燈泡 **sweep the floor** 掃地 **mow the lawn** 修剪草皮 **climb the ladder** 爬梯子 **relax on the grass** 在草地上休息 **along the shore** 沿著海岸 **spend time** 消磨時間 **fish** 釣魚

1.

(A) (B) (C) (D)

2.

(A) (B) (C) (D)

▶ 答案與解析請參考解析本第7頁

1.

(A)   (B)   (C)   (D)

2.

(A)   (B)   (C)   (D)

3.

(A)　　　(B)　　　(C)　　　(D)

4.

(A)　　　(B)　　　(C)　　　(D)

▶ 答案與解析請參考解析本第7頁

聽寫訓練

1. (A) All of the _____ doors _____ _____ _____ open.

   (B) There are _____ in the building's _____.

   (C) The house is _____ _____ flowers.

   (D) There are _____ styles of _____ on the _____.

2. (A) Boats are _____ along the _____.

   (B) Buildings _____ a _____.

   (C) Rocks _____ _____ _____ along the shore.

   (D) A bridge _____ _____ the water.

1. (A) They are _____ _____ the windows of _____ _____.

   (B) One of _____ _____ is _____ a balcony.

   (C) Ladders of different _____ are _____ _____ the wall.

   (D) There is a _____ the buildings.

2. (A) A sail is _____ _____ _____ boat.

   (B) A passenger is _____ a _____ in the air.

   (C) Some people are _____ _____ _____.

   (D) Water is _____ _____ a boat _____.

Review Test   🎧 dictation-06.mp3

1. (A) Rugs _____ against the _____.

   (B) A sofa is _____ _____.

   (C) The _____ are _____.

   (D) The _____ have been _____.

2. (A) A man _____ a piece of _____.

   (B) Pottery _____ on the shelf.

   (C) A man is _____ a workshop.

   (D) A _____ has been _____ the wall.

3. (A) People _____ for an _____.

   (B) Workers are _____.

   (C) There are _____ in the _____.

   (D) _____ from the floor _____.

4. (A) Chairs _____ on _____ of a sofa.

   (B) Some cups are _____ from a table.

   (C) There are _____ on the table.

   (D) _____ above the table.

PART 1

Directions: For each question in this part, you will hear four statements about a picture in your test book. When you hear the statements, you must select the one statement that best describes what you see in the picture. Then find the number of the question on your answer sheet and mark your answer. The statements will not be printed in your test book and will be spoken only one time.

1.

(A)   (B)   (C)   (D)

2.

(A)   (B)   (C)   (D)

3.

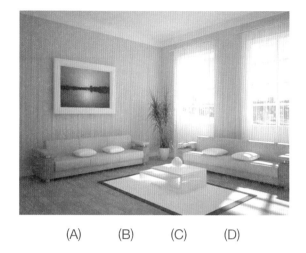

(A)   (B)   (C)   (D)

4.

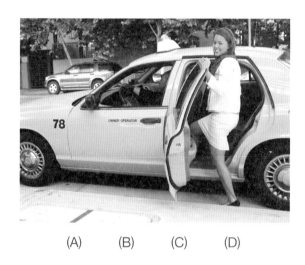

(A)   (B)   (C)   (D)

5.

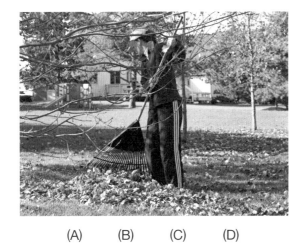

(A)   (B)   (C)   (D)

6.

(A)   (B)   (C)   (D)

▶ 答案與解析請參考解析本第9頁

PART 1

Directions: For each question in this part, you will hear four statements about a picture in your test book. When you hear the statements, you must select the one statement that best describes what you see in the picture. Then find the number of the question on your answer sheet and mark your answer. The statements will not be printed in your test book and will be spoken only one time.

1.

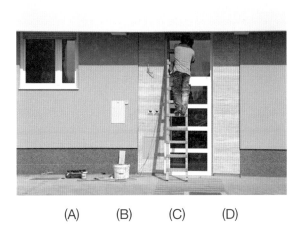

(A)   (B)   (C)   (D)

2.

(A)   (B)   (C)   (D)

3.

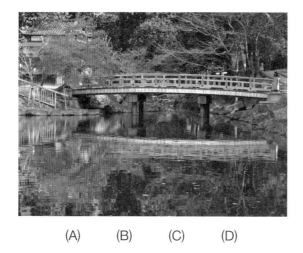

(A)   (B)   (C)   (D)

4.

(A)   (B)   (C)   (D)

5.

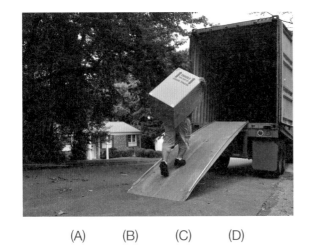

(A)   (B)   (C)   (D)

6.

(A)   (B)   (C)   (D)

▶ 答案與解析請參考解析本第10頁

PART
2

應答問題

第二大題要在聽完題目後，從三個選項中選出最合適的回答。
（共 25 題）

Voca Preview

請勾選不認識的單字，學習完類型分析後再重新確認勾選的單字。

- employment application
  工作申請書
- hiring committee 招聘委員會
- award 獎項
- candidate 候選人
- sponsor 贊助，贊助人
- shame 蒙羞，羞恥
- corporation 企業，公司
- headquarters 總公司
- be in charge of 負責～
- be responsible for 對～負責
- attend the meeting 出席會議
- inform 告知
- organize 籌備
- training session 培訓課程
- go to lunch 去吃午餐
- hold 舉辦
- leave the office 下班，離開辦公室
- volunteer activity 志工活動
- get together 相聚
- submit 提交
- reserve 預約

- employee 員工
- be supposed to
  預計～，應該要～
- merger 合併
- take place 發生，舉行
- architectural firm 建築公司
- get reimbursed
  報銷，拿回報帳金額
- travel expense 旅費
- approve 批准
- accountant 會計師
- respond to 回應～
- bill 帳單
- invoice 發票，發貨單
- form 形式，表格
- give the presentation 做簡報
- storage area 儲藏區
- bookshelf 書櫃
- usually 通常
- fix 使固定
- supervisor 上司

類型分析 **3**

疑問詞問句①

WARMING UP

🎧 13.mp3

診斷評估　聽完 mp3 後，請從 A、B 之中選出合適的回答。

1. Ⓐ (　) 　　　Ⓑ (　)　　　2. Ⓐ (　) 　　　Ⓑ (　)

3. Ⓐ (　) 　　　Ⓑ (　)　　　4. Ⓐ (　) 　　　Ⓑ (　)

填空　再聽一次 mp3 並填空。

1. ＿＿＿ ＿＿＿ ＿＿＿ ＿＿＿ your job at the museum?

   Ⓐ ＿＿＿ ＿＿＿ ＿＿＿.

   　　　　　　　　哪個是適合 When 問句的答覆？

   Ⓑ In customer service.

2. ＿＿＿ ＿＿＿ ＿＿＿ ＿＿＿ an employment application?

   Ⓐ Not much longer.

   　　　　　　　　哪個是適合 Where 問句的答覆？

   Ⓑ ＿＿＿ ＿＿＿ ＿＿＿ ＿＿＿.

3. ＿＿＿ is on the ＿＿＿ ＿＿＿ ＿＿＿.

   Ⓐ ＿＿＿ ＿＿＿, for now.

   Ⓑ Tuesday at 9.

   　　　　　　　　哪個是適合 Who 問句的答覆？

4. Who won the president's award?

   Ⓐ Yes, I heard that.

   Ⓑ ＿＿＿ ＿＿＿ Marketing.

確認解答&要點　確認正確答案，了解疑問詞問句的特徵。　🎧 13.mp3

1. When do you start your job at the museum?
您是何時開始在博物館工作的？

   Ⓐ　On April 11.　4月11日。　⭕

   Ⓑ　In customer service.　在客服部。　❌

以具體的日期或大概的時間點回覆 When 問句。
可以回覆on＋星期／日期、at＋時間、in＋期間。

2. Where can I get an employment application?
我可以在哪裡拿到工作申請書？

   Ⓐ　Not much longer.　不會很久。　❌

   Ⓑ　On the fourth floor.　四樓。　⭕

以 at / on / in ＋具體的場所回覆 Where 問句。

3. Who is on the new hiring committee?
誰在新的招聘委員會內？

   Ⓐ　I am, for now.　現在是我。　⭕

   Ⓑ　Tuesday at 9.　星期二九點。　❌

可以使用姓名、職位、部門或人稱代名詞回覆Who問句。

4. Who won the president's award?
誰獲得總裁獎？

   Ⓐ　Yes, I heard that.　對，我聽說過。　❌

   Ⓑ　Someone from Marketing.　行銷部的人。　⭕

在 Who 問句中聽到 someone from、someone in 的話，提及不特定人物的選項通常是正確答案。

Unit 05 Who問句

Step 1　實戰重點

Who問句通常會問行為或動作的主體，所以必須仔細聆聽答覆中主詞的部分。正確答案通常是包含人名、人稱代名詞、職位、部門或公司名稱的選項。

 代表題型 聽完音檔後請選出合適的正確答案。　🎧 14.mp3

1. (A)　　　(B)　　　(C)

2. (A)　　　(B)　　　(C)

 攻略解題法 了解該如何作答Who問句的題目。

Q1 **Who's interviewing** the job candidate?　誰會去面試求職者？

▶ 務必仔細聆聽以疑問詞為中心的前三、四個單字。這是Who問句，所以能聽到人稱代名詞的選項即為正確答案。

(A) In my office.　在我的辦公室。　✗

▶ 這是適合Where問句的回覆。

(B) I am planning to.　我正打算這麼做。　○

▶ 這是使用了I、we或you等人稱代名詞的正確答案。

(C) She can't do that.　她沒辦法做那個。　✗

▶ 無法具體地知道「她」是誰，所以是錯誤答案。Who問句的答覆中有第三人稱的一定是錯誤答案。

詞彙整理 **interview** 面試　**job candidate** 求職者

Q2 **Who's sponsoring** this event?　誰贊助這個活動？

▶ 務必仔細聆聽以疑問詞為中心的前三、四個單字。這是Who問句，所以能聽到某個人名或公司名稱的選項即有可能為正確答案。

(A) Near the restaurant.　在餐廳附近。　✗

▶ 這是適合Where問句的答覆。

(B) Yes, it's a shame.　對，很可惜。　✗

▶ 在疑問詞問句的答覆中，Yes、No選項是錯誤答案。

(C) The Choice Corporation is.　喬伊斯公司。　○

▶ 這是出現公司名稱的正確答案。

詞彙整理 **sponsor** 贊助　**event** 活動　**shame** 蒙羞，羞恥　**corporation** 企業，公司

攻略POINT 雖然Who問句的答覆中經常出現人名、職責、部門名稱或公司名稱等等，但有時候也會出現「我不清楚；我會確認看看；做～看看」的答覆。

· 包含疑問詞的前三、四個單字通常會決定出題意圖，所以要專心聆聽開頭部分，尤其是一定要聽到疑問詞。

· 出現人名、職責、部門或公司的句子是最常見的Who問句答覆。

· 表示不知道或反問的答覆99%（幾乎）都是正確答案。

 ## Who 問句的正確答案類型

回答人名、職責的類型

Who is visiting our headquarters today? 今天誰會拜訪我們的總公司？	● Mr. Adams. 亞當斯先生。
Who is in charge of the promotional campaign? 誰負責宣傳活動？	● The director of public relations. 公關主任。
Who is responsible for his schedule? 誰負責他的行程？	● The vice president's secretary. 副總裁的祕書。

回答人稱代名詞的類型

Who was the man I saw with Mr. Kim? 我看到的那個跟金先生在一起的男子是誰？	● He is our new supervisor. 他是我們的新上司。
Who will attend the meeting? 誰會出席會議？	● Everyone except Matilda. 每個人，除了瑪蒂達。
Who will help him to move the desk? 誰要幫他搬桌子？	● I can help him. 我可以幫他。

回答部門、公司或組織名稱的類型

Who will inform the staff about the new policy? 誰會通知員工新政策的事？	● The Human Resources Department. 人力資源部。
Who is repairing the air conditioner? 誰會來修理冷氣機？	● The Maintenance Department. 維修部。
Who is organizing this promotion? 誰會來籌備這個活動？	● The BNW Company. BNW 公司。

回答不知道或反問的類型

Who is going to the training session? 誰會參加培訓課程？	● I don't know. 我不知道。
Who should I talk to about the program? 我應該跟誰談這個計畫？	● Which program is it? 你是說哪個計畫？
Who is in the conference room now? 誰現在在會議室？	● You'd better ask your manager. 你最好問問你的經理。

🔊 15.mp3

1. (A)　　　(B)　　　(C)　　　　　　**2.** (A)　　　(B)　　　(C)

3. (A)　　　(B)　　　(C)　　　　　　**4.** (A)　　　(B)　　　(C)

▶ 答案與解析請參考解析本第12頁

Unit 06 When、Where問句

Step 1 實戰重點

When問句是詢問行為發生時間點的題目，所以出現時間副詞（子句）等特定時間的句子即為正確答案。Where問句是詢問行為發生地點的題目，所以出現特定場所的句子即為正確答案。

 代表題型 聽完音檔後請選出合適的正確答案。　　　　　　　　　　　 16.mp3

---

1. (A)　　　　(B)　　　　(C)

2. (A)　　　　(B)　　　　(C)

✏️ 攻略解題法 了解該如何作答When、Where問句的題目。

Q1 **When do employees usually go** to lunch?　員工通常在什麼時候去吃午餐？
▶ 務必仔細聆聽以疑問詞為中心的前三、四個單字。題目問的是一般吃午餐的時間點。

(A) Yes, I know her.　對，我認識她。　✗
▶ 在疑問詞問句的答覆中，Yes、No選項是錯誤答案。

(B) Around noon.　正中午左右。　○
▶ 這是提到「介系詞＋特定時間點／準確的時間／日期／星期」等的正確答案。

(C) They will leave at 10 o'clock.　他們會在十點離開。　✗
▶ 這是利用聯想單字（go - leave）誘導考生選為正確答案的錯誤答案。

詞彙整理 **usually** 通常 **leave** 離開，出發

Q2 **Where do you keep** the coffee?　你把咖啡放在哪裡？
▶ 仔細聆聽前面三、四個單字。題目問的是放置咖啡的地點。

(A) In my cabinet.　在我的櫃子裡。　○
▶ 這是提到「介系詞＋地點」的正確答案。

(B) Every day at 3.　每天三點。　✗
▶ 這是適合答覆When問句的錯誤答案。

(C) Thanks, but I asked him already.　謝謝，但是我已經問過他了。　✗
▶ 這是適合答覆勸說、建議問句的錯誤答案。

詞彙整理 **keep** 保管，維持 **cabinet** 櫃子，櫥櫃 **already** 已經，早就

攻略POINT 反問或是表示「我不知道」的答覆很有可能是包含When、Where問句在內的任何題目的正確答案。在近期的多益測驗中，Where問句的答案通常是某個來源或對象（人物、部門、公司或新聞）等。

- When問句的答覆中若出現「介系詞＋時間表達詞彙／時間名詞／時間副詞」等即是正確答案。
- Where問句的答覆中若出現地點副詞（片語）即是正確答案。
- 無論是什麼題目，反問或表示不知道的答覆都很有可能是正確答案。

 ### When 問句的正確答案類型

回答「介系詞＋時間名詞」的類型

When will the event be held? 活動將在何時舉行？	● On Sunday. 星期日。
When is your vacation? 你何時休假？	● In October. 十月。
When do you finish your work? 你何時會完成工作？	● Around 2 o'clock. 兩點左右。

回答時間名詞或時間副詞的類型

When will you leave the office? 你何時會離開辦公室？	● Later. 等一下。
When do you do a volunteer activity? 你何時做志工活動？	● Every month. 每個月。
When are you planning to visit her? 你打算何時拜訪她？	● Before dinner. 晚餐之前。

回答不知道或反問的類型

When can we get together for a meeting? 我們何時可以見面開會？	● How about on Monday? 星期一怎麼樣？
When can I submit the report? 我何時可以交報告？	● Can I see now? 我現在可以看嗎？
When are you going to leave for vacation? 你何時要去旅遊？	● I don't know yet. 我還不知道。

 ### Where 問句的正確答案類型

回答「介系詞＋地點名詞」的類型

Where can I find the department store? 我可以在哪裡找到百貨公司？	● Near the bank. 銀行附近。
Where is the bus station? 公車站在哪裡？	● In front of the park. 在公園前面。
Where is the museum? 博物館在哪裡？	● Beside the bookstore. 在書店旁邊。

Where will the meeting be held?
會議會在哪裡舉行？

● The register office will help you.
報到處會協助您。

Where is the book?
書在哪裡？

● Right here.
就在這裡。

回答來源或對象（人物、部門、公司、新聞）的類型

Where did you get this coupon?
你在哪裡得到這個折價券的？

● I got it from a magazine.
從雜誌上拿到的。

Where did you learn about it?
你從哪裡得知的？

● I asked Cindy.
我問過辛蒂。

Where can I buy it?
我可以在哪裡買到這個？

● I bought it at the department store.
我在百貨公司買的。

回答不知道或反問的類型

Where is the supermarket?
超市在哪裡？

● I am a stranger here.
我對這裡不熟。

Where should I submit this application?
我應該在哪裡繳交這份申請書？

● You should ask the manager.
你可以詢問經理。

Where do you plan to go this weekend?
這個週末你打算去哪裡？

● I have no idea yet.
我還不知道。

Step 3 實戰演練　　　　🎧 17.mp3

1. (A)　　　(B)　　　(C)

2. (A)　　　(B)　　　(C)

3. (A)　　　(B)　　　(C)

4. (A)　　　(B)　　　(C)

▶ 答案與解析請參考解析本第13頁

REVIEW TEST

一邊解題，一邊應用學到的內容。 18.mp3

1. Mark your answer on your answer sheet.

   (A)   (B)   (C)

2. Mark your answer on your answer sheet.

   (A)   (B)   (C)

3. Mark your answer on your answer sheet.

   (A)   (B)   (C)

4. Mark your answer on your answer sheet.

   (A)   (B)   (C)

5. Mark your answer on your answer sheet.

   (A)   (B)   (C)

6. Mark your answer on your answer sheet.

   (A)   (B)   (C)

7. Mark your answer on your answer sheet.

   (A)   (B)   (C)

8. Mark your answer on your answer sheet.

   (A)   (B)   (C)

9. Mark your answer on your answer sheet.

   (A)   (B)   (C)

10. Mark your answer on your answer sheet.

   (A)   (B)   (C)

▶ 答案與解析請參考解析本第14頁

聽寫訓練

1. Who is _____ new secretary?

(A) Betty Rodman.

(B) _____ an email.

(C) _____ table.

2. _____ coming to the _____ tomorrow?

(A) In the _____.

(B) The _____ team.

(C) Yes, 2 _____.

3. Who _____ the _____?

(A) The _____.

(B) No, she _____.

(C) In _____.

4. Who _____ I call to _____ room?

(A) It's in the _____.

(B) _____ to do it.

(C) For _____.

Unit 06 **When、Where問句** | **Step 3** 實戰演練   🎧 **dictation-08.mp3**

1. _____ the _____?

   (A) A _____.

   (B) On _____.

   (C) Five _____.

2. Where _____ I _____ _____ package?

   (A) By _____ mail.

   (B) After _____ P.M.

   (C) To the _____.

3. When _____ Mr. Erickson _____ _____ arrive?

   (A) _____ the park.

   (B) Yes, she _____.

   (C) At one o'clock.

4. Where should I _____ _____ report?

   (A) _____ before you _____.

   (B) On the _____.

   (C) I _____ _____ him.

聽寫訓練

1. _____ _____ the merger _____ _____?

    (A) _____ _____.

    (B) _____ in November.

    (C) _____, _____ _____.

2. _____ _____ the new office building?

    (A) The Merch _____ _____.

    (B) In the _____ _____.

    (C) _____ _____ _____.

3. _____ _____ Nelson _____ the agenda?

    (A) By _____ _____.

    (B) _____ _____ _____.

    (C) From Chicago.

4. Who will _____ _____ _____?

    (A) _____ _____ _____ _____.

    (B) Ms. Miranda.

    (C) In December.

5. _____ did you _____ _____?

    (A) A _____.

    (B) Isn't it _____ _____ _____?

    (C) I will _____ _____.

6. When do we _____ for travel expenses?

    (A) _____.

    (B) _____ are _____.

    (C) After the _____.

7. Who's _____?

    (A) We only _____.

    (B) Mr. Park is.

    (C) It's _____.

8. _____ should I _____?

    (A) He isn't.

    (B) _____.

    (C) Ask the _____.

9. _____ this department?

    (A) Julie is.

    (B) _____ is too _____.

    (C) _____ to it.

10. _____ does the _____ the project?

    (A) _____.

    (B) _____.

    (C) On August 30.

Voca Preview

請勾選不認識的單字，學習完類型分析後再重新確認勾選的單字。

- [ ] **edit** 編輯
- [ ] **medical conference** 醫學會議
- [ ] **delay** 延期
- [ ] **chef** 廚師
- [ ] **parking fee** 停車費
- [ ] **prefer** 偏好～
- [ ] **leave a message** 留言
- [ ] **housewarming** 喬遷宴
- [ ] **happen** 發生
- [ ] **lose** 遺失
- [ ] **in front of** 在～前面
- [ ] **turn left** 左轉
- [ ] **go straight** 直走
- [ ] **open position** 職缺，空位
- [ ] **work for** 在～工作
- [ ] **one-way ticket** 單程票
- [ ] **hold a meeting** 開會
- [ ] **deliver** 傳達
- [ ] **reach** 聯絡
- [ ] **exhibition** 展覽會

- [ ] **job opening** 職缺
- [ ] **traffic jam** 交通堵塞
- [ ] **in order to** 為了～
- [ ] **take a break** 休息
- [ ] **registration fee** 報名費
- [ ] **job interview** 工作面試
- [ ] **half an hour** 半小時
- [ ] **mailbox** 信箱
- [ ] **remodel** 改建
- [ ] **experience** 經驗
- [ ] **furniture** 家具
- [ ] **reschedule** 重新調整日程
- [ ] **a variety of** 各式各樣的
- [ ] **heater** 加熱器，暖氣機
- [ ] **decisive** 決定性的
- [ ] **advantage** 優點
- [ ] **expire** 滿期
- [ ] **receive** 收到
- [ ] **on the right** 在右邊
- [ ] **leave early** 早點出發

類型分析 4

疑問詞問句②

WARMING UP

WARMING UP

🎧 19.mp3

診斷評估　聽完 mp3 後，請從 A、B 之中選出合適的回答。

1. Ⓐ (　　)　　Ⓑ (　　)　　2. Ⓐ (　　)　　Ⓑ (　　)

3. Ⓐ (　　)　　Ⓑ (　　)　　4. Ⓐ (　　)　　Ⓑ (　　)

填空　再聽一次 mp3 並填空。

1. Which brochure still has to be edited?

   Ⓐ ＿＿＿＿＿ ＿＿＿＿＿ for the medical conference.

   Ⓑ That would be great.

   哪個是適合 Which 問句的答覆？

2. Why was your flight delayed?

   Ⓐ ＿＿＿＿＿＿ ＿＿＿＿＿ the weather.

   Ⓑ Ten minutes ago.

   哪個是適合 Why 問句的答覆？

3. What time does the museum open?

   Ⓐ On Elm Avenue.

   Ⓑ Actually, it's ＿＿＿＿＿＿ ＿＿＿＿ ＿＿＿＿＿＿.

   哪個是適合 What time 問句的答覆？

4. How long have you worked as a chef?

   Ⓐ In the kitchen.

   Ⓑ For ＿＿＿＿＿ ＿＿＿＿＿.

   哪個是適合 How long 問句的答覆？

確認解答＆要點　確認正確答案，了解疑問詞問句的特徵。

1. Which brochure still has to be edited?
   哪本小冊子還需要編輯？

   Ⓐ The one for the medical conference.
   那本醫學會議的。　〇

   Ⓑ That would be great.　那好像很棒。　✗

   > 回答「Which ＋名詞」問句時，選擇其中一個名詞或包含 The one 的回覆來回答。

2. Why was your flight delayed?
   你的班機為什麼延誤了？

   Ⓐ Because of the weather.　因為天氣的緣故。　〇

   Ⓑ Ten minutes ago.　十分鐘前。　✗

   > 以表示理由的介系詞（because of）、表示理由的連接詞（because、to 不定詞、in order to 不定詞）回覆 Why 問句。

3. What time does the museum open?
   博物館幾點開門？

   Ⓐ On Elm Avenue.　在艾姆大道上。　✗

   Ⓑ Actually, it's closed on Mondays.
   事實上，星期一沒開。　〇

   > 將 What time 問句理解成 When 問句，並回覆時間或時間點。

4. How long have you worked as a chef?
   你當廚師多久了？

   Ⓐ In the kitchen.　在廚房。　✗

   Ⓑ For two years.　兩年。　〇

   > 以「for ＋期間」或所需的時間回覆 How long 問句。

Unit 07 What、Which問句

Step 1 實戰重點

What問句的答案取決於What後面的動詞或名詞，所以要練習準確地聽到動詞。Which問句經常以「Which＋名詞」的選擇疑問句出現，選擇Which後面出現過的名詞，並具體說明的選項即為正確答案，所以要仔細聽Which後面的名詞。

 代表題型 聽完音檔後請選出合適的正確答案。　🎧 20.mp3

1. (A)　　　(B)　　　(C)

2. (A)　　　(B)　　　(C)

✏️ **攻略解題法**　了解該如何作答What、Which問句。

Q1　**What** will the **parking fee be**?　停車費多少？
▶ 回答What問句時，須準確地聽到What後面的名詞和動詞。

(A) He is six feet two inches tall.　他的身高是六呎兩吋。　✗
▶ 聽到發音類似的單字（fee－feet）的選項為錯誤答案。

(B) No, she can still drive.　不，她仍可以開車。　✗
▶ 以Yes／No回覆疑問詞問句的選項為錯誤答案。

(C) Twenty dollars a day.　一天二十美元。　⭕
▶ 以金額回覆停車費是多少的正確答案。

詞彙整理 **parking fee** 停車費　**tall** 高的，身高高的　**still** 仍然，還

Q2　**Which color** do you prefer to paint the new house?　你偏好用哪種顏色油漆新房子？
▶ 是「Which＋名詞」結構的題目，所以要準確地聽到Which後面的名詞（color）再選出提及此物的答覆。

(A) The caller left a message.　來電者留言了。　✗
▶ 聽到發音類似的單字（color－caller）的選項為錯誤答案。

(B) Yellow looks good.　黃色看起來很好。　⭕
▶ 提及顏色的正確答案。

(C) It is not the one that I like.　這不是我喜歡的那個。　✗
▶ 利用相關詞彙（prefer－like）造成混淆的錯誤答案。

詞彙整理 **prefer** 偏愛～，偏好～　**paint** 油漆　**leave a message** 留言

攻略POINT What問句中的「What would you like~」句型是有禮貌地詢問對方想要什麼的表達方式。例如：
What would you like for lunch?（午餐想吃什麼？）

· 回答What問句時，What後面出現的名詞或動詞是關鍵線索。

· 回答「Which＋名詞」問句時，要仔細聽Which後面的名詞。選擇具體敘述的名詞並補充說明的選項為正確答案。

· 回答「Which＋名詞」問句時，出現The one的選項99%為正確答案。

 What、Which問句的正確答案類型

What 後面的名詞決定答案的類型

What color did you paint your restaurant? 你用什麼顏色油漆你的餐廳？	● I chose white. 我選了白色。
What time does the meeting start? 會議幾點開始？	● At 10 o'clock. 十點。
What type of business are you in? 您從事什麼行業？	● I work at a design company. 我在設計公司上班。

What 後面的動詞決定答案的類型

What will we **bring to** the seminar? 我們要帶什麼去研討會？	● Some documents. 一些文件。
What did Tommy give you as a housewarming gift? 湯米給你什麼當喬遷宴禮物？	● He gave me a flowerpot. 他給了我一個花盆。
What happened to you yesterday? 你昨天發生什麼事了？	● I lost my bag. 我弄丟了包包。

Which 後面的名詞決定答案的類型

Which car do you want? 你想要哪一台車？	● I want the compact one. 我想要小型汽車。
Which department does she work in? 她在哪個部門工作？	● She works in the Sales Department. 她在銷售部門工作。
Which employee will be going to the meeting tomorrow? 哪個員工會去明天的會議？	● Sally will go. 莎莉會去。

「Which ＋名詞」的問題中，出現 (the) one 的一定會是正解。

Which hotel are you staying at? 你住在哪間飯店？	● **The one** in front of the sea. 海岸前面那間。
Which office has a problem with its photocopier? 哪間辦公室的影印機有問題？	● **The one** next to the restroom. 洗手間旁邊那間。

---

1. (A)　　　(B)　　　(C)　　　　　**2.** (A)　　　(B)　　　(C)

3. (A)　　　(B)　　　(C)　　　　　**4.** (A)　　　(B)　　　(C)

▶ 答案與解析請參考解析本第17頁

How、Why問句

How問句的答案取決於How後面的形容詞、副詞,所以要仔細聆聽形容詞和副詞。在Why問句的答覆中,表示理由或目的的片語和子句為正確答案。出現表示理由的連接詞(because)、表示理由的介系詞(because of、due to、in order to)、to不定詞句子的話,即為正確答案。

 代表題型 聽完音檔後請選出合適的正確答案。　　🎧 22.mp3

1. (A)　　　(B)　　　(C)

2. (A)　　　(B)　　　(C)

 攻略解題法 了解該如何作答How、Why問句的題目。

Q1 **How long** did your job interview take? 你面試了多久?
▶ How後面的形容詞決定了答案。作答How long題目時,表示期間和所需時間的選項為正確答案。

(A) An open position. 一個職缺。 ✗
▶ 提及相關詞彙(job – position)的選項大部分都是錯誤答案。

(B) A new employee. 一個新員工。 ✗
▶ 提及相關詞彙(job interview – employee)的選項大部分都是錯誤答案。

(C) Only half an hour. 只有半小時。 ○
▶ 這是提及所需時間的正確答案。

詞彙整理 **job interview** 工作面試 **take** 花費~

Q2 **Why is the office closed** today? 辦公室為什麼今天關門?
▶ 這是詢問理由的題目,所以要仔細聽包含表示理由的介系詞或to不定詞的句子。

(A) It's close to the park. 離公園很近。 ✗
▶ 聽到發音類似的單字(closed – close)的選項為錯誤答案。

(B) Because it's a holiday. 因為今天是假日。 ○
▶ 這是提及because的正確答案。

(C) Turn left and then go straight. 左轉,然後直走。 ✗
▶ 這是適合答覆How問句的錯誤答案。

詞彙整理 **turn** 旋轉,使轉動 **go straight** 直走

攻略POINT 「How about~」結構的勸誘或建議句也會用到How問句,這種時候表示答應、拒絕或回覆That's good.即可。除了Why問句以外,「For what~?、How come~?、What's the reason for~?」等也是詢問理由的問句。

· How問句的答案取決於How後面出現的形容詞或副詞。

· 回答Why問句時，出現表示理由的連接詞、介系詞或to不定詞的選項很有可能是正確答案。

 How問句的正確答案類型

How 後面的形容詞或副詞決定答案的類型

How long have you worked for this company?
你在這間公司工作多久了？

● About three years.
　大概三年。

How far is the bus station from here?
公車站離這裡多遠？

● Only five minutes away on foot.
　走路只要五分鐘。

How much furniture do you need to move?
你需要搬多少家具？

● Everything in the office.
　辦公室裡的所有家具。

How much is it for a one-way ticket?
單程票多少錢？

● It's $30.
　三十美元。

How often does your department hold meetings?
你的部門多常開會？

● Once a week.
　一週一次。

How soon will you be able to deliver it?
你多快可以寄送這個？

● Before next week.
　下週之前。

回答手段或方法的類型（使用 by、through 的答覆）

How can I get to the airport from here?
我該怎麼從這裡到機場？

● By taxi.
　坐計程車。

How can I reach him? 我該怎麼聯絡他？

● Through email. 透過電子郵件。

回答命令句的類型

How do I get the information?
我該怎麼獲得資訊？

● Just call the information center.
　打電話給諮詢服務中心。

How can I turn on this computer?
我該怎麼打開電腦？

● Press the red button.
　按紅色按鈕。

回答勸誘、建議句的類型

How about this table for my new house?
在我的新家用這張桌子怎麼樣？

● Why don't you look at the other design? 你不看看其他設計嗎？

How would you like your steak?
您要幾分熟的牛排？

● Well-done, please.
　全熟，謝謝。

回答來源的類型

How did you know about the exhibition?
您怎麼知道這個展覽會的？

● I saw an ad for it on TV.
　我在電視上看到廣告。

How did you hear about the job opening?
您怎麼知道這個職缺的？

● I read about in on a website.
　我在網站上看到的。

回答進行狀況的類型（提及說明狀態的形容詞或副詞的選項）	
How did your training session go? 你的培訓課程上得怎樣？	● It was as smooth as I had expected. 跟我預期中的一樣順利。
How did your project go? 你的案子進行得怎樣？	● I can finish it next week. 我可以在下週完成。

 ## Why問句的正確答案類型

以表示理由的連接詞或目的作為回答的類型	
Why were you late? 你為什麼遲到了？	● Because of a traffic jam. 因為交通堵塞。
Why was Mr. Parker here? 帕克先生為什麼在這裡？	● Due to a special seminar. 因為一場特別的研討會。
Why are all of the employees out of the office? 為什麼所有員工都在辦公室外面？	● To remove the old furniture. 為了搬走老舊的家具。
Why did you leave the office early? 你為什麼提早離開辦公室？	● In order to attend a meeting. 為了出席會議。

以藉口或否定的表達方式作為回答的類型	
Why didn't you call me yesterday? 你昨天為什麼沒有打給我？	● I was too busy with my project. 我忙著做案子。
Why isn't he in the office? 他為什麼不在辦公室裡？	● He is taking a short break now. 他現在暫時休息中。

以答應或拒絕作為回答的類型	
Why don't you ask the manager? 你怎麼不問經理？	● That's a good idea. 好主意。
Why don't you take a break? 你怎麼不休息？	● I have to finish this work by today. 我必須在今天完成這個工作。

Step 3　　實戰演練　　🎧 23.mp3

1. (A)　　(B)　　(C)

2. (A)　　(B)　　(C)

3. (A)　　(B)　　(C)

4. (A)　　(B)　　(C)

▶ 答案與解析請參考解析本第18頁

REVIEW TEST

一邊解題，一邊應用學到的內容。 24.mp3

1. Mark your answer on your answer sheet.

   (A)   (B)   (C)

2. Mark your answer on your answer sheet.

   (A)   (B)   (C)

3. Mark your answer on your answer sheet.

   (A)   (B)   (C)

4. Mark your answer on your answer sheet.

   (A)   (B)   (C)

5. Mark your answer on your answer sheet.

   (A)   (B)   (C)

6. Mark your answer on your answer sheet.

   (A)   (B)   (C)

7. Mark your answer on your answer sheet.

   (A)   (B)   (C)

8. Mark your answer on your answer sheet.

   (A)   (B)   (C)

9. Mark your answer on your answer sheet.

   (A)   (B)   (C)

10. Mark your answer on your answer sheet.

   (A)   (B)   (C)

▶ 答案與解析請參考解析本第18頁

聽寫訓練

1. What's the _____ _____?

    (A) It's _____ _____ from today.

    (B) One _____ _____ staff members _____ it.

    (C) On the _____ _____ Bull Street.

2. Which _____ should I _____?

    (A) Only _____ copies.

    (B) The _____ has _____.

    (C) The one _____ _____ the door.

3. What's the _____ _____?

    (A) By _____ Monday.

    (B) Cash will _____ _____.

    (C) It's _____.

4. What are the _____ in the _____ _____?

    (A) In the _____ _____ beside the _____.

    (B) A _____ I'm _____.

    (C) I will _____ _____ later.

| Unit 08 How、Why問句 | Step 3 實戰演練 | 🎧 dictation-11.mp3 |

1. How long _____ _____ _____ us to _____ downtown?

   (A) I'm _____ town.

   (B) It _____ _____ seven P.M.

   (C) About _____ _____ .

2. Why is there _____ _____ ?

   (A) The computer system _____ .

   (B) I _____ _____ today.

   (C) Yes, I guess so.

3. How can I _____ _____ Bruce _____ form?

   (A) I will _____ it.

   (B) _____ _____ his mailbox.

   (C) He _____ New York now.

4. Why is the J&J _____ ?

   (A) Because _____ .

   (B) The restaurant _____ .

   (C) The new _____ .

聽寫訓練

1. _____ _____ _____ _____ do you have _____ _____?
   (A) _____ _____ _____ for five years.
   (B) The sale will _____ _____ _____.
   (C) It will _____ _____ _____.

2. _____ was the _____ _____?
   (A) On Tuesday.
   (B) _____ _____ _____.
   (C) _____ the manager _____ _____ _____.

3. _____ _____ _____ _____?
   (A) _____ _____ _____.
   (B) Yes, it was him.
   (C) It's Monica Ben.

4. _____ _____ has the _____ _____?
   (A) From _____ _____ _____.
   (B) French Coffee House.
   (C) _____ _____ _____.

5. _____ _____ _____ _____ the front desk?
   (A) It's _____ _____ _____.
   (B) _____ _____ _____.
   (C) Yes, it's _____ _____ _____.

6. _____ Mr. Roy _____ you can _____

_____ tomorrow?

(A) _____ .

(B) No, it isn't.

(C) Yes, _____ .

7. _____ the heater?

(A) I sent him yesterday.

(B) The _____ .

(C) No, _____ .

8. _____ to Moil Village?

(A) Yes, very _____ .

(B) _____ to my office.

(C) _____ .

9. _____ of using a _____ ?

(A) Yes, _____ .

(B) You can _____ .

(C) You have to _____ .

10. _____ the computer screen?

(A) If you want to come.

(B) _____ .

(C) _____ .

Voca Preview

請勾選不認識的單字，學習完類型分析後再重新確認勾選的單字。

- ☐ **finish** 結束，完成
- ☐ **online** 線上
- ☐ **put ~ in order** 擺放整齊
- ☐ **fix** 修理
- ☐ **fax machine** 傳真機
- ☐ **table for four** 四人桌
- ☐ **certainly** 當然
- ☐ **attend** 出席
- ☐ **annual party** 週年派對
- ☐ **perfect** 完美的
- ☐ **instead of** 代替～
- ☐ **submit** 繳交
- ☐ **by today** 到今天為止
- ☐ **quit** 放棄
- ☐ **have a chance** 有機會
- ☐ **check on** 確認～
- ☐ **actually** 事實上
- ☐ **succeed** 成功
- ☐ **arrange** 安排，準備
- ☐ **promotion** 升遷

- ☐ **be free** 空閒的，有時間的
- ☐ **whether ~ or not ~** 是否～
- ☐ **financial report** 財務報告
- ☐ **rent** 出租
- ☐ **sign the contract** 簽約
- ☐ **article** 文章
- ☐ **weather** 天氣
- ☐ **probably** 大概
- ☐ **hire** 聘僱
- ☐ **book** 預約
- ☐ **storage space** 儲藏空間
- ☐ **wardrobe** 衣櫥
- ☐ **full-time** 正職的
- ☐ **general manager** 總經理
- ☐ **have an appointment** 有約
- ☐ **appoint** 任命
- ☐ **in advance** 事先
- ☐ **receipt** 收據
- ☐ **make an order** 訂購
- ☐ **directory** 電話簿，名錄

類型分析 **5**

一般問句＆選擇疑問句

WARMING UP

診斷評估　聽完 mp3 後，請從 A、B 之中選出合適的回答。　🎧 25.mp3

1. Ⓐ (　　)　　Ⓑ (　　)　　2. Ⓐ (　　)　　Ⓑ (　　)

3. Ⓐ (　　)　　Ⓑ (　　)　　4. Ⓐ (　　)　　Ⓑ (　　)

填空　再聽一次 mp3 並填空。

1. Have you finished the financial report?

   Ⓐ He reports to Mr. Jones.

   Ⓑ ...., not yet.

   哪個是適合一般問句的答覆？

2. Did you receive the memo?

   Ⓐ Ms. Henderson.

   Ⓑ ...., I read it yesterday.

3. Would you like some coffee or tea?

   Ⓐ Yes, I do.

   Ⓑ .... would be great.

   哪個是適合建議或選擇疑問句的答覆？

4. Should I buy tickets at the theater or order them online?

   Ⓐ Yes, please put them in order.

   Ⓑ .... are okay.

確認解答＆要點　確認正確答案，了解一般問句和選擇疑問句的特徵。　🎧 25.mp3

1. Have you finished the financial report?
你完成財務報告了嗎？

　Ⓐ He reports to Mr. Jones.　他跟瓊斯先生報告。　✗

　Ⓑ No, not yet.　不，還沒。　◯

以 Yes 或 No 回覆一般問句。

2. Did you receive the memo?
你收到備忘錄了嗎？

　Ⓐ Ms. Henderson.　漢德森女士。　✗

　Ⓑ Yes, I read it yesterday.　嗯，我昨天看過了。　◯

以 Yes 或 No 回覆一般問句再補充說明。

3. Would you like some coffee or tea?
您要喝咖啡或茶嗎？

　Ⓐ Yes, I do.　對，我會。　✗

　Ⓑ Coffee would be great.　咖啡好了。　◯

回答建議或選擇疑問句時，選擇兩者其中之一。

4. Should I buy tickets at the theater or order them online?
我應該在電影院還是線上買票？

　Ⓐ Yes, please put them in order.　是的，請依序擺放。　✗

　Ⓑ Both are okay.　兩者都可以。　◯

可以用 either、neither 或 both 回覆建議或選擇疑問句。

Unit 09 一般問句

 Step 1 | **實戰重點**

回答一般問句時，應注意提問者和答覆者的主詞或動詞時態是否一致。可以使用Yes或No答覆，選項如果出現跟題目中的單字發音相似的詞彙，大部分都是錯誤答案。

🎓 **代表題型** 聽完音檔後請選出合適的正確答案。　　　　🎧 26.mp3

> **1.** (A)　　　(B)　　　(C)
>
> **2.** (A)　　　(B)　　　(C)

 攻略解題法 了解該如何作答一般問句的題目。

Q1 **Has the air conditioner been fixed** yet?　冷氣機修好了嗎？
  ▶ 須仔細聆聽一般問句的主詞和動詞時態。這題以現在完成式詢問冷氣機是否修好了。
  (A) No, but someone's coming tomorrow.　不，但是明天會有人來。　○
  ▶ 回覆No後，補充說明之後會修理，所以是正確答案。
  (B) They already fixed the computer.　他們已經修好電腦了。　✗
  ▶ 聽到相同單字（fixed）的選項大部分都是錯誤答案。
  (C) The fax machine is on the desk.　傳真機在桌子上。　✗
  ▶ 聽到發音類似的單字（fixed – fax）的選項大部分都是錯誤答案。

  詞彙整理 **fix** 修理，修繕　**yet** 還（沒）　**already** 已經

Q2 **Do you have a table** for four?　有四個人能坐的桌位嗎？
  ▶ 須仔細聆聽一般問句的主詞和動詞時態。這題問的是現在是否有座位。
  (A) Yes, certainly.　有，當然。　○
  ▶ 給予正面回覆的正確答案。
  (B) On a label.　在標籤上。　✗
  ▶ 聽到發音類似的單字（table– label）的選項大部分都是錯誤答案。
  (C) So do I.　我也是。　✗
  ▶ 這是同意對方的意見的答覆，所以是錯誤答案。

  詞彙整理 **certainly** 當然，沒問題　**label** 標籤

攻略POINT 有時候回覆一般問句時也會省略Yes或No。出現I think~（我認為）、I believe~（我認為）、I suppose~（我想）、I hope~（我希望）、Actually（實際上）或Certainly（當然）等表達方式的選項大部分都是正確答案。

· 提問者和答覆者的主詞必須一致。

· 須確認題目和選項的動詞時態是否一致。

· 如果選項出現發音類似的單字，大部分都是錯誤答案。

 一般問句的正確答案類型

回答 Yes 或 No 後補充說明的類型

Did you attend the meeting?
你有出席會議嗎？

Have you seen Nancy today?
你今天有看到南希嗎？

Should I open the door?
我可以開門嗎？

Are you planning to go to the annual party?
你打算去週年派對嗎？

- Yes, I did.
  是的，我有出席。

- Yes, she just left the office.
  有，她剛離開辦公室。

- No, it's raining outside.
  不行，外面正在下雨。

- No, I haven't finished my project yet.
  不，我還沒完成我的案子。

省略 Yes 或 No，只有補充說明的類型

Didn't you work at another company before?
你之前不曾在其他公司上班過嗎？

Have you heard about the new office?
你聽說新辦公室的事了嗎？

Don't you have the program on your computer?
你的電腦沒有這個程式嗎？

Didn't she ask you about the meeting?
她沒有問你會議的事嗎？

- This is my first job.
  這是我的第一份工作。

- It must be perfect.
  那一定很棒。

- I don't have it.
  我沒有。

- I haven't even met her.
  我甚至還沒見到她。

回答勸誘、建議或請求疑問句的類型

Would you please call the manager?
你可以打電話給經理嗎？

Can you attend the meeting instead of me?
你可以代替我出席會議嗎？

- Of course.
  沒問題。

- Sure, I would be happy to help you.
  當然，我很開心能幫到你。

表示「是的／不是那樣子的」的類型

Do we have to submit this report by today?
我們需要在今天之前交報告嗎？

She is the new manager of our department, right?
她是我們部門的新經理，對吧？

Will Ms. Park quit her job?
帕克女士會辭職嗎？

- I think so.
  我想是吧。

- That's what I believe.
  我是這麼認為的。

- Not that I know of.
  據我所知不會。

Have you ever visited our headquarters?
你拜訪過我們的總公司嗎？

Is Mr. Rey still in the meeting now?
雷伊先生還在開會嗎？

- I haven't had a chance yet.
  我還沒有機會去過。

- Let me check on that for you.
  我幫你確認看看。

回答 Actually、Certainly 的類型

Is he the best employee at our company?
他是我們公司最棒的員工嗎？

Do you think our project will succeed?
你覺得我們的案子會成功嗎？

- Actually, he will leave the company soon.
  事實上，他很快就要離開我們公司了。

- Certainly.
  當然會。

Step 3 | **實戰演練**　🎧 27.mp3

1. (A)　　(B)　　(C)

2. (A)　　(B)　　(C)

3. (A)　　(B)　　(C)

4. (A)　　(B)　　(C)

▶ 答案與解析請參考解析本第21頁

Unit 10 選擇疑問句

選擇疑問句為二選一的題目，所以以回覆Yes或No的選項都是錯誤答案。回答「選擇兩者其中之一」、「兩個都喜歡或討厭」，或是「兩者皆可」的選項為正確答案。

🎓 **代表題型** 聽完音檔後請選出合適的正確答案。 🎧 28.mp3

```
1. (A)        (B)        (C)
2. (A)        (B)        (C)
```

✏️ **攻略解題法** 了解該如何作答選擇疑問句的題目

Q1 Is it faster to go to the airport **by bus or by train**?
搭公車還是火車去機場比較快？

▶ 是選擇疑問句，所以要專心聆聽「or」前後的內容。

(A) Probably by train.　應該是搭火車。　〇

▶ 這個選項選擇了兩種交通方式之中的一種，所以是正確答案。

(B) No, I have no idea.　不，我不知道。　✕

▶ 回答選擇疑問句時，No選項為錯誤答案。

(C) Yes, I think so.　對，我也這樣想。　✕

▶ 回答選擇疑問句時，Yes選項為錯誤答案。

詞彙整理　**probably** 大概　**fast** 快速的　**airport** 機場

Q2 Should we arrange **a lunch or a dinner** for our annual party?
我們應該為週年派對準備午宴或晚宴嗎？

▶ 這是選擇疑問句，所以要專心聆聽「or」前後的內容。

(A) Dinner would be better.　晚宴比較好。　〇

▶ 這個選項選擇了其中一種宴會，所以是正確答案。

(B) All the employees will come.　所有員工都會來。　✕

▶ 這是跟題目的選擇無關的錯誤答案。出現單字all的選項很有可能是錯誤答案。

(C) Yes, I will be there.　是的，我會在那裡。　✕

▶ 回答選擇疑問句時，Yes選項為錯誤答案。

詞彙整理　**arrange** 安排，籌備　**annual party** 週年派對

攻略POINT　在近期的多益測驗中以The one回覆選擇疑問句的情況大增，所以回答選擇疑問句時聽到The one的話，可以先選它當正確答案。雖然選擇疑問句原則上無法以Yes或No回覆，但是勸誘句可以。例如：Would you care for some coffee or tea？（您要喝點咖啡或茶嗎？）→Yes, please.（好，麻煩你。）

· 回答選擇疑問句時，回覆Yes或No的選項為錯誤答案。（勸誘句除外）

· 在A or B之中選擇一個的選項為正確答案。　· A、B兩者都喜歡或討厭的選項為正確答案。

· 對A、B都沒興趣的選項為正確答案。

 選擇疑問句的正確答案類型

回答二者其中之一的類型

Which do you prefer, black or white?
你比較喜歡黑色還是白色？

Did you meet the president or his secretary?
你遇到總裁或他的祕書了嗎？

Should we meet or talk on the phone?
我們要見面還是透過電話談？

● Black will be good.
黑色不錯。

● I met his secretary.
我遇到他的祕書了。

● Let's meet up tomorrow.
我們明天見面吧。

回答兩者都喜歡或討厭的類型

Do you prefer the bigger or smaller furniture?
你偏好大型還是小型家具？

Which would you prefer, coffee or tea?
你比較喜歡咖啡還是茶？

Where would be better to have the promotion, at the restaurant or at the department store?
在餐廳還是百貨公司宣傳比較好？

● Either one will be fine.
任何一種都好。

● Neither, thanks.
都不喜歡，謝謝。

● It doesn't matter.
都沒差。

回答第三種建議的類型

Do you want me to send you an email today or tomorrow?
你想要我今天還是明天寄電子郵件給你？

Can I see Dr. Kim tomorrow or later this week?
我明天或這週稍晚可以見金博士嗎？

● I want you to send it now.
我希望你現在寄出。

● He is free on Friday.
他週五有空。

回答不知道或反問的類型

Is Angela going to the training session today or tomorrow?
安潔拉是今天還是明天要去上培訓課程？

Do you know whether our company will move to the new building or not?
你知道我們公司會不會搬去新大樓嗎？

Which do you prefer, the traveling or hiking club?
你比較喜歡旅遊俱樂部還是健行俱樂部？

● She hasn't told me.
她沒跟我說。

● I'm not sure.
我不清楚。

● Which one is better?
哪個比較好？

Step 3　實戰演練　🎧 29.mp3

1. (A)　　(B)　　(C)　　　**2.** (A)　　(B)　　(C)

3. (A)　　(B)　　(C)　　　**4.** (A)　　(B)　　(C)

▶ 答案與解析請參考解析本第22頁

1. Mark your answer on your answer sheet.

   (A)　　　　　(B)　　　　　(C)

2. Mark your answer on your answer sheet.

   (A)　　　　　(B)　　　　　(C)

3. Mark your answer on your answer sheet.

   (A)　　　　　(B)　　　　　(C)

4. Mark your answer on your answer sheet.

   (A)　　　　　(B)　　　　　(C)

5. Mark your answer on your answer sheet.

   (A)　　　　　(B)　　　　　(C)

6. Mark your answer on your answer sheet.

   (A)　　　　　(B)　　　　　(C)

7. Mark your answer on your answer sheet.

   (A)　　　　　(B)　　　　　(C)

8. Mark your answer on your answer sheet.

   (A)　　　　　(B)　　　　　(C)

9. Mark your answer on your answer sheet.

   (A)　　　　　(B)　　　　　(C)

10. Mark your answer on your answer sheet.

   (A)　　　　　(B)　　　　　(C)

▶ 答案與解析請參考解析本第23頁

聽寫訓練

1. Have ＿＿＿＿＿＿＿＿＿＿＿＿＿＿ apartment to rent?

   (A) Yes, I ＿＿＿＿ have to ＿＿＿＿ the ＿＿＿＿.

   (B) It's in the ＿＿＿＿ ＿＿＿＿.

   (C) He ＿＿＿＿＿＿＿＿ yesterday.

2. ＿＿＿＿ Paul ＿＿＿＿＿＿＿＿ the train station?

   (A) No, ＿＿＿＿＿＿＿＿ raining.

   (B) ＿＿＿＿ the ＿＿＿＿＿＿＿＿.

   (C) He was ＿＿＿＿ to go.

3. ＿＿＿＿ Mr. Smith ＿＿＿＿ the papers ＿＿＿＿＿＿＿＿ yesterday?

   (A) Anywhere ＿＿＿＿ here.

   (B) From a ＿＿＿＿＿＿＿＿.

   (C) Yes, they're ＿＿＿＿＿＿＿＿.

4. Will ＿＿＿＿＿＿＿＿＿＿＿＿ nice today?

   (A) I ＿＿＿＿＿＿＿＿.

   (B) ＿＿＿＿ you can.

   (C) I'm sorry.

Unit 10 選擇疑問句 ┊ **Step 3 實戰演練** @ dictation-14.mp3

1. Do you ＿＿＿＿＿ ＿＿＿＿＿ home ＿＿＿＿＿ ＿＿＿＿＿ address?

   (A) Yes, I will ＿＿＿＿＿ ＿＿＿＿＿.

   (B) He ＿＿＿＿＿ ＿＿＿＿＿ ＿＿＿＿＿ office soon.

   (C) Could I ＿＿＿＿＿ ＿＿＿＿＿?

2. Are you ＿＿＿＿＿ ＿＿＿＿＿ ＿＿＿＿＿ or renting?

   (A) 110 ＿＿＿＿＿ ＿＿＿＿＿.

   (B) We're ＿＿＿＿＿ ＿＿＿＿＿ two years.

   (C) No, it is.

3. Would ＿＿＿＿＿ ＿＿＿＿＿ ＿＿＿＿＿ or coffee?

   (A) He ＿＿＿＿＿ ＿＿＿＿＿ yesterday.

   (B) She will ＿＿＿＿＿ ＿＿＿＿＿.

   (C) ＿＿＿＿＿ ＿＿＿＿＿ ＿＿＿＿＿.

4. Are the ＿＿＿＿＿ ＿＿＿＿＿ ＿＿＿＿＿ ＿＿＿＿＿ or in the balcony?

   (A) At the ＿＿＿＿＿ ＿＿＿＿＿.

   (B) I'll ＿＿＿＿＿ ＿＿＿＿＿ later.

   (C) You can ＿＿＿＿＿ ＿＿＿＿＿ the balcony.

1. Have you _____ ?

    (A) Yes. He'll _____ .

    (B) I will _____ .

    (C) It is the _____ .

2. Does this building _____ ?

    (A) Yes, there's more _____ .

    (B) I bought _____ .

    (C) He will _____ .

3. Is this a _____ ?

    (A) About _____ .

    (B) We're hoping to _____ .

    (C) James is the _____ .

4. _____ we have _____ ?

    (A) _____ .

    (B) Sorry, _____ .

    (C) Mary was _____ .

5. Did you pay for _____ ?

    (A) Yes, _____ .

    (B) No, there is _____ .

    (C) She didn't _____ .

6. _____ would you prefer, _____?

    (A) _____.

    (B) In the office.

    (C) _____, thank you.

7. Do you have the _____?

    (A) _____ of a document.

    (B) _____.

    (C) _____ is here.

8. Did you know that _____?

    (A) I hope _____.

    (B) No, I have _____.

    (C) I will _____.

9. Have you already _____?

    (A) Yes, there is.

    (B) _____, _____.

    (C) I'll read it.

10. Is the _____?

    (A) Oh, the _____.

    (B) He'll be _____.

    (C) Yes, all of _____.

Voca Preview

請勾選不認識的單字，學習完類型分析後再重新確認勾選的單字。

- [ ] **drop off** 轉交（文件等）
- [ ] **run out of** 用完～
- [ ] **office supply** 辦公用品
- [ ] **at the same time** 同時
- [ ] **tax** 稅金
- [ ] **for a while** 暫時，一會兒
- [ ] **mobile phone** 手機
- [ ] **previous engagement** 有約在先
- [ ] **business trip** 出差
- [ ] **proposal** 提議，提案書
- [ ] **review** 檢閱
- [ ] **disconnect** 使分離
- [ ] **document** 文件
- [ ] **curious** 好奇的
- [ ] **announce** 宣布
- [ ] **at least** 至少
- [ ] **suggest** 建議
- [ ] **product** 產品
- [ ] **have an idea** 有個想法
- [ ] **consider** 考慮

- [ ] **hand** 傳遞
- [ ] **loud noise** 噪音
- [ ] **extend** 延長
- [ ] **window latch** 窗鉤
- [ ] **attachment** 附件
- [ ] **take a look** 查看
- [ ] **missing** 遺失
- [ ] **director** 主任
- [ ] **put together** 組合
- [ ] **inventory** 庫存，清單貨品
- [ ] **fax** 傳真
- [ ] **application** 申請（書）
- [ ] **cashier** 收銀員
- [ ] **with cash** 以現金
- [ ] **blueprint** 藍圖，設計圖
- [ ] **profit** 利潤
- [ ] **withdraw** 取消，撤退
- [ ] **job offer** 工作機會
- [ ] **sales figure** 銷售額，銷售量
- [ ] **expensive** 昂貴的

類型分析 **6**

建議（請求）句 & 陳述句

WARMING UP

REVIEW TEST

聽寫訓練

WARMING UP

31.mp3

診斷評估　聽完 mp3 後，請從 A、B 之中選出合適的回答。

1. Ⓐ（　　）　　Ⓑ（　　）　　2. Ⓐ（　　）　　Ⓑ（　　）
3. Ⓐ（　　）　　Ⓑ（　　）　　4. Ⓐ（　　）　　Ⓑ（　　）

填空　再聽一次 mp3 並填空。

1. Would you like me to drop those files off for you?

   Ⓐ No, none of them broke.

   Ⓑ ＿＿＿＿. I'd appreciate it.

   哪個是適合建議／請求句的答覆？

2. Could I please speak with a mechanic?

   Ⓐ I ＿＿＿＿ ＿＿＿＿ ＿＿＿＿.

   Ⓑ Actually, a group of salespeople.

3. We're running out of pens and pencils.

   Ⓐ ＿＿＿＿ order supplies tomorrow.

   Ⓑ She runs every day.

   哪個是適合陳述句的答覆？

4. I am going to the staff meeting.

   Ⓐ So ＿＿＿＿ ＿＿＿＿.

   Ⓑ At the same time as yesterday.

確認解答＆要點　確認正確答案，了解建議（請求）句和陳述句的特徵。　🔊 **31.mp3**

1. Would you like me to drop those files off for you?
　　要替你轉交這些檔案嗎？

　　Ⓐ　No, none of them broke.　不，一個也沒損壞。　✗

　　Ⓑ　Thanks. I'd appreciate it.　謝謝，我會很感激的。　⭕

> 回答建議、請求句時，表示同意或接受的話，回覆 Yes、Okay、Sure、Thanks 等；表示拒絕的話，回覆 No, thanks.、I don't think so. 等。

2. Could I please speak with a mechanic?
　　我可以跟技工談一下嗎？

　　Ⓐ　I don't think so.　應該不行。　⭕

　　Ⓑ　Actually, a group of salespeople.　事實上，是一群銷售員。　✗

3. We're running out of pens and pencils.
　　我們的鋼筆和鉛筆快用完了。

　　Ⓐ　I'll order supplies tomorrow.
　　　　我明天會訂購辦公用品。　⭕

　　Ⓑ　She runs every day.　她每天跑步。　✗

> 陳述句的回答最常以 I will~（=I am going to~）的句型出現，也可以回答附和陳述句的 so、too、either 或 neither 等。

4. I am going to the staff meeting.
　　我要去參加員工會議。

　　Ⓐ　So am I.　我也是。　⭕

　　Ⓑ　At the same time as yesterday.　跟昨天同樣的時間。　✗

建議（請求）句

回答建議（請求）句時，想表示接受的話，可以回覆Sure~、Okay~、Let's~、That's good.、That sounds great. 等；想表示拒絕的話，可回覆I'm sorry~、I'm afraid~、Thanks but~、No, thanks.等。

🎓 **代表題型** 聽完音檔後請選出合適的正確答案。　　　　　　　　　🎧 32.mp3

1. (A)　　　(B)　　　(C)

2. (A)　　　(B)　　　(C)

✏️ **攻略解題法** 了解該如何作答建議（請求）句的題目。

Q1 **Would you like to** join our club?　你要加入我們的俱樂部嗎？
▶ 聆聽前三、四個單字並確認是不是建議句。

(A) Thanks. I'd like that.　謝謝，我很高興能參加。　⭘
▶ 說完Thanks後給予正面的答覆。

(B) No, he's not a member.　不，他不是會員。　✗
▶ 出現聯想單字（club – member）的錯誤答案。

(C) I need her.　我需要她。　✗
▶ 跟題目無關的錯誤答案。

詞彙整理 **join** 加入，入會 **member** 會員

Q2 **Can you** call a taxi for me?　你可以替我叫計程車嗎？
▶ 聆聽前三、四個單字並確認是不是建議句。

(A) The tax will be paid.　稅金將會被繳納。　✗
▶ 聽到發音類似的單字（taxi – tax）的選項大部分都是錯誤答案。

(B) I'd be glad to.　我很樂意。　⭘
▶ 若聽到表示同意的表達方式即為正確答案。

(C) She called me last night.　她昨晚打電話給我了。　✗
▶ 聽到發音類似的單字（call – called）的選項大部分都是錯誤答案。

詞彙整理 **tax** 稅金

攻略POINT 在近期的多益測驗中，建議（請求）句的正確答案經常出現反問或要求對方等待的回答，表示「不清楚」的回答，出現的頻率也很高。

· 表示同意／接受的Yes、Okay、Sure、Thanks、Certainly、Absolutely等表達方式為正確答案。

· 表示拒絕的Thanks、But no thanks、Unfortunately、I don't think so.等表達方式為正確答案。

· 表示樂意做某事的I'd be happy / glad / love / like to~等表達方式為正確答案。

· 反問或要求對方等待的選項為正確答案。

 ## 建議（請求）句的正確答案類型

表示接受的類型

Could I read your magazine? 我可以看你的雜誌嗎？	● Yes, it's on the table. 可以，在桌上。
Would you like to join us for dinner? 你要和我們一起吃晚餐嗎？	● Okay, please wait for a while. 好，請等我一下。
Can I borrow your mobile phone for a while? 我可以借一下你的手機嗎？	● Sure. 沒問題。
Do you need any help? 你需要幫忙嗎？	● Thanks. I appreciate it. 太感謝了。
Can you tell our manager that I will be late? 你可以跟我們的經理說我會晚到嗎？	● I'd be glad to tell him. 我很樂意告訴他。
Could you attend the meeting instead of me? 你能代替我出席會議嗎？	● I'd be happy to do it. 我很樂意這麼做。
Can you help me send this email? 你可以幫我寄這封電子郵件嗎？	● I'd love/like to help you. 我很樂意幫你。
How about finishing this project? 結束這個案子怎麼樣？	● That's a good idea. 好主意。
Why don't you go to the bank after lunch? 你何不在午餐後去銀行？	● That would be nice. 那樣應該不錯。
Why don't we have dinner later? 我們等一下去吃晚餐吧？	● That sounds great. 聽起來很棒。

表示拒絕的類型

Would you like some coffee? 你要喝點咖啡嗎？	● No, thanks. 不用，謝謝。
Could you tell me about the meeting? 你可以跟我說會議的事嗎？	● Sorry, but I have to meet my client now. 抱歉，我現在要見客戶。
Would you like to go to the concert tomorrow? 你明天要去看演場會嗎？	● I would, but I have a previous engagement. 我很想，但我有約在先了。
Can I see Susan? 我可以見蘇珊嗎？	● Unfortunately, she just left. 很不巧，她剛離開。
Are you going to attend the speech today? 你會參加今天的演講嗎？	● I don't think so. 應該不會。

When does the new staff member start working? 新員工何時開始工作？	● I'm not sure. 我不確定。
Where did Mr. Roy go on his business trip? 羅伊去哪出差了呢？	● Let me check. 我確認一下。
Can we start our new project now? 我們可以現在開始做新案子嗎？	● Let's finish this first. 我們先完成這個吧。

Step 3 　│　實戰演練　　　　　　　　　　　　　　🎧 33.mp3

1. (A)　　　　(B)　　　　(C)

2. (A)　　　　(B)　　　　(C)

3. (A)　　　　(B)　　　　(C)

4. (A)　　　　(B)　　　　(C)

▶ 答案與解析請參考解析本第26頁

陳述句

回答陳述句時，務必記住附和對方以及說明接下來會做什麼事的表達方式。「I will~」的句型特別常出現。

🎓 **代表題型** 聽完音檔後請選出合適的正確答案。　　　　　　　🎧 34.mp3

1. (A)　　　　(B)　　　　(C)

2. (A)　　　　(B)　　　　(C)

✏️ **攻略解題法** 了解該如何作答陳述句的題目。

Q1　**I sent you** the **latest sales proposal.**　　我寄最新的銷售提案給你了。
▶ 回答陳述句時，須聽完整句並記住關鍵字。

(A) Sorry, but we will leave soon.　抱歉，我們很快就要離開了。　✗
▶ 意思不符合題目的錯誤答案。

(B) I'll mail a letter to you.　我會寄信給你。　✗
▶ 這是適合答覆Who問句的錯誤答案。

(C) All right. I'll review it this afternoon.　好，我會在下午檢閱。　○
▶ 「I'll~」的句型是陳述句的回答中最常出現的正確答案。

詞彙整理 latest 最新的　**proposal** 提議，提案書　**review** 檢閱

Q2　**Our call** must have been **disconnected.**　　我們的通話應該是被斷訊了。
▶ 回答陳述句時，須聽完整句並記住關鍵字。

(A) I think you're right.　你說得對。　○
▶ 以正面的回覆代替Yes的正確答案。

(B) I'll have dinner with him.　我會跟他吃晚餐。　✗
▶ 這是適合答覆Who問句的錯誤答案。

(C) Nobody received a call.　沒人接到電話。　✗
▶ 利用相同的詞彙（call）造成混淆的錯誤答案。

詞彙整理 disconnect 切斷（電話），使分離　**receive a call** 接電話

攻略POINT 「I'll~」的句型是陳述句的回答中最常出現的正確答案，也可以使用建議或請求句來回答陳述句。

· 表示同意或附和的選項為正確答案。

· 出現I will（I'm going to）句型的選項為正確答案。

· 以建議（請求）作為回答的選項即為正確答案。

 陳述句的正確答案類型

反問的類型

I lost my file this morning. 我今天早上弄丟我的資料夾了。	● Is that yours? 那是你的嗎？
I want you to send the documents to Vera. 希望你能寄這些文件給薇拉。	● Where can I find them? 在哪裡呢？

以建議或請求句回答的類型

We should finish this project by this week. 我們要在這週之前完成這個案子。	● Okay, let's start tomorrow. 好，我們明天開始吧。
Please tell Gloria about the meeting. 請跟葛羅莉亞說會議的事。	● Okay, I'll talk to her. 好，我會跟她說。

回答不知道的類型

I'm curious why the meeting has been delayed. 我很好奇會議為什麼延遲了。	● I don't know either. 我也不知道。
I think the seminar will be held next week. 我想研討會將在下週舉行。	● Let me check for you. 我幫你確認看看。
I wonder why Ms. George will change departments. 我很好奇喬治女士為什麼要換部門。	● She didn't tell me anything. 她什麼也沒跟我說。
The president will announce the new policy. 總裁將會宣布新政策。	● Actually, that hasn't been decided yet. 其實，那個還沒決定好。

回答事實或意見的類型

The meeting today was very boring. 今天的會議很無聊。	● Yes, but at least it finished early. 對啊，但是至少提早結束了。
Cathy will leave the company soon. 凱西就快要離開公司了。	● I'll miss her. 我會想念她的。

1. (A)   (B)   (C)   **2.** (A)   (B)   (C)

3. (A)   (B)   (C)   **4.** (A)   (B)   (C)

▶ 答案與解析請參考解析本第27頁

1. Mark your answer on your answer sheet.

   (A)   (B)   (C)

2. Mark your answer on your answer sheet.

   (A)   (B)   (C)

3. Mark your answer on your answer sheet.

   (A)   (B)   (C)

4. Mark your answer on your answer sheet.

   (A)   (B)   (C)

5. Mark your answer on your answer sheet.

   (A)   (B)   (C)

6. Mark your answer on your answer sheet.

   (A)   (B)   (C)

7. Mark your answer on your answer sheet.

   (A)   (B)   (C)

8. Mark your answer on your answer sheet.

   (A)   (B)   (C)

9. Mark your answer on your answer sheet.

   (A)   (B)   (C)

10. Mark your answer on your answer sheet.

   (A)   (B)   (C)

▶ 答案與解析請參考解析本第28頁

聽寫訓練

1. Would you _____ see our _____ ?

   (A) I'll _____ .

   (B) In five _____ .

   (C) Do you _____ ?

2. May I _____ for a new _____ ?

   (A) _____ for you.

   (B) I _____ for you.

   (C) _____ to _____ your ideas.

3. Why _____ travel together?

   (A) At the _____ .

   (B) When _____ ?

   (C) I _____ call him.

4. Can you _____ this project?

   (A) Sure, _____ there.

   (B) We _____ document.

   (C) I _____ .

聽寫是提高聽力能力的最佳學習方法。
請聆聽實戰演練與REVIEW TEST的音檔並填空。音檔將播放三次。

Unit 12　陳述句　│　**Step 3 實戰演練**　　　　🎧 dictation-17.mp3

1. Today's meeting _____ _____ _____ long.

(A) I _____ _____.

(B) What _____ _____ _____ talking about?

(C) This is _____ _____ _____.

2. The copy machine is _____ _____ _____.

(A) I _____ _____ you.

(B) You _____ _____ come.

(C) I think _____ _____.

3. Maybe we _____ _____ _____ deadline.

(A) _____ _____ the office.

(B) Okay, _____ _____ that.

(C) No, I don't want _____ _____.

4. I _____ _____ this window _____.

(A) They _____ _____ 7 P.M.

(B) I _____ _____ _____ an attachment.

(C) Let me _____ _____ _____.

Review Test

🎧 dictation-18.mp3

1. The directory is _____ _____ _____ _____.
   (A) _____?
   (B) _____ are _____.
   (C) No, _____ the office.

2. _____ an inventory of our merchandise?
   (A) _____.
   (B) Sure, I have some time.
   (C) _____.

3. I need _____ by this afternoon.
   (A) _____ for you?
   (B) He is _____.
   (C) No, I have it already.

4. _____ to you?
   (A) No, _____ on education.
   (B) Yes, that _____.
   (C) The interview _____.

5. _____ you to the _____.
   (A) No, _____.
   (B) It's the old one I have.
   (C) Thanks, but _____.

6. _____ of our newsletter?

(A) I'm _____.

(B) _____.

(C) In the newspaper.

7. _____ for the Liael Project?

(A) It is _____.

(B) Those _____.

(C) I think Bob has them.

8. I think _____ Mr. Davidson.

(A) _____.

(B) Our _____ to be _____.

(C) Unfortunately, he _____.

9. Could you _____?

(A) Yes, _____.

(B) I have to take the bus.

(C) I'm afraid the _____.

10. I'd like to _____.

(A) I have to _____.

(B) Would you like me _____?

(C) _____.

PART 2 FINAL TEST - 1

🎧 **Part2-final1.mp3**

PART 2

Directions: You will hear a question or statement and three responses spoken in English. They will not be printed in your test book and will be spoken only one time. Select the best response to the question or statement and mark the letter (A), (B), or (C) on your answer sheet. Now let us begin with question number 7.

7. Mark your answer on your answer sheet.   (A)   (B)   (C)

8. Mark your answer on your answer sheet.   (A)   (B)   (C)

9. Mark your answer on your answer sheet.   (A)   (B)   (C)

10. Mark your answer on your answer sheet.   (A)   (B)   (C)

11. Mark your answer on your answer sheet.   (A)   (B)   (C)

12. Mark your answer on your answer sheet.   (A)   (B)   (C)

13. Mark your answer on your answer sheet.   (A)   (B)   (C)

14. Mark your answer on your answer sheet.   (A)   (B)   (C)

15. Mark your answer on your answer sheet.   (A)   (B)   (C)

16. Mark your answer on your answer sheet.   (A)   (B)   (C)

17. Mark your answer on your answer sheet.   (A)   (B)   (C)

18. Mark your answer on your answer sheet.   (A)   (B)   (C)

19. Mark your answer on your answer sheet.   (A)   (B)   (C)

20. Mark your answer on your answer sheet.   (A)   (B)   (C)

21. Mark your answer on your answer sheet.   (A)   (B)   (C)

22. Mark your answer on your answer sheet.   (A)   (B)   (C)

23. Mark your answer on your answer sheet.   (A)   (B)   (C)

24. Mark your answer on your answer sheet.   (A)   (B)   (C)

25. Mark your answer on your answer sheet.   (A)   (B)   (C)

26. Mark your answer on your answer sheet.   (A)   (B)   (C)

27. Mark your answer on your answer sheet.   (A)   (B)   (C)

28. Mark your answer on your answer sheet.   (A)   (B)   (C)

29. Mark your answer on your answer sheet.   (A)   (B)   (C)

30. Mark your answer on your answer sheet.   (A)   (B)   (C)

31. Mark your answer on your answer sheet.   (A)   (B)   (C)

▶ 答案與解析請參考解析本第31頁

PART 2 FINAL TEST - 2

PART 2

Directions: You will hear a question or statement and three responses spoken in English. They will not be printed in your test book and will be spoken only one time. Select the best response to the question or statement and mark the letter (A), (B), or (C) on your answer sheet. Now let us begin with question number 7.

7. Mark your answer on your answer sheet. (A) (B) (C)
8. Mark your answer on your answer sheet. (A) (B) (C)
9. Mark your answer on your answer sheet. (A) (B) (C)
10. Mark your answer on your answer sheet. (A) (B) (C)
11. Mark your answer on your answer sheet. (A) (B) (C)
12. Mark your answer on your answer sheet. (A) (B) (C)
13. Mark your answer on your answer sheet. (A) (B) (C)
14. Mark your answer on your answer sheet. (A) (B) (C)
15. Mark your answer on your answer sheet. (A) (B) (C)
16. Mark your answer on your answer sheet. (A) (B) (C)
17. Mark your answer on your answer sheet. (A) (B) (C)
18. Mark your answer on your answer sheet. (A) (B) (C)
19. Mark your answer on your answer sheet. (A) (B) (C)
20. Mark your answer on your answer sheet. (A) (B) (C)
21. Mark your answer on your answer sheet. (A) (B) (C)
22. Mark your answer on your answer sheet. (A) (B) (C)
23. Mark your answer on your answer sheet. (A) (B) (C)
24. Mark your answer on your answer sheet. (A) (B) (C)
25. Mark your answer on your answer sheet. (A) (B) (C)
26. Mark your answer on your answer sheet. (A) (B) (C)
27. Mark your answer on your answer sheet. (A) (B) (C)
28. Mark your answer on your answer sheet. (A) (B) (C)
29. Mark your answer on your answer sheet. (A) (B) (C)
30. Mark your answer on your answer sheet. (A) (B) (C)
31. Mark your answer on your answer sheet. (A) (B) (C)

▶ 答案與解析請參考解析本第36頁

PART
3

簡短對話

第三大題為聽完兩人或三人對話後作答三道題目的類型，
總共13則對話（39題）。

Voca Preview

請勾選不認識的單字，學習完類型分析後再重新確認勾選的單字。

- [ ] **officially** 官方地
- [ ] **launch** 上市
- [ ] **supplier** 供應商
- [ ] **be familiar with** 對～熟悉
- [ ] **data entry** 資料輸入
- [ ] **take away** 拿走，取走
- [ ] **additional** 附加的
- [ ] **renovate** 改造，翻修
- [ ] **totally** 完整地
- [ ] **plumbing** 配管，配管系統
- [ ] **toilet** 沖水馬桶
- [ ] **quickly** 快速地
- [ ] **restroom** 洗手間
- [ ] **notice** 注意到～
- [ ] **overflow** 溢出
- [ ] **get stuck** 困住，堵住
- [ ] **traffic jam** 交通堵塞
- [ ] **quite** 相當地
- [ ] **colleague** 同事
- [ ] **carpool** 共乘汽車

- [ ] **rough map** 簡圖，草圖
- [ ] **office furniture** 辦公家具
- [ ] **painting work** 油漆作業
- [ ] **make sure** 確定
- [ ] **printing plant** 印刷廠
- [ ] **appointment** 約會
- [ ] **leave a message** 留言
- [ ] **business card** 名片
- [ ] **purchase** 購買
- [ ] **place an order** 下單
- [ ] **confirm** 確認
- [ ] **real estate** 房地產
- [ ] **inspector** 檢查員
- [ ] **electrical wiring** 電線
- [ ] **pedestrian** 行人
- [ ] **exhibit** 展示品，展示
- [ ] **art class** 美術課
- [ ] **commute** 通勤
- [ ] **drop in** 順便拜訪
- [ ] **leak** （液體、氣體）滲漏

類型分析 7

各大題型攻略

WARMING UP

1. Where does this conversation most likely take place? _____
2. When will the event begin? _____
3. What is the woman looking for? _____

W : Excuse me. I'm looking for the International Business Association Center.

M : It is right over there. The seminar will begin at 10 o'clock, and now it's 9 o'clock.

W : Oh, thanks. Is there any place I can get a cup of coffee while I'm waiting?

M : You can go downstairs and find Coffee and Bread Cafe.

確認解答&要點　確認正確答案，了解第三大題的題目特徵。

診斷評估：掌握題目的重點

1. Where does this conversation most likely take place?　此對話最有可能在哪裡發生？
   ▶對話發生的地點

2. When will the event begin?　活動何時開始？　▶活動開始的時間

3. What is the woman looking for? 女子在找什麼？ ▶女子在找的東西

尋找線索：分析測驗內容

W : Excuse me. I'm looking for the International Business Association Center.
   ▶ 1. 對話地點的第一個答題依據／3. 女子正在找東西的答題依據

   女：不好意思。我正在找國際商務協會中心。

   詢問對話地點的題目，通常會在對話開頭提到特定地點的單字。
   對話中的女子正在路上或建築物內尋找國際商務協會中心。

M : It is right over there. The seminar will begin at 10 o'clock, and now it's
   9 o'clock.　　　▶2. 活動開始時間的答題依據

   男：就在那邊。研討會十點開始，現在是九點。

   特定時間或具體資訊的相關線索會在對話的中間出現。

W : Oh, thanks. Is there any place I can get a cup of coffee while I'm waiting?

M : You can go downstairs and find Coffee and Bread Cafe.
   ▶ 1. 對話地點的第二個答題依據

   女：噢，謝謝。我在等的時候，有地方可以讓我喝杯咖啡嗎？
   男：你可以到樓下找找看「咖啡和麵包店」。

   雖然對話的地點或目的通常會放在開頭，但是就算錯過第一句，也
   可以在聽完整個對話後掌握到重點，所以這題也可以放在三道題目
   中的最後再作答。在這裡可以知道對話地點是在建築物內。

   詞彙整理 look for 尋找～ **international** 國際的 **association** 協會，聯盟 **right over there** 就在那
   邊 **downstairs** 在樓下，往樓下

Unit 13 詢問主題、目的的題目

Step 1 | 實戰重點

詢問主題或目的的題目線索 99% 以上會在對話的第一句提到，所以不要錯過第一句。

 代表題型 先閱讀題目再聆聽音檔後，請選出合適的正確答案。 37.mp3

Q. What are the speakers discussing?

(A) A new store opening

(B) The price of a new product

(C) Packaging some samples

(D) Changing suppliers

 攻略解題法 了解該如何作答詢問主題、目的的題目。

🧑 聆聽對話前閱讀題目時

Q. What are the speakers discussing? 說話者正在討論什麼？

▶ 要在對話開始前快速了解題目再聆聽對話。這是詢問主題的題目，所以要仔細聆聽第一句。

(A) A new store opening 新店開幕

(B) The price of a new product 新產品的價格

(C) Packaging some samples 包裝一些樣品

(D) Changing suppliers 換供應商

🎧 聆聽對話時

Refer to the following conversation. 請參照以下的對話。

W: Have you heard that Mr. Park wanted to change the packaging materials for our new laptop samples? ▶從第一句話可以知道目前正在討論跟「包裝」有關的事，所以(C)為正確答案。

女：你有聽說帕克先生想換掉我們的新筆記型電腦樣品的包裝材料嗎？

M: No, I haven't heard about it yet. When do we need to finish the work?
男：沒有，我還沒聽說。我們什麼時候得完成這個工作？

W: Well, the laptop will be officially launched on July 1, so all of them will have to be ready by then. 女：嗯，筆記型電腦會在七月一日正式上市，所以全部都得在那時候準備好。

M: Okay, I'll contact our supplier. 男：好，我會聯絡我們的供應商。

詞彙整理 **packaging** 包裝 **laptop** 筆記型電腦 **sample** 樣品 **officially** 官方地 **launch** 開始，上市 **supplier** 供應商

攻略POINT ❶ 詢問主題或目的的題目線索會在對話的第一句提到。
　　　　 ❷ 若只聽第一句還是不確定主題的話，也可以在聽完整個對話後再選出合適的正確答案。

Step 2　核心理論＆基礎形式

🔤 詢問主題或目的的題型

- What are the speakers talking about? 說話者正在談論什麼？
- What is the topic / subject of the report? 報告主旨是什麼？
- What is the main topic of the conversation? 此對話的主題是什麼？
- What are the speakers discussing? 說話者正在討論什麼？
- What is the conversation about? 此對話與什麼有關？
- Why is the woman calling? 女子為什麼打電話？
- What is being advertised? 廣告的東西是什麼？
- What is the purpose of the woman's call? 女子打電話的目的是什麼？

Step 3　實戰演練　　　🎧 38.mp3

1. What is the conversation about?

    (A) Using a computer program
    (B) Purchasing a new computer
    (C) Inviting customers
    (D) Hiring requirements

2. What is the purpose of the woman's call?

    (A) To place an order
    (B) To ask for repairs
    (C) To buy a new refrigerator
    (D) To confirm a delivery

▶ 答案與解析請參考解析本第41頁

Unit 14 詢問職業／對話地點的題目

雖然關於說話者的職業線索大部分會在對話開頭的前一、兩句出現，但若是沒有出現的話，則要聽到最後才行。考慮到這一點，最後再作答詢問職業的題目比較好。詢問對話地點的題目，答案也會在對話開頭前一、兩句出現，但有時候也得聽完整個對話，在綜合線索後推敲出答案，所以解題攻略是留到最後再作答。

 代表題型 先閱讀題目再聆聽音檔後，選出合適的正確答案。 39.mp3

Q. What is the woman's job?

(A) Real estate agent

(B) Building inspector

(C) Lawyer

(D) Interior designer

 攻略解題法 了解該如何作答詢問職業／對話地點的題目。

> **聆聽對話前閱讀題目時**

Q. What is the woman's job?　女子的職業是什麼？

> ▶ 要在對話開始前快速了解題目再聆聽對話。這題是詢問女子的職業，所以要仔細聆聽對話開頭的前一、兩句。沒聽到的話，也可以在聽完整個對話後再作答。

(A) Real estate agent　房地產仲介

(B) Building inspector　建物檢查員

(C) Lawyer　律師

(D) Interior designer　室內設計師

> **聆聽對話時**

Refer to the following conversation.　請參照以下的對話。

W: Mr. Bryan, I just contacted the owner of the apartment. I'm pleased to tell you that the owner wants to sign a contract with you.

> ▶ 第一句的內容是「跟公寓屋主通過電話後，屋主願意簽約」，這裡出現了關於女子的職業的線索，可以知道女子是一名「房地產仲介」。(A)為正確答案。若沒有聽到這個部分，聽完整個對話再作答也可以。
>
> 女：布萊恩先生，我剛才連絡過公寓屋主了。很高興能告訴您，屋主想跟您簽約。

M: That's great news. Actually, we are concerned about the electrical wiring in the living room.　男：真是個好消息。事實上，我們很擔心客廳的電線。

W: You don't have to worry about it. The owner will renovate every single part of the apartment.　女：您不用擔心。屋主會翻修公寓的每個角落。

攻略POINT ❶ 對話的前一、兩句會出現跟詢問職業和對話地點的題目直接相關的線索。
　　　　 ❷ 若在前半段錯過了線索，可以透過在整個對話中聽到的職業和地點相關單字來推敲答案。
　　　　 ❸ 須事先熟悉跟特定職業、地點有關的詞彙。

 詢問職業或對話地點的題型

* Who most likely is the man? 男子最有可能是誰？

* Who most likely are the speakers? 說話者最有可能是誰？

* Who is the man speaking / talking to? 男子正在跟誰說話？

* What do the speakers probably do? 說話者可能會做什麼？

* Where does the man probably work? 男子可能在哪裡工作？

* What is the woman's job / occupation? 女子的工作／職業是什麼？

* Where does the conversation take place? 此對話發生的地點在哪？

Voca Check - up! 地點、職業相關詞彙

‧ **museum** 博物館：**exhibit** 展示品 **painting** 畫作 **pottery** 陶器 **curator** 館長 ‧ **airport** 機場：**departure** 出發 **landing** 著陸 **boarding** 登機 **gate** 登機門 **check-in counter** 報到櫃檯 **customs** 海關 **cabin** 機艙 **cart** 推車 **boarding pass** 登機證 **carry-on baggage** 手提行李 ‧ **post office** 郵局：**mail** 郵件 **package** 包裹 **parcel** 包裹 **express mail** 快捷郵件 **courier** 快遞員 **courier service** 快遞服務 **fragile** 易碎的 ‧ **restaurant** 餐廳：**special** 特選料理 **menu** 菜單 **dish** 菜餚 **chef** 廚師 **cafeteria** 自助餐廳 **plate** 盤子 ‧ **hotel** 飯店：**room** 房間 **single** 單人房 **double** 雙人房 **suite** 套房 **check in** 辦理入住手續 **check out** 辦理退房手續 ‧ **library** 圖書館：**librarian** 圖書館員 **check out** 借書 **overdue** 逾期的 **late fee** 逾期罰金 ‧ **bookstore** 書店：**aisle** 通道，走道 **section** 區塊 **writer / author** 作者 ‧ **hospital** 醫院／ **pharmacy** 藥局：**physician** 醫生 **examine** 診察 **prescribe** 開藥方 **dentist** 牙醫 **fill** 補（牙） **pick up** 拿（藥） **take pills** 吃藥 ‧ **real estate agency** 房地產公司：**apartment** 公寓 **property** 房地產 **real estate** 房地產 **landlord** 房東 **tenant** 承租人 **deposit** 保證金 ‧ **bank** 銀行：**account** 帳戶 **balance** 餘額 **teller** 出納員 **loan** 貸款 **deposit** 存款 **transfer money** 轉帳 **ATM** 提款機 ‧ **plumber** 水管工／ **electrician** 電工：**toilet** 沖水馬桶 **faucet** 水龍頭 **sink** 水槽 **leak** 滲漏 **install** 安裝 **electricity** 電力 **light** 燈 **wire** 電線 **power** 電力 ‧ **travel agency** 旅行社：**itinerary** 行程 **accommodation** 住處 **book** 預訂 **cancel** 取消 **reserve** 預約

其他職業相關詞彙

caterer 外燴業者 **landscaper** 造景師 **representative** 員工，代表 **staff** 員工 **boss** 老闆 **president** 總裁 **CEO** 首席執行官 **head** （部門）部長 **chief** （部門）主管 **director** 主任 **executive officer** 執行長 **supervisor** 上司 **manager** 部長，經理 **agent** 代理人

1. Who most likely is the man?

(A) A pedestrian

(B) A bus driver

(C) A salesperson

(D) A tour guide

2. Where does the conversation most likely take place?

(A) At a plumbing office

(B) At a computer store

(C) At a restaurant

(D) At a hotel

▶ 答案與解析請參考解析本第42頁

Unit 15　詢問說話者的建議的題目

此類詢問說話者對聆聽者提出什麼請求、建議或拜託的題目，聆聽對話內容的時候，要仔細聽「Why don't~?、Could you~?」等表達方式，因為接在這種表達後面的句子是此類題型的答題線索。

 代表題型 先閱讀題目再聆聽音檔後，選出合適的正確答案。　　 41.mp3

> Q. What does the woman suggest that the man do?
>
> (A) Buy a membership
>
> (B) Return on another day
>
> (C) Take a tour
>
> (D) Join an art class

 攻略解題法 了解該如何作答詢問說話者的建議的題目。

> 聆聽對話前閱讀題目時
>
> Q. What does the woman suggest that the man do?　女子建議男子做什麼？
>
> ▶ 要在對話開始前快速了解題目再聆聽對話。這是詢問建議內容的題目，所以要仔細聽後面的「Why don't~?、Could you~?」的部分。
>
> (A) Buy a membership　買會員
>
> (B) Return on another day　改天再來
>
> (C) Take a tour　參加導覽
>
> (D) Join an art class　報名美術課
>
> 聆聽對話時
>
> Refer to the following conversation.　請參照以下的對話。
>
> M: Hi. This is the first time for me to visit the gallery, so could I learn more about the paintings on this floor?
> 男：嗨。這是我第一次逛美術館，我可以多了解一點這層樓的畫作嗎？
>
> W: Well, why don't you take a tour? It goes to all of our exhibits. The next one begins in 20 minutes.　▶ 作答建議題時，why don't的下一句是正確答案的線索。女子提議「參加導覽」，所以(C)為正確答案。
> 女：嗯，參加導覽怎麼樣呢？您可以逛到所有的展示品。下一場在二十分鐘後開始。
>
> M: Unfortunately, I don't have enough time today.　男：很可惜，我今天時間不夠。

詞彙整理 **gallery** 美術館，畫廊 **painting** 畫作 **floor** 樓層 **exhibit** 展示

攻略POINT ❶ Why don't~?、Would you~?、Could you~?、Would you like me to~?、I suggest~、I can~等後面的句子會出現正確答案的線索。

❷ 對話開始前務必先看過題目和選項，以便在聆聽對話途中出現答案的時候可以立刻選出來。

Step 2 ┃ **核心理論＆基礎形式**

🔤 詢問建議內容的題型

- What does the man / woman suggest / recommend?　男子／女子建議／推薦做什麼？
- What does the man offer / want / say to do?　男子建議／想要／說做什麼？
- What does the man ask / encourage the woman to do?　男子要求／鼓勵女子做什麼？
- What does the man ask for?　男子要求什麼？

🔤 預想答案
接在這些表達方式後面的句子，是詢問「建議做什麼」的題目的線索。

- Why don't you ~?　你何不～？
- What about / How about~?　～怎麼樣？
- Would / Could / Should you ~?　你可以～嗎？
- Shall / Can / May I ~?　我可以～嗎？
- You would / should / could / must / have to ~.　你應該～
- You want / need / hope to ~.　你想要／需要／希望～
- I (We) can ~.　我（我們）可以～
- I suggest / recommend ~.　我建議／推薦～
- Please＋原形動詞～.　請～

Step 3 ┃ **實戰演練**　　　　　　　　　　　　🎧 **42.mp3**

1. What problem are the speakers discussing?

(A) Traffic congestion

(B) A new employee

(C) A training session

(D) A new system

2. What does the man suggest that the woman do?

(A) Buy a car

(B) Take the subway

(C) Speak with her colleagues

(D) Commute to work by walking

▶ 答案與解析請參考解析本第42頁

詢問接下來會做什麼事的題目

next題型（詢問接下來會做什麼事的題目）是一種推論題，也就是詢問對話結束後，說話者會做什麼的題目，所以要專心聆聽最後面的對話。

 代表題型 先閱讀題目再聆聽音檔後，選出合適的正確答案。 43.mp3

Q. What will the man probably do next?

(A) Go to another shop

(B) Pay for a gift

(C) Fill out a form

(D) Call his wife

 攻略解題法 了解該如何作答詢問接下來會做什麼事的題目。

> 聆聽對話前閱讀題目時

Q. What will the man probably do next? 男子接下來可能會做什麼？

▶ 這是next題型，所以要專注於最後面的對話。

(A) Go to another shop 去另一間店

(B) Pay for a gift 付禮物的錢

(C) Fill out a form 填寫表格

(D) Call his wife 打電話給他的妻子

> 聆聽對話時

Refer to the following conversation. 請參照以下的對話。

W: Welcome to Mandi Gift Shop! May I help you, sir?

女：歡迎光臨曼蒂禮品店！有什麼我能為您效勞的嗎？

M: Yes, please. I just dropped by here to look for a birthday gift for my wife. Oh, this should be nice. 男：是的，麻煩你了。我順路來這裡想找我老婆的生日禮物。喔，這個應該不錯。

W: Good choice! If you just fill out this application form, you'll receive 15% off on any purchase. ▶ 女子說「只要填寫這份申請書，任何一筆消費就能享有15%的折扣」之後，男子回覆 Okay，所以可以推論出男子接下來會填寫表格。正確答案為(C)。

女：選得好！您只要填寫這份申請書，任何一筆消費就能享有十五％的折扣。

M: Okay. That sounds like a great deal. 男：好，聽起來很不錯。

詞彙整理 **drop by** 順便拜訪 **look for** 尋找，尋求 **fill out** 填寫，撰寫 **application form** 申請書

攻略POINT ❶ 此類詢問接下來會做什麼事的題目，最後面的對話會出現正確答案的線索，所以要專心聆聽這個部分。
❷ 在提出請求或建議的對話中很可能會出現線索。

Step 2 | **核心理論&基礎形式**

 詢問接下來會做什麼事的題型

- What will the man do next? 男子接下來會做什麼？
- What will the woman probably do next? 女子接下來可能會做什麼？
- What will the speakers probably do next? 說話者接下來可能會做什麼？
- Where will the speakers go next? 說話者接下來會去哪裡？

Step 3 | **實戰演練**

1. What are the speakers mainly discussing?

   (A) The restaurant on Main Street
   (B) The guide map of the city
   (C) The new office building
   (D) The location of the post office

2. What will the woman probably do next?

   (A) Give the man an address
   (B) Show a city map
   (C) Take the man to the post office
   (D) Draw a rough map

▶ 答案與解析請參考解析本第43頁

Unit 17 詢問細節的題目

多益測驗中有像詢問主題、目的等一般內容的題目，此外，也有詢問行為、地點、人物等細節的題目。詢問細節的題目的出現順序很重要。若是對話中的第一題，正確答案的線索通常會在對話前半段出現；若是第二題，會在中間出現；若是第三題，則會在後半段出現。

 代表題型 先閱讀題目再聆聽音檔後，選出合適的正確答案。 45.mp3

> **Q2.** What does the man say about the building?
>
> (A) He likes how it was renovated.
>
> (B) He likes how it was designed.
>
> (C) He likes the size of the office.
>
> (D) He likes the conference room.

 攻略解題法 了解該如何作答詢問細節的題目。

聆聽對話前閱讀題目時

Q1. 詢問主題的題目

Q2. What does the man say about the building?

▶ 詢問細節的題目在這裡是第二題。可以猜測正確答案的線索會在對話的中間出現。請記住這題的關鍵字是man say about the building，線索可能會在男子中間的發言中出現。

(A) He likes how it was renovated. ▶ 所有選項都是以He likes開頭。請仔細聆聽男子提到的大樓優點。

(B) He likes how it was designed.

(C) He likes the size of the office.

(D) He likes the conference room.

Q3. 詢問接下來會做什麼事的題目

▶ 如果第三題是詢問細節的題目，那麼正確答案的線索將出現在對話的下半部分。

聆聽對話時

Refer to the following conversation. 請參照以下的對話。

W: Hi, James. I found a really nice office space for our new start-up. It's in the old First National Bank. They have turned it into an office building. ▶ 女子正在說大樓的事。接下來男子的發言會透露出男子的想法。

女：嗨，詹姆斯。我替我們的新創公司找到了一個很棒的辦公空間。在舊的第一國家銀行裡。他們把它改成一棟辦公大樓了。

M: I've always admired the architecture of that bank, but the building is almost a hundred years old.　▶ 男子提到大樓時表示雖然自己很欣賞那棟建築，但是建築物太過老舊。也就是說，該大樓的優點是設計得很好。正確答案為(B)。

男：我一直都很欣賞那間銀行的建築風格，但那棟大樓的屋齡幾乎快一百年了。

W: Don't worry. The building has been completely renovated. Do you want to look at it with me this afternoon?　女：別擔心。大樓整個翻修過了。今天下午要不要跟我一起去看看？

M: I'd like to, but I have to meet the investors this afternoon. Could we go tomorrow morning?　男：我很想去，但我今天下午要見投資人。我們可以明天早上去嗎？

詞彙整理 **downtown**（在）市區 **start-up** 新創企業 **turn A into B** 把A改成B（使脫胎換骨） **admire** 欣賞，欽佩，讚賞 **architecture** 建築，建築風格 **completely** 完整地 **renovate** 改造，翻修

攻略POINT ❶ 詢問細節的題目的出現順序很重要。若是第一題，線索很可能會在對話前半段出現；若是第二題，會在中間出現；若是第三題，則會在後半段出現。
　　　　　 ❷ 事先注意題目的關鍵字，對話途中提到關鍵字時要專心聆聽。正確答案的線索經常以改述（用其他單字表達意思）的方式出現。不過，數字、星期、地名等不會改變。

| Step 2 | 核心理論&基礎形式 |

 詢問細節的題型

1. 關於時間、地點的題目

事先注意題目的關鍵字，聆聽對話時專心聽時間、地點的表達方式（5 P.M.、Tuesday、in front of the center、Richmond Street等）。不過，時間或地點可能會提到很多次，答題重點在於選出跟題目相符的內容。

- When is the woman's appointment?　女子有約的時間是何時？
- What will begin at 5 p.m.?　什麼會在下午五點開始？
- Where can the woman catch the bus?　女子可以在哪裡搭公車？
- Where does the man anticipate traffic jam?　男子預期哪裡會塞車？

2. 關於特定人物的題目

事先注意題目的關鍵字，聆聽對話時專心聽提到人物名稱的部分。

- Who are the workers waiting for?　工人在等誰？
- Who is the man going to meet?　男子要去見誰？
- What does the man mentioned about Michael?　男子提到關於麥可的什麼？
- How does Frank feel about the new rule?　法蘭克對於新規定有什麼感覺？

3. 詢問方法、原因、問題的題目

牢記關鍵字後聆聽對話。對話內容經常在改述後出現於選項中，所以要熟悉常見的改述表達。

- How can a visitor get discount? 訪客要怎麼享有折扣？
- What problem do the man have? 男子有什麼問題？
- What is the woman concerned about? 女子擔心什麼？
- Why is the man unable to find Amanda? 為什麼男子無法找到亞曼達？
- What solution does the woman offer? 女子提供的解決方案是什麼？

4. 詢問行為、提過或陳述過的內容的題目

牢記關鍵字後聆聽對話。一樣要留意改述的內容，從選項中選出正確答案。

- What does the woman mention about the agency? 女子提到關於代理商的什麼？
- What does the man tell the women? 男子告訴女子什麼？
- What does the man say about the computer? 男子說了關於電腦的什麼事？

 細節的改述範例

對話中的內容	正確答案的內容
website is going to be redesigned 網站會被重新設計	• updating website　更新網站
recruited several new people 招募了一些新員工	• hired some new staff members 　僱用了一些新員工
airport limousine bus　機場接駁巴士	• transportation　交通工具
get in touch with a courier company 跟快遞公司聯絡	• call a delivery company 　打電話給快遞公司
personal fitness equipment in my house 我家的個人健身器材	• a home exercise machine 　家庭用運動器材
the founder of the company　公司創始人	• a company's owner　公司所有人
the style seems to be over now 這個風格好像已經過時了	• the style is no longer popular 　這個風格不再流行
corporate meeting　企業會議	• company gathering　公司聚會
go to see the head of the project 去見專案負責人	• visit an organizer 　拜訪主辦人

a large screen　大螢幕	• a big monitor　大型顯示器
the machine is not working properly 機器運作不正常	• a product is faulty 產品有缺陷
use the back door　使用後門	• exit through the rear door　從後門離開
plane tickets and passport　機票和護照	• travel document　旅行文件
attracting new people　吸引新的人潮	• finding new customers　找尋新客人
handout flyers　傳單	• a publicity campaign　宣傳活動

Step 3 ｜ 實戰演練　　🔊 46.mp3

1. What does the man want to do?

   (A) Sign a lease

   (B) Find an apartment

   (C) Join a gym

   (D) Make some copies

2. What does the woman require?

   (A) Proof of residence

   (B) A security deposit

   (C) A late registration fee

   (D) Some exercise equipment

3. What does the man receive from the woman?

   (A) A signed lease

   (B) A registration form

   (C) Schedule information

   (D) A utility bill

▶ 答案與解析請參考解析本第43頁

Unit 18 掌握句子意圖的題目

此類掌握句子意圖的題目，必須從對話鋪陳中掌握句子隱含的意思。對於「吃飯了嗎？」的提問，回答「我不餓」時，包含了「肚子不餓，而且不想一起吃飯」的意思。若想這樣準確地理解對話中的特定句子含義，就要了解對話的前後文。而且，我們無法知道該句子會在哪裡出現，所以要非常專心地聆聽。

 代表題型 先閱讀題目再聆聽音檔後，選出合適的正確答案。　　　 47.mp3

Q. Why does the man say, "I'm really busy with the presentation slides for tomorrow"?

(A) To ask for assistance

(B) To postpone a presentation

(C) To make an excuse

(D) To make some changes

 攻略解題法 了解該如何作答掌握句子意圖的題目。

 聆聽對話前閱讀題目時

Q. Why does the man say, "I'm really busy with the presentation for tomorrow"?

男子為什麼說「I'm really busy with the presentation for tomorrow」？

▶ 聆聽對話前先看過該句子一遍。「I'm really busy with the presentation for tomorrow」的意思是「我因為明天的簡報而非常忙碌」。必須掌握並判斷句子的鋪陳，才能準確地理解這句話隱含的意思。

(A) To ask for assistance　為了請求協助

(B) To postpone a presentation　為了推遲簡報

(C) To make an excuse　為了找一個藉口

(D) To make some changes　為了做一些改變

 聆聽對話時

Refer to the following conversation.　請參照以下的對話。

W: Hi, Thomas. I have to enter some sales figures in our network database, but I'm having trouble signing in. My password keeps being rejected. Can you come over here and help me?

女：嗨，湯姆士。我得在我們的網絡資料庫輸入一些銷售額，但我登入時遇到問題。我的密碼一直顯示有誤。你可以過來這裡幫幫我嗎？

M: I'm really busy with the presentation for tomorrow. If you can't sign in, it's probably a problem with the server. Why don't you ask one of the IT technicians to take a look at it? ▶ 對於女子的請求，男子表示現在因為明天的簡報很忙，可以將這視為拒絕女子請求的藉口。正確答案為(C)。

男：我因為明天的簡報而非常忙碌。如果你不能登入，可能是伺服器有問題。你何不請資訊科技部的技術人員幫你看看？

W: Oh, yes, I should do that. Do you know who our contact in the IT Department is?

女：啊，好，我是該那樣做。你知道資訊科技部裡負責跟我們聯絡的人是誰嗎？

M: Umm... I don't know. You should just call and ask for someone who's available right now.

男：嗯……我不知道。你應該直接打電話找現在有空的人。

詞彙整理 sales figure 銷售額 **reject** 拒絕 **take a look at** 查看 **contact** 聯絡 **excuse** 藉口

攻略POINT ❶ 掌握句子意圖的題目有可能在第一題、第二題或第三題出現。出題順序是該句子會何時出現的提示。若是三題中的第一題，很可能會在對話前半段出現該句子；若是第二題，可能會在中間出現；若是第三題，則可能會在對話的最後面出現。

❷ 可以利用連接詞來判斷後者對於前者所說的意見，抱持肯定還是否定的想法。出現否定連接詞But、I'm sorry、Actually、I'm afraid、Unfortunately、However的話，句子內容會是反駁對方的意見；出現肯定連接詞Okay、therefore、so、sure、right、certainly等等的話，句子內容會是贊同對方的意見。

Step 2 | 核心理論＆基礎形式

 掌握句子意圖的題目中可能會出現的口語表達

1. 肯定／同意對方的意見 vs 反對的時候

- I think so. 我也這樣想。
- You're right. 你說得對。
- It sounds proper. 聽起來很妥當。
- I agree with you on that point.
  我同意這一點。
- It's quite a good idea. 這是個不錯的主意。
- I'm of the same opinion.
  我和你的意見一樣。
- That's exactly what I'm saying.
  那正是我想說的。
- You're talking sense. 你說得有道理。
- Just as you say. 正如你所說的。

- I can't agree with you. 我不同意你。
- I'm sorry, but I have a different opinion.
  抱歉，我有不一樣的看法。
- That's not my idea of... 這不是我對於～的想法。
- I don't think so. 我不這樣想。
- Certainly not. [Absolutely not. Surely not.]
  當然不。
- Nothing at all. 絕對不是那樣。
- I'm against... / I object to.... /
  I am opposed to... 我反對……。
- I have a different opinion about it.
  我對此的意見不一樣。

2. 對於對方的意見有共鳴／理解時 vs 沒有共鳴／無法理解時

- I see. 我懂。
- I see what you mean. 我明白你的意思。
- I see your point. 我明白。
- I understand what you mean.
  我了解你的意思。
- I can catch the point of what you're saying. 我可以理解你所說的重點。

- I don't know what you mean.
  我不明白你的意思。
- What do you mean? 你的意思是什麼？
- Would you come again, please?
  可以請你再說一次嗎？
- I have no idea of what he says.
  我不知道他在說什麼。

3. 提醒已知的事實時

- Please think ... over again.
  請再回想一次……。
- As you see[know], ... 如你所知，……。
- I think you are well aware of…
  我想你很清楚……。

4. 請對方再說一次時

- Excuse me? 你說什麼？
- Pardon (me)? 你說什麼？
- Would you say that again?
  可以請你再說一遍嗎？
- I didn't catch what you said.
  我沒聽到你說的話。

5. 為犯錯致歉時

- I'm not sure, but I think…is a ridiculous mistake.
  我不確定，但我覺得……是很荒唐的錯誤。
- I apologize for my mistake.
  我為我的錯誤道歉。
- It's my fault/mistake. 這是我的錯。

6. 表示跟自己沒關係的時候

- I have nothing to do with…
  ……跟我沒關係。
- I have no connection with…
  ……跟我沒關係。
- …is irrelevant to… ……跟……沒關係。
- It's none of your business. 不關你的事。

7. 鄭重拒絕請求或提議的時候

- I'm afraid I can't accept…
  我恐怕無法接受……。
- That's absolutely unacceptable.
  這真的令人難以接受。
- It would be difficult. 這很困難。

8. 追究責任的時候

- You have to be responsible for…
  你要對……負責。
- You are to blame. 都怪你。
- That's your fault. 那是你的錯

9. 因為意料之外的情況而感到驚訝時

- You surprise me. 嚇我一跳。
- I hardly expected to…
  我幾乎不抱……的期待。
- I'm really surprised to hear…
  我很驚訝聽到……。

10. 指出對方離題時

- I think your statement is out of the point.
  我覺得你的發言離題了。
- Would you give me a straight answer?
  你能說重點嗎？
- So, what's your point?
  所以你的重點是什麼？

1. What is the conversation mainly about?

   (A) A recent performance

   (B) An upcoming show

   (C) A sold-out concert

   (D) The breakup of a band

2. Why does the woman say, "How shocking"?

   (A) She thinks the quality of a performance was poor.

   (B) She heard that a show was overbooked.

   (C) She found out about a low turnout.

   (D) She found out a concert was canceled.

3. Why does the woman say, "I can't believe it"?

   (A) She is surprised that an employee left the company.

   (B) She does not trust the man.

   (C) She has received some false information.

   (D) She is happy to hear some news.

4. What does the man suggest the woman do?

   (A) Have an account number ready

   (B) Speak with Ms. Lemoute's replacement

   (C) Mail an application form

   (D) Visit the bank in person

▶ 答案與解析請參考解析本第44頁

結合視覺資料的題目

視覺資料題目是要結合題目和視覺資料才能解題的類型，通常會在Part 3的最後出現兩到三題。測驗中的視覺資料非常多元，包含表格、圖表、行程表、地圖等等。視覺資料題目的解題關鍵是，根據視覺資料的類型事先猜測對話內容。還要事先掌握視覺資料的重要內容，一邊聆聽對話一邊對照來解題。

 代表題型 先閱讀題目再聆聽音檔後，選出合適的正確答案。 🎧 49.mp3

Q. Look at the graphic. When will Ron make his presentation?

(A) At 9:00

(B) At 10:00

(C) At 11:00

(D) At 12:00

Presenter Time
Susan 9:00
Jack 10:00
Jackie 11:00
Ron 12:00

 攻略解題法 了解如何作答結合視覺資料的題目。

🗨 聆聽對話前閱讀題目時

Q. Look at the graphic. When will Ron make his presentation?

請看圖表。榮恩什麼時候會做簡報？

▶ 在聆聽對話之前，一定要先確認圖表的內容並預測對話內容。這題要問的是榮恩的簡報時間，所以要記住榮恩的簡報時間。我們可以猜測因為某人發生突發事件，榮恩會在其他時段做簡報，而不是在十二點進行，所以請專心聆聽簡報時間變動的部分。

(A) At 9:00　9點

(B) At 10:00　10點

(C) At 11:00　11點

(D) At 12:00　12點

發表者時間
蘇珊 9點
傑克 10點
潔姬 11點
榮恩 12點

 聆聽對話時

Refer to the following conversation and schedule.　請參照以下的對話和日程。

M: Hello, Jackie. I'm just calling to remind you about the presentation schedule for this morning's meeting. You know you're scheduled for 11:00, right?

男：哈囉，潔姬。我打電話給你是想提醒你今天早上的會議簡報日程。你知道你被排在十一點吧？

W: About that... I need to change my presentation time because a client is coming to see me for an urgent meeting at 10:30, and I think it will take a little longer than 30 minutes to deal with her.

女：關於那個……我需要更改我的簡報時間，因為十點三十分有個客戶要來找我開緊急會議，我覺得會花三十分鐘以上跟她討論。

M: Okay... Well, Jack is scheduled for right before you while Ron is speaking as soon as you're done. Do you want to change sessions with one of them?

男：好……嗯，傑克被排在你前面，你結束後由榮恩發表。你要跟他們其中一人換時間嗎？

W: Yes. I think I'll take the later time since I need some time to get prepared.

▶ 必須了解整個對話內容才能解題。原定十一點發表的潔姬（女子）因為十點三十分有客戶要來，可能會耗時半小時以上，所以想要換時間。男子建議她換成前面或後面的時段，女子選擇了後者。潔姬之後是榮恩，所以可以猜到潔姬會跟榮恩換時間。因此，榮恩會在十一點做簡報。正確答案為(C)。

女：嗯，我要換到晚一點的時段，因為我需要一些時間做準備。

M: Okay, I'll revise the timetable right away.　男：好，我會立刻修改時程表。

詞彙整理 remind 提醒　**urgent** 緊急的　**as soon as** 一～就～　**get prepared** 準備好的

攻略POINT ❶ 遇到有行程表的題目時，就要預想到會發生某件事，行程表因此有變動。整個對話會出現與問題起因、已變更的行程表有關的線索，所以必須理解整個內容。

❷ 在上述的對話中，行程表發生變動不是因為榮恩，而是因為其他人，榮恩的時間才發生變動。所以不能只聽關於榮恩的內容，要仔細聆聽整個行程表的變更內容。

Step 2 ｜ 核心理論&基礎形式

視覺資料題型

1. 須在視覺資料中尋找並對照對話內容的題目

Q. Look at the graphic. Which storage capacity will the man probably order?

請看圖表。男子可能會訂購哪個儲存容量？

(A) 16GB

(B) 32GB

(C) 64GB

(D) 128GB

Storage Capacity	Price
16GB	$199.00
32GB	$249.00
64GB	$299.00
128GB	$399.00

結合對話與表格

M: The PC prices greatly vary according to the storage capacity. I'm not sure which one I should order.　男：桌上型電腦的價格會根據儲存容量而有大幅變動。我不確定我該訂購哪一個。

W: Well, the more storage space, the better. But let's not exceed 300 dollars per PC.

女：嗯，儲存空間越多越好。但是每台桌上型電腦不要超過三百美元吧。

▶ 透過表格可以知道符合功能與價格要求，意即不超過三百美元，且容量最大的桌上型電腦是64GB的。多益測驗中會出現這種需要尋找符合對話內容的物品的題型。

2. 觀察地圖或構造後尋找位置的題目

Q. Look at the graphic. Which booth will the woman reserve? 請看圖表。女子會預訂哪個攤位？

(A) Booth 5
(B) Booth 6
(C) Booth 8
(D) Booth 9

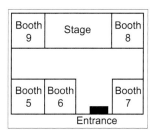

結合對話與圖表

W: We wanted to reserve the two booths next to the entrance, but booth 6 has already been taken. So I signed up for booth 7, and now we have to choose one more spot. 女：我們本來想預訂入口旁邊的兩個攤位，但是六號攤位已經被訂走了。所以，我想申請七號攤位，現在我們要再選一個地點。

M: Okay. Let's just go with the one close to booth 7. It's also right next to the stage, so I think it'll get plenty of attention as well.
男：好。我們就選接近七號攤位的吧。這剛好就在舞台旁邊，所以我覺得也會獲得很多關注。

▶ 接近七號攤位又在舞台旁邊的是八號攤位。多益測驗中會出現這種看平面圖或地圖再找位置的題目。

3. 利用圖表的最高或最低點出題的題目

Q. Look at the graphic. What was the sales figure when the company held a discount event?
請看圖表。公司舉辦折扣活動時的銷售額是多少？

(A) $1,000,000
(B) $600,000
(C) $400,000
(D) $200,000

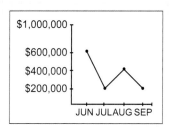

結合對話與圖表

M: Did you see our sales figures for the last few months? Our most successful month was June, but after that, the figures dropped dramatically and are still maintaining a downward tendency. 男：你看到我們前幾個月的銷售額了嗎？我們最成功的月份是六月，但在那之後數字就大幅下降了，而且還保持下滑的趨勢。

W: Yes, I saw it. The figures rose a bit when we had that discount event in August, but it wasn't enough to set a record. So we need to come up with some new and innovative ideas. 女：嗯，我看到了。數字在我們八月舉辦折扣活動時上升了一點，但還是不足以創造紀錄。所以我們需要想出一些新的創新點子。

▶ 對話提到八月舉辦了折扣活動，那時候銷售額上升了一點。八月的銷售額是四十萬美元，所以正確答案是 (C)。多益測驗中會出現這種需要結合銷售比較、產品占有率或數量增減率的圖表題目。

4. 與表格、收據、票券或優惠券相關且詢問價格的題目

Q. Look at the graphic. What discount will the man most likely receive?

請看圖表。男子最有可能獲得什麼折扣？

(A) $3
(B) $20
(C) $25
(D) $50

Discount coupon	
Monitor Sizes	
20~24 inch	$30 Value
25 inch and above	$50 Value
Gilbut Tech	
Expiration Date 10/30	

結合對話與圖表

M: Excuse me. I'm looking for a 27-inch computer monitor, but I can only see 21 and 24-inch. Do you have any larger monitors in stock? And I have this discount coupon. Is it valid for your store? 男：不好意思，我正在找一台二十七吋的電腦螢幕，但是我只有看到二十一和二十四吋的。你們有更大的螢幕現貨嗎？我有這張優惠券，你們的店適用嗎？

W: Yes, you can get a discount. The monitors used to be all together, but we recently moved the larger displays to a separate aisle. I'll show you. 女：是的，您可以享有折扣。螢幕通常都放在一起，但是我們最近把更大的螢幕搬到不同的走道上了。我帶您去看。

▶ 男子正在找二十七吋的螢幕，大於二十四吋的螢幕有五十美元的折扣。多益測驗中也有這種跟表格、收據、優惠券，或門票的折扣率或日期有關，要選出正確金額的類型。

Step 3　　實戰演練　　🎧 50.mp3

1. What kind of event are the speakers sponsoring?

   (A) An auction
   (B) A running race
   (C) A design competition
   (D) An art show

2. Look at the graphic. Which firm will the speakers do business with?

   (A) Fine Art
   (B) W Design
   (C) Varizon
   (D) Griffino

Company	Location
Fine Art	New Jersey
W Design	San Francisco
Varizon	San Diego
Griffino	Los Angeles

3. What is the man's problem?

   (A) He has not received extra payment.
   (B) He needs a phone number for Human Resources.
   (C) He cannot use his ID card.
   (D) He cannot remember a password for a computer system.

4. Look at the graphic. What location is the man told to go to?

   (A) Room 1
   (B) Room 2
   (C) Room 3
   (D) Room 4

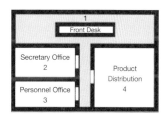

▶ 答案與解析請參考解析本第45頁

REVIEW TEST

1. What are the speakers mainly discussing?

   (A) Moving an office
   (B) Removing some old furniture
   (C) Painting an office
   (D) Hiring a new staff member

2. Where does the conversation probably take place?

   (A) In a museum
   (B) In an office
   (C) In a restaurant
   (D) In an airport

3. According to conversation, what will the woman probably do next?

   (A) Remove all the documents
   (B) Leave the office
   (C) Send an email to Ms. Bunny
   (D) Contact a particular department

4. Why was the woman late for the meeting?

   (A) She was using public transportation.
   (B) She just came back from her vacation.
   (C) She was stuck in traffic.
   (D) She lives far from the company.

5. When will the speakers install the new program?

   (A) On Monday
   (B) On Tuesday
   (C) On Wednesday
   (D) On Thursday

6. According to the conversation, what does the man suggest?

   (A) To come early on Thursday
   (B) To visit the Sales Department
   (C) To buy an airplane ticket
   (D) To leave for a business trip

7. Where is this conversation most likely taking place?

   (A) In an office
   (B) At a healthcare seminar
   (C) At a fitness center
   (D) In a sporting goods store

8. What do the men say about the new facility?

   (A) It has some secondhand sports equipment.
   (B) It was more crowded on the first floor.
   (C) It has been upgraded in many ways.
   (D) It has more expensive machines than before.

9. What does the woman say she will do?

   (A) Visit the first floor
   (B) Go to a facility
   (C) Work out at the park
   (D) Call a fitness center

10. What does the woman like about her album?

    (A) It can interest people in all age groups.
    (B) It is her bestselling album yet.
    (C) It focuses only on traditional jazz music.
    (D) It is her first album.

11. What is the woman planning to do?

    (A) Release her next album
    (B) Give a performance
    (C) Visit her hometown
    (D) Take a break from music

12. What does the woman mean when she says, "Thanks for asking"?

    (A) She wants to ask the same question.
    (B) She wants to talk about a new topic.
    (C) She has heard the question many times.
    (D) She cannot give an answer now.

DIRECTORY

Suite No.
401 Dr. Young's clinic
402 Reed and Ken Marketing
403 R&J Architecture
405 FOR RENT
406 Carson's Law Office

---

13. Who most likely is the man?

    (A) An interviewer
    (B) A repair technician
    (C) A front desk clerk
    (D) A painter

14. Look at the graphic. Where most likely will the woman have an interview?

    (A) At a doctor's clinic
    (B) At a marketing company
    (C) At an architecture firm
    (D) At an attorney's office

15. What will the man probably do next?

    (A) Relocate a ladder
    (B) Sign his name
    (C) Repaint a wall
    (D) Use a stairway

▶ 答案與解析請參考解析本第46頁

聽寫訓練

Unit 13 詢問主題、目的的題目　　Step 3 實戰演練　　　　　⊕ dictation-19.mp3

Question 1 refers to the following conversation.

M : How are you doing ＿＿＿＿＿＿＿＿＿＿＿ program you ＿＿＿＿＿＿＿
＿＿＿＿＿ customer data?

W : I'm ＿＿＿＿＿＿＿＿＿＿＿＿＿＿＿. I did the same ＿＿＿＿＿＿＿＿＿
＿＿＿＿＿＿＿ at my last job.

M : That sounds really great! If you ＿＿＿＿＿＿＿＿＿＿, don't ＿＿＿＿＿＿ call me.

Question 2 refers to the following conversation.

W : Hello. I ＿＿＿＿＿＿＿＿＿＿＿ at your store this morning, and I heard from the store that
＿＿＿＿＿＿＿＿＿＿＿ my new refrigerator today.

M : Yes, ＿＿＿＿＿＿＿＿. ＿＿＿＿＿＿＿＿ Mrs. Jackson, right?

W : Yes, ＿＿＿＿＿＿＿＿. ＿＿＿＿＿＿＿＿＿ take away my old refrigerator as well?

M : Sure. There will ＿＿＿＿＿＿＿＿＿＿＿＿＿＿ for that service ＿＿＿＿＿.

Unit 14 詢問職業／對話地點的題目　　Step 3 實戰演練　　　　　⊕ dictation-20.mp3

Question 1 refers to the following conversation.

W : Excuse me. ＿＿＿＿＿＿＿＿＿＿＿＿ go to the Central Shopping Mall. Will your bus
＿＿＿＿＿＿＿＿＿＿＿?

M : No, ＿＿＿＿＿＿＿. You'll have to take the ＿＿＿＿＿＿＿＿＿. It will bring you there.

W : Thank you. ＿＿＿＿＿＿＿＿＿＿＿＿ at this station? I totally ＿＿＿＿＿
＿＿＿＿＿＿＿＿ about taking the bus.

M : You have to ＿＿＿＿＿＿＿＿＿＿＿＿＿＿＿.
You can see the bus station ＿＿＿＿＿＿＿＿＿＿＿＿ roof.

Question 2 refers to the following conversation.

M : Hi. This is Kim from _____. We _____ from the restaurant

manager saying that _____ problem with _____.

W : Oh, thanks for _____. I was cleaning the restroom and _____

_____ water in the toilet _____.

M : Okay. I _____ some equipment from my truck. I'll be back

in a minute.

Unit 15 詢問說話者的建議的題目 ┊ **Step 3** 實戰演練 ⊙ dictation-21.mp3

Question 1-2 refer to the following conversation.

W : I _____ again this morning. I _____ a

terrible _____.

M : Really? It's _____ taking the subway.

W : I wish I could _____, too, but my house is _____

_____ the subway station.

M : Maybe _____ near you would like to _____ to the station. Why

don't you talk _____?

Unit 16 詢問接下來會做什麼事的題目 ┊ **Step 3** 實戰演練 ⊙ dictation-22.mp3

Questions 1-2 refer to the following conversation.

M : Doris, _____ that the post office on Park Avenue _____

_____? Now, a restaurant is _____.

W : Yes. The post office _____ a new location on Main Street _____

_____.

M : Oh, really? Do you _____ I have to _____ today.

W : No, I don't, but I can _____.

聽寫訓練

Unit 17 詢問細節的題目 · **Step 3** 實戰演練

🅐 dictation-23.mp3

Questions 1-3 refer to the following conversation.

M : Hello there. I moved in to the apartment complex last month. I'd like to _____ _____ _____ _____ _____.

W : No problem. _____ _____ or a utility bill _____ you are currently _____.

M : Unfortunately, _____ with me. _____ _____ _____ after work?

W : Of course. We _____ though, so _____ _____ _____. This information _____ _____ and the office hours.

Unit 18 掌握句子意圖的題目 · **Step 3** 實戰演練

🅐 dictation-24.mp3

Questions 1-2 refer to the following conversation with three speakers.

M1 : Did you hear the _____ _____?

W : Yes, I did. _____ the show would definitely _____. _____ _____!

M2 : I know. Everyone was so excited about the concert. _____ that _____ _____?

W : _____ do you think _____ was?

M1 : Well, the critics are saying that the _____. The venue, the Golden Lion Theater, does have high prices.

Questions 3-4 refer to the following conversation.

W : Hello. I'd like to discuss _____. _____ Marianne Lemoute, please?

M : I'm sorry, but Ms. Lemoute _____.

W : Really? I can't believe it! I have always gotten _____ _____

_____ _____ as my financial advisor.

M : _____ anymore from

what I understand.

W : Oh, that's too bad. Well, then _____

_____?

M : It's best if you _____ Flooder. He is the _____

_____.

Unit 19 結合視覺資料的題目 | Step 3 實戰演練 🎧 dictation-25.mp3

Questions 1-2 refer to the following conversation and list.

W : Charles, I'm really _____ we're sponsoring

next month. I bet it'll _____.

M : Yeah, I'm excited, too. We need to _____

_____ that we'll give out to the participants. Have you looked over the list of

design firms? We have to _____

_____.

W : I know. I think Fine Art does a very good job, but _____

_____. And management has _____ to spend on

souvenirs this year.

M : That's true. Let's just _____

_____. We can reduce the shipping costs, and _____

_____, too.

Questions 3-4 refer to the following conversation and map.

M : Excuse me, Amanda. I have a _____. _____

_____ to the building, so I have to get someone on the

front desk staff to let me in. Could you _____

_____?

W : Well, the staff in _____

_____ for our building, Why don't you _____

_____? Someone there should be able to save you on the database.

M : Okay. I'll try. Thanks.

聽寫訓練

🔊 dictation-26.mp3

Questions 1-3 refer to the following conversation.

W : Hi, Michael. Did you hear that _____

_____? The workers will _____

_____, so we have to _____

before we leave today.

M : Really? I heard from Ms. Bunny that _____

_____.

W : Hmm. _____ to make

sure.

Questions 4-6 refer to the following conversation.

W : Hi, Mr. Anderson. I'm sorry. I was _____ this morning

_____. What did I miss?

M : Oh, on Thursday, _____

_____ for all of the computers in the Sales Department.

W : So is there _____ we have to do to _____?

M : No, but I suggest that _____. We

will have a lot of work to do.

Questions 7-9 refer to the following conversation with three speakers.

M1 : Have you guys _____ on the

15th floor?

W : _____, but I heard that it's gotten much

_____.

M2 : Yeah, it has. I started working out there this Monday, and I was really _____

_____.

M1 : And _____. It's fantastic! You can _____

_____.

M2 : I know. _____

_____ up from the first floor.

W : Wow, it sounds amazing. I'm definitely _____

today.

Questions 10-12 refer to the following conversation.

M : Welcome back to Music Hour. _____ with our special guest,

Michelle O'Conner. Michelle, can you tell us more _____

_____?

W : Sure! It's a contemporary _____

, and I think the best part is that you can all enjoy the songs _____

_____.

M : That sounds great. Now, I heard that you're planning to _____

_____. Which states will you be visiting?

W : Thanks for asking. Right now, we're still _____.

The details _____.

Questions 13-15 refer to the following conversation and directory.

W : Hello. _____ at noon. The person

I spoke to told me I need to _____

to gain access to the building.

M : Well, you're in the right place. Please sign your name here and show me your ID. _____

_____?

W : Office 406. I'm meeting with Mr. Landon.

M : Okay, you can use the elevator. Our building is _____ in the hallway

right now, and there's a lot of _____. Hold on… Let me

_____ out of your way. Otherwise, _____

_____.

Voca Preview

請勾選不認識的單字，學習完類型分析後再重新確認勾選的單字。

☐ **sales report** 銷售報告

☐ **run** 運作

☐ **beverage** 飲料

☐ **meal** 用餐

☐ **vegetarian** 素食主義者

☐ **go over** 檢閱，查看

☐ **chef** 廚師

☐ **refreshments** 輕食，茶點

☐ **frequent** 慣常的

☐ **seasoned** 調味過的

☐ **broiled** 烤過的

☐ **organic** 有機的

☐ **complain** 抱怨

☐ **starter** 開胃菜

☐ **appetite** 食慾

☐ **cater** 承辦宴席

☐ **cuisine** 烹飪，烹飪方法

☐ **attract** 吸引，引誘

☐ **take an order** 接單

☐ **set the table** 擺桌

☐ **eat out** 外食

☐ **reserve a table** 訂位

☐ **advance reservation** 事先預約

☐ **suitable** 合適的

☐ **resonable price** 合理的價格

☐ **laundry service** 洗衣服務

☐ **inconvenience** 不便

☐ **access** 連線

☐ **accommodation** 住宿

☐ **capacity** 容納能力

☐ **key deposit** 鑰匙保證金

☐ **nonsmoking room** 禁菸室

☐ **page** 廣播叫（人）

☐ **room rate** 房價，住宿費

☐ **service charge** 服務費

☐ **valuables** 貴重物品

☐ **clearance sale** 清倉拍賣

☐ **happy hour** 特別折扣時段

☐ **belongings** 隨身物品

☐ **concierge** 接待專員

類型分析 **8**

各大主題攻略—服務

WARMING UP

REVIEW TEST

聽寫訓練

WARMING UP

診斷評估　閱讀題目後，在兩秒內掌握題目重點。

1. What is the conversation mainly about? ....
2. Where probably are the speakers? ....
3. What does the woman suggest? ....

尋找線索　觀察對話，找出上述題目的線索。

M : I should stay late tonight because I have to finish the sales report by today.

W : Don't forget to leave the computer on after you finish work. All the security software on the computers will be upgraded by seven p.m.

M : That's right. I forgot. I think I will have to finish the report at home.

W : Or you could get here early tomorrow. The computers will be running by 7 o'clock.

確認解答＆要點　確認正確答案，了解與服務有關的對話特徵。

診斷評估：掌握題目的重點

1. What is the conversation mainly about?　此對話主要跟什麼有關？　▶詢問主題
2. Where probably are the speakers?　說話者有可能在哪裡？　▶詢問對話地點
3. What does the woman suggest?　女子建議做什麼？　▶詢問建議內容

尋找線索：分析測驗內容

M :　I should stay late tonight because I have to finish the sales report by today.
　　　▶1. 對話主題的答題依據／2. 對話地點的答題依據

　　　男：我今晚應該會留到很晚，因為我必須在今天完成銷售報告。

　　可以從第一句話猜測整個對話的鋪陳，第一句是跟主題／目的有
　　關的句子。可以得知男子就算得熬夜，也想在今天寫完報告。

W :　Don't forget to leave the computer on after you finish work. All the
　　　▶3. 女子的建議的答題依據／2. 對話地點的第二個答題依據

　　　security software on the computers will be upgraded by seven p.m.
　　　女：工作結束後別忘記開著電腦。電腦裡所有的防毒軟體會在晚上七點更新。

　　對話地點的直接相關線索會在對話的第一、二句出現，所以要專心聆聽這個部分和
　　跟地點有關的詞彙。跟地點有關的詞彙大部分會在三、四個地方出現，這有助於
　　推敲對話地點。透過這句提到的 computer、after you finish work 和第一句的 sales
　　report，我們可以猜測對話地點是公司或辦公室。女子建議對方離開前不要關電腦。

M :　That's right. I forgot. I think I will have to finish the report at home.

W :　Or you could get here early tomorrow. The computers will be running by
　　　7 o'clock.

　　　男：對耶！我忘了。我想我應該會需要在家裡完成報告。
　　　女：或是你明天早點到。電腦會在七點運作。

　　詞彙整理　**finish the report** 完成報告　**security software** 防毒軟體　**run** 運作

155

Step 1 | 實戰重點

與餐廳有關的對話，會出現詢問「對話場所、請求／建議、說話者的職業」等題目。

 代表題型 先在十秒內讀完三道題目，聆聽音檔後選出正確答案。 52.mp3

1.Where does this conversation most likely take place?

    (A) In an office

    (B) In a restaurant

    (C) In a department store

    (D) In a supermarket

2.What does the woman ask for?

    (A) A sales receipt

    (B) A beverage

    (C) A magazine

    (D) A menu

3.What will the woman do next?

    (A) Watch TV

    (B) Read a magazine

    (C) Scan a menu

    (D) Contact a colleague

攻略解題法 了解該如何作答與餐廳相關的題目。

聆聽對話前閱讀題目時

1. Where does this conversation most likely take place? 這則對話最有可能在哪裡發生？

   ▶ 這題是詢問對話地點的題目，所以要專心聆聽第一句。

   (A) In an office   在辦公室

   (B) In a restaurant   在餐廳

   (C) In a department store   在百貨公司

   (D) In a supermarket   在超市

2. What does the woman ask for?   女子要求什麼？

   ▶ 這題是建議／請求題，所以要仔細聆聽女子提出請求後的句子。

   (A) A sales receipt   銷貨收據

   (B) A beverage   飲料

   (C) A magazine   雜誌

   (D) A menu   菜單

3. What will the woman do next?   女子接下來會做什麼？

   ▶ 這題是next題型，所以要專心聆聽最後的對話。

   (A) Watch TV   看電視

   (B) Read a magazine   看雜誌

   (C) Scan a menu   看菜單

   (D) Contact a colleague   聯絡同事

聆聽對話時

Questions 1-3 refer to the following conversation.   第1-3題請參照以下的對話。

W: Hi. I'm from the Nature Design Company. [1] **We're supposed to meet here for lunch at noon.**   ▶ 這是詢問對話地點的題目。這句出現跟地點有關的詞彙（lunch），所以(B)為正確答案。

女：嗨，我來自自然設計公司。我們預定中午時在這裡見面吃午餐。

M: Nobody has arrived yet. Would you like to be seated now?

男：還沒有人到。您現在要先入座嗎？

W: Yes, please. And [2] **could I have some juice while I'm waiting?**

   ▶ 這是請求題，所以要仔細聆聽請求問句後面的對話。女子要求對方給果汁，所以意思是「要喝的東西、飲料」，因此(B)為正確答案。

女：好，麻煩你。在我等人的時候可以給我果汁嗎？

M: Of course. [3] **Here is a menu with our daily specials for you to look at while you are waiting.**   ▶ 這是next題型，所以要專心聆聽最後的對話。男子提議「邊等人邊看特選菜單」，由此可推論出女子接下來會做的事是看菜單，所以正確答案為(C)。

男：沒問題。您在等人的時候可以先看看本日的特選菜單。

攻略POINT ❶ 詢問地點的題目會在開頭第一、二句出現直接的相關提示，所以要專心聆聽這個部分。但即使錯過這邊的線索，聽完整個內容再解題也可以。

❷ 請求題要專心聆聽「could / would~?」這類的請求問句。

❸ 此類詢問接下來會做什麼事的題目，須專注於最後面的對話。

 與餐廳有關的常見表達方式

- Hello. I'd like to see if I can make a reservation for lunch on Monday at noon.
  你好，我想知道能不能預約禮拜一中午的午餐。

- What did you think about Carla's Steakhouse? 你覺得卡拉牛排館怎麼樣？

- I want to know what else is on the menu. 我想知道菜單上還有什麼其他的選項。

- I believe you've given me the wrong meal. 你好像上錯菜了。

- I requested a vegetarian meal. 我點了素食餐。

- Are you ready to order? 您要點餐了嗎？

- Could we have a minute to go over the menu? 我們可以看一下菜單嗎？

- Do you have a table available for tonight at 8:00? 你們今晚八點有位置嗎？

- You can only make a reservation for more than 20 people. 只有二十人以上可以預約。

- We're supposed to meet here for lunch at one. 我們約好一點在這裡見面用午餐。

- Would you like to be seated now? 您要現在入座嗎？

Voca Check - up! **order** 點菜 **chef** 廚師 **dessert** 點心 **refreshments** 輕食，茶點 **frequent** 時常的，頻繁的 **seasoned** 調味過的 **broiled** 烤過的 **fillet** 里肌肉，菲力 **vegetarian** 素食（主義）者 **organic** 有機的 **complain** 抱怨 **popular** 受歡迎的 **starter** 開胃菜 **appetite** 食慾 **luncheon** 午餐會 **dine** 用餐 **cater** 承辦宴席 **cuisine** 烹飪，烹飪方法 **amount** 總額，總計 **attract** 吸引，引誘 **take an order** 接單 **set the table** 擺桌 **great location** 好位置 **famous for** 以～聞名 **daily special** 本日特選料理 **eat out** 外食 **look over** 瀏覽～ **reserve a table** 訂位 **advance dining reservation** 事先訂餐廳 **be invited**＋名詞 被邀請至～

1. Where probably are the speakers?

   (A) In a restaurant

   (B) In an office

   (C) In a cinema

   (D) In a bookstore

2. According to the conversation, what does the man request?

   (A) A suitable place

   (B) A special menu

   (C) A discount

   (D) A resonable price

3. What does the woman recommend?

   (A) A menu for children

   (B) A new menu

   (C) A special set menu

   (D) A happy hour menu

▶ 答案與解析請參考解析本第51頁

Unit 21 飯店

Step 1 實戰重點

與飯店有關的對話，會出現抱怨、要求事項、問題解決方法、辦理入住或退房手續、服務等相關內容。

 代表題型 先在十秒內讀完三道題目，聆聽音檔後選出正確答案。 54.mp3

1.Why is the woman calling?

(A) To book a room

(B) To call housekeeping

(C) To check on a reservation

(D) To find a hotel guest

2.Who most likely is the woman talking to?

(A) A waiter

(B) A repairman

(C) A housekeeper

(D) A hotel receptionist

3.When will the woman arrive?

(A) On Thursday

(B) On Friday

(C) On Saturday

(D) On Sunday

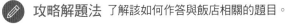 攻略解題法 了解該如何作答與飯店相關的題目。

聽聽對話前閱讀題目時

1. Why is the woman calling? 女子為什麼打電話？

   ▶ 詢問理由的題目，相關線索通常會在對話的前半段出現。

   (A) To book a room　為了訂房

   (B) To call housekeeping　為了請人打掃房間

   (C) To check on a reservation　為了確認預約

   (D) To find a hotel guest　為了找房客

2. Who most likely is the woman talking to?　女子最有可能正在跟誰談話？

   ▶ 這題問的是男子的職業，所以要在對話的前半段找提示。

   (A) A waiter　服務生

   (B) A repairman　維修人員

   (C) A housekeeper　房務人員

   (D) A hotel receptionist　飯店接待員

3. When will the woman arrive?　女子會在何時抵達？

   ▶ 選項中的星期在對話中提及一次以上時，要先記住對話中出現過的星期，之後專心聆聽可參考的關鍵字，選出最終的答案。

   (A) On Thursday　星期四

   (B) On Friday　星期五

   (C) On Saturday　星期六

   (D) On Sunday　星期日

聽聽對話時

Questions 1-3 refer to the following conversation.　第1-3題請參照以下的對話。

W: My name is Victoria, and ¹ I'm calling to confirm my room reservation for this weekend.　▶ 這是詢問理由的題目，所以要專心聆聽第一句。句子內容是「確認訂房預約」的來電，所以(C)為正確答案。

女：我叫做維多利亞，我打電話是想確認我在這週末的訂房預約。

M: ² Please wait a second. Let me check for you, ma'am. ³ Will you be arriving on Saturday morning?　▶ 這是出現男子職業的第二句話。男子說會幫忙確認預約，所以他的職業是飯店接待員。(D)為正確答案。

男：請稍候。我替您確認一下，女士。您會在星期六早上抵達嗎？

W: ³ No, the day before. I'd like to know about the facilities at the hotel as well. Could you tell me about them briefly?

   ▶ 男子詢問抵達日期是不是星期六，女子則回覆是前一天抵達，所以(B)為正確答案。

女：不是，是前一天。我還想了解飯店裡的設施。你可以簡單地跟我說一下嗎？

詞彙整理 call 打電話 **confirm** 確認 **reservation** 預約 **check** 確認 **facility** 設施

攻略POINT ❶ 詢問理由的題目，相關線索通常會在對話前半段出現。

　　　　 ❷ 詢問職業的題目，相關提示會在對話前半段出現。

　　　　 ❸ 選項中的星期在對話中提及一次以上時，要先記住對話中出現過的星期，之後專心聆聽可參考的關鍵字，選出最終的答案。

與飯店有關的常見表達方式

- We have our own laundry service here at the hotel. 我們飯店提供洗衣服務。
- I'm terribly sorry for the inconvenience. 很抱歉給您造成不便。
- I'd like to check in(out), please. 我想辦理入住（退房）手續，麻煩你。
- I'm calling about my room reservation. 我打電話是為了訂房的事。
- I'd like to make a reservation for this weekend. 我想訂這個週末的房間。
- I want to know about the facilities at this hotel. 我想了解飯店的設施。
- How can I access the Internet in my room? 我要怎麼在房間裡上網？
- Let me check your reservation. 讓我確認看看您的預約。
- Please wait a second. 請稍候。
- How many people does the suite accommodate? 套房可以容納多少人？
- I'd like to speak to housekeeping, please. 我想跟房務人員說話，麻煩你。

Voca Check - up! **accommodation** 住處 **booked up** 全部被訂完的 **capacity** 容納能力 **check-in** 入住，投宿 **check-out** 退房 **conference room** 會議室 **doorman** 看門人 **fitness center** 健身房 **key deposit** 鑰匙保證金 **lobby** 大廳 **lounge** 休息室 **maid** （飯店的）女服務員 **maid service** 打掃服務 **meeting room** 會議室 **nonsmoking room** 禁菸房 **page** 廣播叫（人）**receptionist** 接待員 **registration form** 住宿登記表 **reservation number** 預約號碼 **reserve** 預約 **room rate** 房價，住宿費 **room service** 客房服務 **safety deposit box** 保險櫃 **sauna** 桑拿 **service charge (= tip)** 服務費，小費 **single** 單人房 **double** 雙人房 **suite** 套房 **twin** 雙床房 **valuables** 貴重物品 **wake-up call** 電話喚醒服務

1. Who does the woman want to have stay at the Manchester Hotel?

   (A) Her coworkers

   (B) Her family

   (C) Her friends

   (D) Her clients

2. What does the man want to know about the hotel?

   (A) Its location

   (B) Its profits

   (C) Its facilities

   (D) Its prices

3. Why does the woman suggest going to her office?

   (A) To check a website

   (B) To meet with clients

   (C) To make a reservation

   (D) To prepare for a meeting

▶ 答案與解析請參考解析本第51頁

REVIEW TEST

1. Where did the woman get the coupon?

   (A) A book
   (B) A magazine
   (C) A newspaper
   (D) A website

2. What problem does the man mention about the coupon?

   (A) It can only be used at lunch.
   (B) It can only be used on the weekend.
   (C) It has expired.
   (D) It's for another restaurant.

3. What does the man say is happening now?

   (A) A grand opening sale
   (B) A clearance sale
   (C) A happy hour
   (D) A special offer

4. Why is the man calling?

   (A) To make a reservation
   (B) To find his lost belongings
   (C) To cancel a reservation
   (D) To make a payment

5. How long will the man stay at the hotel?

   (A) 1 week
   (B) 2 weeks
   (C) 3 days
   (D) 5 days

6. What will the man most likely do next?

   (A) Send an email about his reservation
   (B) Go to the front desk at the hotel
   (C) Give his credit card information
   (D) Mention his contact information

7. Who most likely is the man?

(A) A salesperson
(B) An office worker
(C) A hotel employee
(D) A hotel guest

8. According to the conversation, where is the concierge?

(A) Around the swimming pool
(B) Beside the front desk
(C) Near the man's room
(D) Near the entrance

9. What will the woman do after the conversation?

(A) Go to the concierge
(B) Find a driver
(C) Call a travel agency
(D) Speak with another guest

10. Where are the speakers?

(A) In a restaurant
(B) In a hotel
(C) In an office
(D) In an electronics store

11. What does the man mean when he says, "I can't put up with the noise"?

(A) He hopes that the fridge will be fixed immediately.
(B) He cannot speak with the woman for long.
(C) He is satisfied with the room service.
(D) He will cancel his reservation.

12. What will the woman most likely do next?

(A) Serve a dessert
(B) Cancel an order
(C) Bring some water
(D) Check a schedule

▶ 答案與解析請參考解析本第51頁

聽寫訓練

dictation-27.mp3

Unit 20　餐廳　｜　**Step 3** 實戰演練

Questions 1-3 refer to the following conversation.

M : Excuse me. Do you _____ for large groups? I want to

_____ who are visiting my company this weekend here for

dinner.

W : Yes, we have _____ that _____

_____ 20 people.

M : That's great. But before I _____, I need to _____

_____ first.

W : Then you should _____ menu for groups. It's _____

_____, but the price _____.

Unit 21　飯店　｜　**Step 3** 實戰演練

dictation-28.mp3

Questions 1-3 refer to the following conversation.

W : Our _____ are here next week. I'd like to _____ in the

Manchester Hotel for them. _____ think about that hotel?

M : I like it, but I want to _____ at the hotel.

W : We can _____ to find out about them. We can use the computer in my

office _____.

Review Test

dictation-29.mp3

Questions 1-3 refer to the following conversation.

W : Hi. Before we order our meal, could you please _____ that I printed out

_____? It indicates that if we order _____

_____, we can _____.

M : I'm so sorry, but that coupon is _____.

W : Really? I thought I can use this coupon. That's a shame.

M : But don't be disappointed. We are having _____, so you

can _____.

Questions 4-6 refer to the following conversation.

M : Hi. My name is Dean, and I'm calling to _____ _____ _____ .

W : Thank you for calling the WD Hotel. For how long would you like to stay, sir?

M : _____. How much is _____, _____ ?

W : It's $500, and _____. Could you please give me your name and phone number?

Questions 7-9 refer to the following conversation.

W : Excuse me. Where can I _____ around your hotel?

M : You could _____ _____. He can give you a travel map.

W : How about transportation? Do you provide any transportation services?

M : Yes. You can get a _____ _____ as well. It runs _____ _____ .

Questions 10-12 refer to the following conversation.

M : Hello. _____ _____. I can't put up with the noise. I think it's broken.

W : I am very sorry about the inconvenience. _____ _____to check it out. _____ I can do for you?

M : _____ _____? All the water in the fridge is getting warm.

W : Of course. I'll get that for you right away.

Voca Preview

請勾選不認識的單字，學習完類型分析後再重新確認勾選的單字。

- [ ] **describe** 說明，描述
- [ ] **book** 預約
- [ ] **sold out** 售罄的，賣完的
- [ ] **unique** 獨特的
- [ ] **fitting room** 更衣室
- [ ] **be made of** 以～製作的
- [ ] **certainly** 當然，沒問題
- [ ] **try on** 試穿
- [ ] **negotiate** 協商
- [ ] **retailer** 零售商
- [ ] **outfit** 服裝，裝備，用品
- [ ] **affordable** （價格等）可負擔的
- [ ] **refund** 退款
- [ ] **ready-made** 現成的
- [ ] **commodity** 日常用品，生活必需品
- [ ] **regular customer** 常客
- [ ] **under warranty** 保固期間內的
- [ ] **in stock** 有庫存的
- [ ] **latest trend** 最新潮流
- [ ] **tailor-made** 訂製的

- [ ] **voucher** 兌換券
- [ ] **exhibition** 展覽
- [ ] **half price** 半價
- [ ] **round trip** 來回旅行
- [ ] **departure** 出發
- [ ] **charge** 收費
- [ ] **blowout sale** 促銷特賣
- [ ] **refundable** 可退還的
- [ ] **replacement** 取代
- [ ] **performance** 表演
- [ ] **ticket booth** 售票處
- [ ] **print out** 列印
- [ ] **family vacation** 家族旅遊
- [ ] **complimentary** 免費的
- [ ] **tourist attraction** 觀光景點
- [ ] **main entrance** 正門
- [ ] **rechargeable** 可再充電的
- [ ] **clothing store** 服飾店
- [ ] **aisle seat** 走道座位
- [ ] **make a payment** 付款

類型分析

9

各大主題攻略—購物

WARMING UP

1. What is the purpose of the call?　--------------------------------

2. What problem does the woman describe?　--------------------------------

3. When will the man leave?　--------------------------------

尋找線索　觀察對話，找出上述題目的線索。

W : Thank you for calling Banassy Airline. May I help you?

M : Oh, yes. I'd like to book a flight to Chicago early in the morning on September 1.

W : Unfortunately, all the early flights are sold out on September 1. If you don't mind, I recommend that you take an early flight the next day.

M : Yes, I'd like that.

確認解答＆要點　確認正確答案，了解與購物有關的對話特徵。

診斷評估：掌握題目的重點

1. What is the purpose of the call?　這通電話的目的是什麼？　▶ 詢問打電話的目的

2. What problem does the woman describe?　女子描述了什麼問題？　▶ 詢問女子描述的問題

3. When will the man leave?　男子何時出發？　▶ 詢問男子的出發時間

尋找線索：分析測驗內容

W : Thank you for calling Banassy Airline. May I help you?

女：謝謝您打電話到貝納西航空公司。我能為您效勞嗎？

M : Oh, yes. I'd like to book a flight to Chicago early in the morning on September 1.

▶ 1. 打電話的目的

男：啊，是的。我想訂九月一日清晨飛往芝加哥的班機。

前半段出現「I'm calling~、I'd like to~、I want / hope~」等句型的部分會出現來電目的相關線索，所以要仔細聆聽這個部分。

W : Unfortunately, all the early flights are sold out on September 1. If you

▶ 2. 女子描述問題的答題依據

don't mind, I recommend that you take an early flight the next day.

▶ 3. 男子出發時間的答題依據

女：很遺憾的是，所有九月一日的早班班機都賣完了。如果您不介意，建議您搭隔天的早班班機。

雖然關於問題的線索會在前半段出現，但是題目的出題順序為第二題的話，正確答案的答題依據通常會在對話的中間部分出現。

關於未來的行程會在後半段出現，所以要專心聆聽後半段。

M : Yes, I'd like that.　男：好，就那樣吧。

詞彙整理　**book** 預約　**early in the morning** 清晨　**unfortunately** 遺憾地，不幸地　**sold out** 售罄的，賣完的

Unit 22　購物

與購物有關的題目，要專心聆聽對話發生的地點、請求、接下來會做的事等。

 代表題型 先在十秒內讀完三道題目，聆聽音檔後選出正確答案。　 57.mp3

1. Where probably are the speakers?

(A) In an office

(B) In a clothing shop

(C) In a restaurant

(D) In a shoe shop

2. What does the woman ask for?

(A) Different patterns

(B) Something longer

(C) A unique design

(D) Some other colors

3. What is the man going to do next?

(A) Take the woman to the fitting room

(B) Show the woman some other pants

(C) Bring the woman a glass of water

(D) Get some more items

攻略解題法 了解該如何作答與購物有關的題目。

聆聽對話前閱讀題目時

1. Where probably are the speakers?　說話者可能在哪裡？

　　▶ 這是詢問地點的題目，所以要仔細聽開頭前兩句。

　　(A) In an office　　在辦公室

　　(B) In a clothing shop　　在服飾店

　　(C) In a restaurant　　在餐廳

　　(D) In a shoe shop　　在鞋店

2. What does the woman ask for?　女子要求提供什麼？

　　▶ 這是詢問請求內容的題目，所以要專心聆聽提供建議的句子。

　　(A) Different patterns　　不一樣的花紋

　　(B) Something longer　　長一點的

　　(C) A unique design　　獨特的設計

　　(D) Some other colors　　其他顏色

3. What is the man going to do next?　男子接下來會做什麼？

　　▶ 這是詢問接下來會做什麼事的題目，所以要專心聆聽最後面的對話。

　　(A) Take the woman to the fitting room　　帶女子去更衣室

　　(B) Show the woman some other pants　　向女子展示其他褲子

　　(C) Bring the woman a glass of water　　給女子一杯水

　　(D) Get some more items　　拿更多物品

聆聽對話時

Questions 1-3 refer to the following conversation.　第1-3題請參照以下的對話。

M: **¹** Here are some skirts you might be interested in, Ms. Stephenson. They are made of silk.　▶ 聽到關於對話地點的線索「skirts、silk」時，可以知道對話地點是「服飾店」。(B)為正確答案。

　　男：這些是史蒂芬生女士您可能會喜歡的裙子。它們是用絲綢製成的。

W: They're very nice, but **²** I was hoping to get something in red or wine. Do you have anything else in those colors?　▶ 女子拒絕對方建議的款式，正在找其他的。女子想要紅色或酒紅色的，所以(D)為正確答案。

　　女：那些很好，但我想找紅色或酒紅色的。有其他這些顏色的衣服嗎？

M: Certainly. **³** I'll be back in a second with some more skirts for you to try on.

　　▶ 這是next題型，所以要在最後面的對話找線索。男子說「我這就去拿更多的裙子給您試穿」，所以(D)為正確答案。

　　男：當然。我這就去拿更多的裙子給您試穿。

詞彙整理 **be interested in** 對～感興趣 **be made of** 以～製作的 **silk** 絲綢 **certainly** 沒問題，當然 **try on** 試穿

攻略POINT ❶ 此類詢問地點的題目，要仔細聆聽開頭前兩句。

　　　　　 ❷ 回答請求題時，須留意提供建議的部分（why don't you~?、you could~、you'd better~）。

　　　　　 ❸ 此類詢問接下來會做什麼事的題目，要在最後面的對話找線索。

與購物有關的常見表達方式

- Were you able to negotiate a better price? 你能給我更好的價格嗎？
- You must show us the receipt. 您必須出示收據。
- They are used on all kinds of clothing. 它們被使用於所有種類的服飾上。
- They are having a clearance sale. 他們正在辦清倉大拍賣。
- Here are some skirts you might be interested in. 這些是您可能感興趣的裙子。
- Do you have anything else? 還有其他的嗎？
- I'll be back with some more shirts for you to try on. 我這就去拿更多的裙子給您試穿。
- I'm looking for yellow pants. 我正在找黃色的褲子。
- Do you have any special events that are going on now? 你們現在有在做什麼特別的活動嗎？
- It is displayed at the front of the store. 擺在商店的前面。
- Let me show you. 我帶您去看。

Voca Check - up! **retailer** 零售商 **price** 價格 **outfit** 服裝，裝備，用品 **outlet** 暢貨中心 **receipt** 收據 **affordable**（價格等）可負擔的 **refund** 退款 **clothing** 服飾 **dress shirt** 正式襯衫 **clearance** 清倉 **ready-made** 現成的 **commodity** 日常用品，生活必需品 **regular customer** 常客 **guarantee** 保證 **expire** 滿期 **auction** 拍賣 **valuables** 貴重物品 **under warranty** 保固期內的，受保障的 **appeal to** 對～有吸引力，向～呼籲 **on the condition that** 在～條件之下 **take place**（活動）舉辦，舉行 **be in stock** 有庫存 **take advantage of** 利用～ **latest trend** 最新潮流 **tailor-made** 訂製的，特製的

1. What does the woman want to know about the camera?

   (A) How much it is
   (B) Which battery to use with it
   (C) What color it is
   (D) Where it was made

2. What can the woman receive if she buys the camera?

   (A) A membership card
   (B) A movie ticket
   (C) A discount voucher
   (D) A free product

3. What will the woman probably do next?

   (A) Pay for the camera
   (B) Look at some cases
   (C) Contact her friend
   (D) Shop for another product

▶ 答案與解析請參考解析本第55頁

Unit 23　購票

購票的對話主題經常跟票券種類（機票、參觀票券等）、對話地點、預約（取消）等有關。

 代表題型 先在十秒內讀完三道題目，聆聽音檔後選出正確答案。 59.mp3

1. Where is the conversation most likely taking place?

    (A) At a cinema

    (B) At a museum

    (C) At a TV station

    (D) At a gallery

2. What does the man tell the woman?

    (A) An exhibition has not opened.

    (B) Tickets are sold out.

    (C) An event has finished.

    (D) The building is about to close.

3. What does the man suggest?

    (A) Attending another exhibition

    (B) Purchasing a ticket

    (C) Visiting the information center

    (D) Returning another day

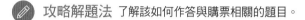 攻略解題法 了解該如何作答與購票相關的題目。

1. Where is the conversation most likely taking place?　此對話最有可能在哪裡發生？

   ▶ 這是詢問對話地點的題目，所以要仔細聆聽前半段。

   (A) At a cinema　電影院

   (B) At a museum　博物館

   (C) At a TV station　電視台

   (D) At a gallery　畫廊

2. What does the man tell the woman?　男子跟女子說什麼？

   ▶ 這題問的是男子跟女子說話的內容，所以要專心聆聽男子的發言。

   (A) An exhibition has not opened.　展覽還沒開放。

   (B) Tickets are sold out.　票賣完了。

   (C) An event has finished.　活動結束了。

   (D) The building is about to close.　大樓要關門了。

3. What does the man suggest?　男子建議做什麼？

   ▶ 這是詢問提供什麼建議的題目，所以要專心聆聽提供建議的部分（I suggest~、Why don't you~等）。

   (A) Attending another exhibition　參加另一個展覽

   (B) Purchasing a ticket　購票

   (C) Visiting the information center　拜訪諮詢服務中心

   (D) Returning another day　改天再來

聆聽對話時

Questions 1-3 refer to the following conversation.　第1-3題請參照以下的對話。

W: Hi. **¹** I saw on TV that there's a graphic artist exhibition here at the gallery this month.　▶ 這句提到地點的相關線索，可以得知對話地點是畫廊。(D)為正確答案。

女：嗨，我在電視上看到這個畫廊這個月有繪圖畫家的展覽。

M: Yes, you're at the right place, but, actually, **²** that exhibition doe<u>s</u>n't start <u>till</u> next
   Friday.　▶ 男子跟女子說展覽下星期五才開始，所以(A)為正確答案。

   ³ Why don't you visit next weekend?

   ▶ 這是提供建議的問句，所以包含關於建議的線索。男子提議「下週再來」，所以(D)為正確答案。

   男：是的，您來對地方了。不過，其實展覽下星期五才開始。您要不要下週再來？

W: Okay. I'll be back next week. Oh, and how much are the tickets?

   女：好，我下週再來。啊，票價是多少？

M: I'm not sure. But give me a second to ask the manager, and I'll let you know.

   男：我不確定。請稍候，我問一下經理再跟您說。

詞彙整理　**graphic artist** 繪圖畫家　**exhibition** 展覽　**gallery** 畫廊　**not~ until~** 在～之前不～，到～才～

攻略POINT ❶ 詢問對話地點的題目，答題線索會在開頭前兩句出現。

　　　　　 ❷ 詢問建議內容的題目，答題線索會在提供建議的部分（I suggest~、Why don't you~?、
　　　　　　　 Could you~）後面出現。

與購票有關的常見表達方式

- I'm sorry. All the window seats are taken. 抱歉，所有靠窗座位都賣完了。
- I'm calling to reserve tickets for Saturday's concert. 我打電話是想訂星期六音樂會的票。
- You can pay with either cash or a credit card. 您可以付現金或刷卡。
- The tickets are limited in number. 門票數量有限。
- You should arrive at the concert 30 minutes before it starts. 您必須在音樂會開始前三十分鐘到場。
- This exhibition doesn't start till next week. 此展覽下週才開始。
- The tickets are all sold out. 票全都賣完了。
- Are the seats next to each other? 座位是連在一起的嗎？
- You can get your tickets at the box office. 您可以在售票處取票。
- Admission is half price on Saturday. 星期六入場費半價。

Voca Check - up! **purchase** 購買 **seat** 座位 **trip** 旅行 **round trip** 來回旅行 **one-way trip** 單程旅行 **recommendation** 推薦 **departure** 出發 **arrival** 抵達 **charge** 收費 **blowout sale** 促銷特賣 **for sale** 販售中 **discount coupon / voucher** 折價券 **receipt** 收據 **refund** 退款 **replacement** 取代 **rate** 費用，價格 **performance** 表演 **exhibition** 展覽 **hold** 舉辦 **be crowded with** 擠滿 **ticket booth** 售票處 **gallery** 畫廊 **museum** 博物館 **be on display** 展示中 **make a reservation** 預約～ **be in line** 排隊 **brochure** 小冊子 **on show** ～展示中 **be out of** 沒有～ **be low in price** 價格低廉 **be over** 結束 **be assembled in a stadium** 在體育場集合 **at a great price** 以絕佳價格 **additional charge** 額外費用 **sold out** 賣完的 **popular** 受歡迎的 **theater** 電影院 **music concert** 音樂會

Step 3 ｜ 實戰演練 60.mp3

1. What does the woman want to do?

  (A) Make a reservation

  (B) Shop at the online store

  (C) Cancel her tickets

  (D) Buy some tickets

2. Why does the man say he cannot help the woman?

  (A) He has been on leave since last week.

  (B) He can sell tickets only at the ticket booth.

  (C) He is not in charge of selling tickets.

  (D) He needs to get approval from a manager.

3. What does the man tell the woman about?

  (A) Limited seats

  (B) Restricted tickets

  (C) The reservation system

  (D) The payment method

▶ 答案與解析請參考解析本第55頁

REVIEW TEST

1. Where most likely are the speakers?

   (A) At a restaurant
   (B) At an office
   (C) At a clothing store
   (D) At a hotel

2. What is the man's occupation?

   (A) Secretary
   (B) Librarian
   (C) Office worker
   (D) Salesperson

3. What does the man suggest the woman do?

   (A) Speak to another staff member
   (B) Visit another store
   (C) Buy the item from the online store
   (D) Fill out a form

4. Why is the man calling?

   (A) To make a reservation
   (B) To change his seat
   (C) To confirm a reservation
   (D) To make a payment

5. What does the man ask for?

   (A) A discount
   (B) A window seat
   (C) An aisle seat
   (D) A vegetarian meal

6. According to the conversation, what will the man probably do next?

   (A) Provide his personal information
   (B) Pay for his flight ticket
   (C) Go to the airport
   (D) Call another airline

7. Where most likely is the conversation taking place?

(A) At a supermarket
(B) At a furniture store
(C) At an electronics store
(D) At a clothing store

Leslie Furniture Discount Coupon for Spring Season			
5% off	10% off	15% off	20% off
~$300	$301~$400	$401~$500	$501~$600

* Valid until April 30

8. What does the man say is going on at the store?

(A) Maintenance work
(B) A grand opening sale
(C) A clearance sale
(D) A special promotion

10. What does the woman say she plans to do?

(A) Renovate her house
(B) Move to a new house
(C) Start her own business
(D) Design some furniture

9. What does the woman request?

(A) The newest laptop
(B) The cheapest laptop
(C) The lightest laptop
(D) The smallest laptop

11. Look at the graphic. Which discount will the woman receive?

(A) 5% off
(B) 10% off
(C) 15% off
(D) 20% off

12. What will the man most likely do next?

(A) Speak with a manager
(B) Check a delivery date
(C) Request a document
(D) Give a product demonstration

▶ 答案與解析請參考解析本第56頁

聽寫訓練

Unit 22 購物 | **Step 3 實戰演練**

🔊 dictation-30.mp3

Questions 1-3 refer to the following conversation.

W : I am looking _____. Can you tell me
_____ this one uses?

M : It _____ battery. And the battery is _____
_____ of any digital camera.

W : Wow, _____. Do you have any special events _____
_____ now?

M : Yes, we _____ camera cases _____ for
free. They _____ the store. Let me
show you where they are.

Unit 23 購票 | **Step 3 實戰演練**

🔊 dictation-31.mp3

Question 1 refers to the following conversation.

W : Hello. I'm calling _____ the concert tomorrow. Can I buy
them _____?

M : I'm sorry, but _____ over the phone. Why don't you
_____ them tomorrow?

W : Then can I _____ them?

M : Sure, but you _____ tomorrow. The discounted tickets
_____.

Review Test

🔊 dictation-32.mp3

Questions 1-3 refer to the following conversation.

W : Excuse me. _____. Could you please help me
_____ just like these?

M : Oh, all of the ones with _____. Do you want to
see another design?

W : No, thanks. Is there _____?

M : Um... _____ on Brit
Street? Or if you can wait until next week, I can order them and have them delivered to your house.

Questions 4-6 refer to the following conversation.

M : Hello. I'm calling _____

_____ on October 1.

W : Okay, let me check to see _____. Sometimes

it's full _____.

M : Oh, and could you please check _____

_____ ?

W : Sure. But before I do that, could you please _____

_____, _____, and phone number?

Questions 7-9 refer to the following conversation.

W : Hi. I need to _____,

and my friend recommended your store.

M : You are lucky because _____. You

can _____ everything.

W : Wow, that sounds great! So _____ ?

M : Sure. _____ that just arrived. I'm

sure you'll love it.

Questions 10-12 refer to the following conversation.

W : Hi. _____. And I'd like to

_____ that I saw in

your catalog.

M : What price range do you have in mind?

W : I am planning to spend _____. And I need to make sure the

furniture _____.

M : I think _____ the color of the wall. The model

in the window display costs $570. It comes in three colors, white, beige, and brown. It has been very

popular since last year.

W : I like the design and the size. And I'll go with the model in beige. _____

_____ ?

M : One moment, please. Let me check the computer _____

_____.

Voca Preview

請勾選不認識的單字，學習完類型分析後再重新確認勾選的單字。

- [ ] **have a problem with** 有～的問題
- [ ] **retirement** 退休
- [ ] **financial difficulty** 財務困難
- [ ] **inauguration** 就職（典禮）
- [ ] **applicant** 應徵者
- [ ] **contribution** 貢獻，捐獻
- [ ] **previous** 先前的
- [ ] **apply for** 應徵～，申請～
- [ ] **replace** 替換
- [ ] **job opening** （工作）空缺
- [ ] **application form** 申請書
- [ ] **resume** 履歷
- [ ] **recommendation letter** 推薦函
- [ ] **background** 背景
- [ ] **qualified** 有資格的
- [ ] **requirement** 要求事項
- [ ] **benefit** 福利，津貼
- [ ] **lay off** 解僱
- [ ] **auditor** 稽核員
- [ ] **assign** 分派

- [ ] **temporary** 暫時的，臨時的
- [ ] **inquire** 詢問
- [ ] **unavailable** 無法使用的
- [ ] **attendee** 出席者
- [ ] **handout** 傳單，印刷品
- [ ] **revise** 變更，修正
- [ ] **organize** 組織，籌備
- [ ] **behind schedule** 進度落後的
- [ ] **ahead of schedule** 進度提前的
- [ ] **achievement** 成果，成就
- [ ] **attractive** 有魅力的，引人注目的
- [ ] **authorize** 授權，認可
- [ ] **public relations** 公共關係
- [ ] **maintenance** 維護，維持
- [ ] **electronic power** 電力
- [ ] **shut down** 關閉
- [ ] **go wrong** 故障
- [ ] **pay period** 支薪期間
- [ ] **cut costs** 削減費用
- [ ] **budget proposal** 預算案

類型分析 **10**

各大主題攻略—職場

WARMING UP

診斷評估　閱讀題目後，在兩秒內掌握題目重點。

1. Who most likely is the woman talking to? ---------------------------
2. How long will the man take to go to Erica's office? ---------------------------
3. What does the woman say she will do? ---------------------------

尋找線索　觀察對話，找出上述題目的線索。

M : Hi, Erica. This is Bryan Wilson from the technical support team. I just received your email explaining that you are having a problem with your computer.

W : Yeah, I had to stop working due to the problem. When can you come to check it?

M : I'll be there as soon as possible, but it will take me another half an hour to get there.

W : Hmm... Since I have to leave the office to meet a client, I'll tell my secretary that you are coming.

確認解答 & 要點　確認正確答案，了解與職場相關的題目特徵。

診斷評估：掌握題目的重點

1. Who most likely is the woman talking to?

女子最有可能在跟誰說話？　▶ 詢問說話對象

2. How long will the man take to go to Erica's office?

男子到艾麗卡的辦公室要花多久時間？　▶ 詢問所需時間

3. What does the woman say she will do?

女子說她會做什麼？　▶ 詢問女子會做的事

尋找線索：分析測驗內容

M : Hi, Erica. This is Bryan Wilson from the technical support team. I just

　　　　　　　　▶ 1. 說話對象的答題依據

received your email explaining that you are having a problem with your

computer.　男：嗨，艾麗卡。我是技術支援組的布萊恩・威爾森，我剛收到你說電腦有問題的信。

　關於職業、公司、部門等的線索會在前半段出現。

W : Yeah, I had to stop working due to the problem. When can you come to check

it?　女：對，因為這個問題，我不得不停止工作。你什麼時候可以過來檢查？

M : I'll be there as soon as possible, but it will take me another half an hour to get

there.　▶ 2. 所需時間的答題依據

男：我會盡快過去，但我到那邊需要半小時。

　詳細的資訊通常在中間出現。

W : Hmm... Since I have to leave the office to meet a client, I'll tell my secretary that

you are coming.　▶ 3. 女子會做什麼事的答題依據

女：嗯……我得離開辦公室去見客戶，我會跟我的祕書說你要過來。

必須特別注意最後面的對話中，關於未來的日程和資訊。

徵人、辭職

關於徵人、辭職的對話中，經常出現跟說話對象、職位、請求和建議有關的題目。

 代表題型 先在十秒內讀完三道題目，聆聽音檔後選出正確答案。 62.mp3

1. What are the speakers discussing?

   (A) The retirement of a staff member

   (B) The hiring of a new manager

   (C) The financial difficulties of the company

   (D) The inauguration of the new president

2. What position does Mr. Victor have at the company?

   (A) Director

   (B) Manager

   (C) Supervisor

   (D) President

3. What does the man ask the woman to do?

   (A) Take Mr. Victor's position

   (B) Find a new employee

   (C) Train the new staff member

   (D) Interview a job applicant

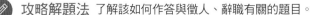 攻略解題法 了解該如何作答與徵人、辭職有關的題目。

聆聽對話前閱讀題目時

1. What are the speakers discussing? 說話者正在討論什麼？

 ▶ 這是詢問對話主題的題目，所以要專心聆聽第一句。

 (A) The retirement of a staff member　員工的退休

 (B) The hiring of a new manager　新經理的聘僱

 (C) The financial difficulties of the company　公司的財務困難

 (D) The inauguration of the new president　新總裁的就職典禮

2. What position does Mr. Victor have at the company?　維克多先生在此公司的職位是什麼？

 ▶ 題目提及特定人物的名稱並詢問該人的職業或職責時，須專心聆聽對話中出現該名稱的部分。通常會在人物名稱的後面使用同位語來提到職責。

 (A) Director　主任

 (B) Manager　經理

 (C) Supervisor　主管

 (D) President　總裁

3. What does the man ask the woman to do?　男子要求女子做什麼？

 ▶ 這是詢問建議／請求內容的題目，所以要專心聆聽跟建議有關的表達方式。

 (A) Take Mr. Victor's position　接手維克多先生的職位

 (B) Find a new employee　找新員工

 (C) Train the new staff member　訓練新員工

 (D) Interview a job applicant　面試求職者

聆聽對話時

Questions 1-3 refer to the following conversation.　第1-3題請參照以下的對話。

M: Did you hear that [1/2] Mr. Victor, the manager of the Sales Department, is retiring?

 ▶ 聆聽對話前先看過三道題目的話，只聽第一句就能作答兩道題目。這句跟銷售部的經理維克多先生「退休」有關，所以第一題的正確答案是(A)，第二題的正確答案是(B)。

 男：你有聽說銷售部的經理維克多先生要退休的事嗎？

W: Yes, he made a lot of contributions to our company. It is really sad news that he is leaving. 女：有，他為我們公司貢獻良多。他要離開是讓人很傷心的消息。

M: Well, [3] I came here to ask you to replace him. You have done quite a lot of things

 ▶ 這句提到要求（ask），所以是出現正確答案的線索的句子。男子要求女子「代替維克多接下該職位」，所以(A)是正確答案。

 at our company as well. I believe you can do more than him.

 男：嗯，我來這裡是想叫你接手他的位置。你也替公司做了很多事。我相信你能做得比他好。

詞彙整理 retire 退休 **contribution** 貢獻，捐獻 **replace** 替換

攻略POINT ❶ 題目提及特定人物的名稱並詢問該人的職業或職責時，要專心聆聽對話中出現該名稱的部分。通常會在人物名稱的後面使用同位語來提到職責。

🔤 與徵人、辭職有關的常見表達方式

- Thanks for applying for the position of manager in the Human Resources Department.
  謝謝您應徵人力資源部經理一職。

- Could you tell us about your previous experience?
  可以說說您以前的工作經歷嗎？

- I'd like to apply for this position.
  我想應徵這個職位。

- Are you interested in applying?
  您有興趣應徵嗎？

- The position is still open.
  這個職位還在開缺中。

- We're looking for someone with experience selling computers.
  我們正在找有電腦銷售經驗的人。

- I've worked in the Customer Service Department for five years.
  我在客服部門工作了五年。

- Have you heard Mr. Bryan is retiring?
  你有聽說布萊恩先生要退休嗎？

- She will leave the company by next month.
  她會在下個月離職。

- We need someone to replace her.
  我們需要代替她的人。

Voca Check - up! hire 聘僱 **apply for a position** 應徵職位 **job opening** 職缺 **applicant** 應徵者 **fill out an application form** 填寫申請書 **resume** 履歷 **recommendation letter** 推薦函 **interview** 面試 **background** 背景 **qualified** 有資格的 **qualification** 資格證明 **requirement** 要求事項 **benefit** 福利，津貼 **transfer** 轉調 **lay off (= fire / dismiss)** 解僱 **retire** 退休 **retirement** 退職 **get a promotion** 升遷 **performance** 工作成果 **review** 工作評價 **auditor** 稽核員 **recommend** 推薦 **replace** 代替 **new employee** 新員工 **Personnel (Human Resources) Department** 人事部 **resignation** 辭職 **medical benefit** 醫療福利 **notice** 公告 **assign** 分派 **be in charge of** 負責～ **duty** 職責 **intern** 實習生 **temporary** 臨時的 **part-time** 兼職的 **full-time** 正職的

1. What are the speakers mainly discussing?

   (A) Inquiring about a computer

   (B) Complaining about a staff member

   (C) Purchasing a computer

   (D) Applying for a position

2. Where does the woman probably work?

   (A) At a supermarket

   (B) At an office

   (C) At an electronics store

   (D) At a computer factory

3. What does the woman suggest that the man do?

   (A) Visit the store

   (B) Call another day

   (C) Come in for an interview

   (D) Submit a document

▶ 答案與解析請參考解析本第59頁

教育、宣傳

與教育、宣傳有關的對話中，會出現詢問教育對象、活動種類、教育目的等題目。

 代表題型 先在十秒內讀完三道題目，聆聽音檔後選出正確答案。 64.mp3

---

1. What type of event are the speakers discussing?

   (A) An employee meeting

   (B) A staff training session

   (C) A company picnic

   (D) A festival

2. Why was the training rescheduled?

   (A) A meeting room was unavailable.

   (B) The food did not arrive on time.

   (C) A different event hadn't finished.

   (D) The person in charge hadn't arrived yet.

3. How will the training be different from last year's?

   (A) It will be held in a different location.

   (B) A new program will be introduced.

   (C) The managers will train the staff.

   (D) Senior employees will attend the training.

攻略解題法 了解該如何作答與教育、宣傳有關的題目。

 聆聽對話前閱讀題目時

1. What type of event are the speakers discussing? 說話者在討論什麼類型的活動？

   ▶ 這是詢問對話主題的題目，所以要專心聆聽第一句。

   (A) An employee meeting 員工會議

   (B) A staff training session 員工培訓課程

   (C) A company picnic 公司郊遊

   (D) A festival 節慶

2. Why was the training rescheduled? 為什麼重新調整了培訓時間？

   ▶ 這是詢問理由的題目，線索會在because或to不定詞子句中出現。

   (A) A meeting room was unavailable. 會議室無法使用。

   (B) The food did not arrive on time. 食物沒有準時抵達。

   (C) A different event hadn't finished. 另一個活動還沒結束。

   (D) The person in charge hadn't arrived yet. 負責人還沒到。

3. How will the training be different from last year's? 培訓跟去年有什麼不一樣？

   ▶ 這是詢問培訓方式細節的題目，而且是三道題目中的最後一題，所以線索很可能會在後半段出現。

   (A) It will be held in a different location. 會在另一個地點舉辦。

   (B) A new program will be introduced. 會介紹一個新活動。

   (C) The managers will train the staff. 經理們會培訓員工。

   (D) Senior employees will attend the training. 資深員工會出席培訓。

聆聽對話時

Questions 1-3 refer to the following conversation. 第1-3題請參照以下的對話。

M: Sarah, do you know [1] whether the training session for the new employees has been cancelled or not? ▶ 對話主題是員工培訓是否取消，所以(B)為正確答案。
男：莎拉，你知道新員工的培訓課程有沒有取消嗎？

W: No, it was not cancelled. It was just postponed until next week [2] because the conference room is being renovated now. ▶ because子句中出現了培訓日程變更的原因。女子表示會議室「正在翻修」，所以無法使用會議室，日程有變動。正確答案為(A)。
女：不，沒有取消。只是延到下週了，因為會議室正在翻修。

M: So is there anything else you know about the training session?
男：那你還知道其他什麼關於培訓課程的事嗎？

W: I think there will be something different this year. [3] All the managers will train the new staff members. The senior employees won't do it.

   ▶ 今年跟去年的培訓差別在於，今年「所有經理都會培訓新員工」，所以(C)為正確答案。

   女：我覺得今年會有些不一樣。所有經理都會培訓新員工，而不是由資深員工來培訓。

詞彙整理 **training** 培訓，訓練 **postpone** 延期 **conference room** 會議室 **senior** 資深的，前輩 **whether~or not~** 是否～

攻略POINT 詢問理由的題目會藉由「because~」或「to~」等表達方式來給予提示。

與教育、宣傳有關的常見表達方式

- The new employee training session has been canceled. 新員工培訓課程取消了。
- The workshop has been postponed until next week. 工作坊延到下週了。
- Did you hear anything about the training session? 你聽說過任何關於培訓課程的事嗎？
- Would you like to come to the staff training session? 你要參加員工培訓課程嗎？
- How was your first training session last week? 上週的第一堂培訓課程怎麼樣？
- You should check the schedule for your workshop tomorrow. 你必須確認你明天的工作坊日程。
- We have to discuss the script for the advertisement. 我們必須討論廣告腳本。
- I have an idea to promote your company. 我有個宣傳貴公司的點子。
- We should advertise more. 我們應該多做廣告。

Voca Check - up! **staff meeting** 員工會議 **company policy** 公司政策 **attendee** 出席者 **discussion** 討論 **seminar** 研討會 **workshop** 工作坊 **training session** 培訓課程 **conference** 會議 **handout** 傳單，印刷品 **make / give / deliver a presentation** 做簡報 **make / give / deliver a speech** 演講 **revise** 變更，修正 **organize** 籌備，組織 **postpone** 延期 **behind schedule** 進度落後的 **ahead of schedule** 進度提前的 **achievement** 成果，成就 **according to** 根據～，按照～ **arrange for** 安排 **attractive** 有魅力的，引人注目的 **authorize** 授權，認可 **public relations** 公共關係 **be doing well**（人／公司）狀況良好 **be made public** 公開 **be due to do** 預計～ **be going on**（事情）進行中 **be too costly** 花費太高 **branch store** 分店 **be supposed to** 應該～ **be planned for** 計劃～ **be similar to** 跟～類似

Step **3** 實戰演練 65.mp3

1. What do the speakers mainly discuss?

 (A) A remodeled restaurant
 (B) An advertising company
 (C) A new restaurant
 (D) An advertising campaign

2. What does the man suggest?

 (A) Taking a look at the restaurant
 (B) Visiting her advertising company
 (C) Discussing the script by next week
 (D) Having dinner at her restaurant

3. What will the speakers do next?

 (A) Negotiate the payment
 (B) Visit a competing restaurant
 (C) Renovate the restaurant
 (D) Talk about an advertisement

▶ 答案與解析請參考解析本第60頁

Unit 26　設施、網絡管理

Step 1　實戰重點

與設施、網絡管理有關的對話中，會出現設施的維修、故障、修理等內容。

代表題型　先在十秒內讀完三道題目，聆聽音檔後選出正確答案。 66.mp3

1. What problem are the speakers discussing?

   (A) A presentation has been delayed.

   (B) An office will move overseas.

   (C) Some customers haven't arrived yet.

   (D) An office machine is not working well.

2. What does the woman suggest?

   (A) Delaying the presentation

   (B) Notifying a coworker

   (C) Calling a photocopier company

   (D) Borrowing something from another department

3. What does the man have to do tomorrow?

   (A) Attend a meeting

   (B) Go on a business trip

   (C) Give a presentation

   (D) Invite a client to an event

攻略解題法 了解該如何作答與設施、網絡管理有關的題目。

 聆聽對話前閱讀題目時

1. What problem are the speakers discussing? 說話者正在討論什麼問題？
   ▶ problem題型會在否定句或帶有否定含義的對話中出現線索。

   (A) A presentation has been delayed. 發表會被延期了。

   (B) An office will move overseas. 辦公室會搬到海外。

   (C) Some customers haven't arrived yet. 有些客人還沒抵達。

   (D) An office machine is not working well. 辦公室機器未正常運作。

2. What does the woman suggest? 女子建議做什麼？
   ▶ 這是詢問建議內容的題目，要專心聆聽提出建議的部分（why don't you~?、you should / could~）。

   (A) Delaying the presentation 延後發表會

   (B) Notifying a coworker 通知同事

   (C) Calling a photocopier company 打電話給影印機公司

   (D) Borrowing something from another department 從另一個部門借東西

3. What does the man have to do tomorrow? 男子明天得做什麼？
   ▶ 這是詢問男子明天要做什麼事的題目，要專心聆聽男子的發言中出現時間點的部分。跟未來有關的題目，提示通常會在後半段出現。

   (A) Attend a meeting 參加會議

   (B) Go on a business trip 出差

   (C) Give a presentation 做簡報

   (D) Invite a client to an event 邀請客戶參加活動

🎧 聆聽對話時

Questions 1-3 refer to the following conversation. 第1-3題請參照以下的對話。

M: Karen, [1] the photocopier isn't working well. The words are all blurry.
   ▶ 這句否定句是problem題型的答題線索。男子說「影印機的運作不正常」，所以(D)為正確答案。

   男：凱倫，影印機的運作不正常。字都很模糊。

W: [2] You should talk to Harry, the manager of the Maintenance Department, about the
   ▶ 這是詢問建議內容的題目，提出建議的部分（you should）會出現線索。(B)為正確答案。

   problem. He will come and repair it.
   女：你應該跟維修部經理哈利說這個問題。他會過來修理。

M: Okay. I hope he can fix it as soon as possible. [3] I have a presentation tomorrow, and I need to prepare a lot for it.
   ▶ 這句出現題目提及的時間點（tomorrow）。(C)為正確答案。

   男：好，我希望他可以盡快修好。我明天有個簡報，我得做好準備。

詞彙整理 photocopier 影印機 **blurry** 模糊的，不清楚的 **Maintenance Department** 維修部門 **repair** 修理，修補 **fix** 修理 **as soon as** 盡快

攻略POINT ❶ problem題型會在否定句或帶有否定含義的對話中出現線索。
   ❷ 作答跟時間點有關的題目時，要專心聆聽出現該時間點的部分。跟未來有關的時間點線索通常會在後半段出現。

與設施、網絡有關的常見表達方式

- There will be a interruption in Internet service today at 2 p.m.
  網路服務預計在今天下午兩點中斷。

- You should tell the technical support team.　你應該跟技術支援組說。

- He is in charge of repairs.　他負責維修。

- I'm having difficulty accessing my email account.　我登入電子郵件帳戶時遇到問題。

- I'm having some trouble with my computer.　我的電腦有問題。

- The photocopier isn't working very well.　影印機的運作不正常。

- When will the maintenance man come to fix the air conditioner?
  維修人員什麼時候會過來修冷氣機？

- Did you ask the technician?　你問過技師了嗎？

- The software will be upgraded by tonight.　軟體會在今晚更新。

- The computer will be running by tomorrow morning.　電腦會在明天早上運作。

Voca Check - up! **photocopier** 影印機 **data management software** 資料管理軟體 **facilities coordinator** 廠務協調員 **technical support** 技術支援 **technician** 技師 **maintenance** 維修，維持 **repair** 修理 **renovation** 改造，翻修 **have trouble with** 遇到～問題 **work** 運作 **go out** （火）熄滅，停電 **electric power** 電力 **shut down** 關閉 **deal with** 處理 **equipment** 裝備 **go wrong** 故障 **replace** 更換 **fix** 修理，使固定 **available** 可使用的，可利用的 **upgrade** 升級 **software** 軟體 **run** 運作

Step 3　實戰演練 67.mp3

1. What does the man ask about?

   (A) A meeting with an employee

   (B) A new secretary

   (C) A repair problem

   (D) An international meeting

2. What does the man say he wants to delay?

   (A) A reservation

   (B) A training

   (C) A business trip

   (D) A meeting

3. What will the woman probably do next?

   (A) Submit a report

   (B) Call a maintenance man

   (C) Prepare for a meeting

   (D) Open a window

▶ 答案與解析請參考解析本第60頁

Unit 27　會計、預算

與會計、預算有關的對話內容通常是企業種類、購買的辦公用品、經費等。

 代表題型 先在十秒內讀完三道題目，聆聽音檔後選出正確答案。 68.mp3

1. What type of business is the woman calling?

   (A)　An office supply store

   (B)　A bookstore

   (C)　A restaurant

   (D)　An electronics store

2. What problem does the woman mention?

   (A)　A bill has an unexpected fee.

   (B)　The wrong photocopiers were delivered.

   (C)　Some photocopiers were delivered late.

   (D)　There are some broken parts.

3. What does the man say about Ms. Park?

   (A)　She made an order.

   (B)　She signed a contract.

   (C)　She will receive a new bill.

   (D)　She will go to the restaurant.

攻略解題法 了解該如何作答與會計、預算有關的題目。

聆聽對話前閱讀題目時

1. What type of business is the woman calling? 女子打電話給什麼類型的店家？
   ▶ 這是詢問行業類別和店家類型的題目，要專心聆聽前半段的對話。

   (A) An office supply store 辦公用品店

   (B) A bookstore 書店

   (C) A restaurant 餐廳

   (D) An electronics store 電子產品店

2. What problem does the woman mention? 女子提到什麼問題？
   ▶ 這是詢問有什麼問題的題目，要專心聆聽出現否定句或帶有否定含義的詞彙的對話。

   (A) A bill has an unexpected fee. 帳單上有意料之外的費用。

   (B) The wrong photocopiers were delivered. 影印機送錯台了。

   (C) Some photocopiers were delivered late. 某些影印機很晚才送來。

   (D) There are some broken parts. 有些壞掉的零件。

3. What does the man say about Ms. Park? 男子提到關於帕克女士的什麼？
   ▶ 這是詢問第三者的事的題目，要專心聆聽提到第三者的名字（Park）的對話。

   (A) She made an order. 她下單了。

   (B) She signed a contract. 她簽約了。

   (C) She will receive a new bill. 她會收到新的帳單。

   (D) She will go to the restaurant. 她會去餐廳。

聆聽對話時

Questions 1-3 refer to the following conversation. 第1-3題請參照以下的對話。

W: Hi. I'm calling from the SMC Company. [2] I am calling because we just received a bill, and it is far more than what we had expected. ▶ 這是詢問遇到什麼問題的題目，所以要專心聆聽帶有否定含義詞彙的部分。女子說「費用比我們預期的多」，所以(A)為正確答案。

女：嗨，這是 SMC 公司。我打電話來是因為我們剛收到一筆帳單，而費用比我們預期的多。

M: Oh, [1] I remember that you ordered 10 photocopiers for your new office, right? The bill includes the service charge as well.
   ▶ 公司的種類通常會在開頭第一、二句出現。男子上班的企業跟辦公用品有關，所以(A)為正確答案。

   男：噢，我記得您替新辦公室訂了十台影印機，對吧？帳單還包含了服務費。

W: Service charge? I didn't know anything about that.
   女：服務費？我對此毫不知情。

M: [3] The fee was included in the contract that Ms. Park signed with our company.
   ▶ 這句提到了題目中提過的第三者。男子說「費用包含在帕克女士跟我們公司簽訂的合約裡」，所以(B)為正確答案。

   男：費用包含在帕克女士跟我們公司簽訂的合約裡。

詞彙整理 **bill** 帳單 **expect** 預期 **service charge** 服務費 **contract** 合約

攻略POINT ❶ 作答詢問行業類別和店家類型的題目時，要專心聆聽開頭前兩句。
         ❷ 作答詢問有什麼問題的題目時，要專心聆聽出現否定句或帶有否定含義的詞彙的對話。
         ❸ 此類詢問第三者的事的題目，要專心聆聽提到第三者名字的對話。

與會計、預算有關的常見表達方式

- We have to reduce our expenses by 10 percent.　我們必須減少十％經費。

- I need to set the budget.　我需要編預算。

- The fee was included in the contract Rachel signed with our company.
  費用包含在瑞秋跟我們公司簽訂的合約裡。

- We received the bill, and it cost more than we had expected.
  我們收到帳單了，而費用比我們預期的多。

- I haven't received the check yet.　我還沒收到支票。

- I requested a cost estimate from some office suppliers.　我跟某些辦公用品供應商索取了估價。

- We can't arrange the project due to the budget limitations.
  因為預算有限，我們無法籌備這個案子。

- We won't be able to buy it due to the lack of money in the budget.
  因為預算不足，我們應該無法買這個。

- Do you have any questions about any particular charges?
  您有對哪筆特定收費有任何問題嗎？

Voca Check - up!　**pay period** 支薪期間　**color printer** 彩色列印機　**cut costs** 削減費用　**order** 訂購　**receive** 收到　**distributor** 經銷商　**be on one's way** 在路上　**manufacturer** 製造商　**reasonable price** 合理的價格　**charge** 收費　**confirm** 確認　**invoice** 發票　**bill** 帳單　**Finance Department** 財務部　**sales report** 銷售報告　**on time** 準時　**shipment** 運輸的貨物　**delivery service** 寄送服務　**listing** 清單　**office supply** 辦公用品　**send** 發送　**online ordering system** 線上訂購系統　**client** 客人　**purchase** 購買　**accounting manager** 會計經理　**sales conference** 銷售會議　**fare** 費用　**budget proposal** 預算案　**approve** 批准　**moving fee** 搬遷費用　**contract** 合約　**supplier** 供應商，供應者

Step **3** | 實戰演練　　　🎧 69.mp3

1. What are the speakers discussing?

   (A) Making a reservation

   (B) Reducing the cost of dinner

   (C) Rescheduling dinner

   (D) Renovating the restaurant

2. What does the man suggest?

   (A) Booking another restaurant

   (B) Redoing an estimate

   (C) Asking for a donation

   (D) Canceling dinner

3. What will the woman probably do next?

   (A) Contact the restaurant

   (B) Inform all of the employees

   (C) Visit another department

   (D) Cancel the reservation

▶ 答案與解析請參考解析本第61頁

Unit 28　事業規劃

Step 1　實戰重點

與事業規劃有關的對話內容是行業類別與店家、問題、解決方法、預算等等。

代表題型 先在十秒內讀完三道題目，聆聽音檔後選出正確答案。　 70.mp3

1. Why is the woman calling?

   (A) To ask about the location of the cafe

   (B) To request some workers

   (C) To invite the man to her cafe

   (D) To inquire about a property

2. What type of business does the woman want to open?

   (A) A supermarket

   (B) A restaurant

   (C) A coffee shop

   (D) A hair salon

3. What are the workers doing today?

   (A) Painting the place

   (B) Cleaning the windows

   (C) Renovating the kitchen

   (D) Removing the furniture

攻略解題法 了解該如何作答與事業規劃有關的題目。

聆聽對話前閱讀題目時

1. Why is the woman calling? 女子為什麼打電話？

    ▶ 此題是詢問打電話的目的，前半段的I'm calling to~後面會出現提示。

    (A) To ask about the location of the cafe 為了詢問咖啡廳的位置

    (B) To request some workers 為了要幾名工人

    (C) To invite the man to her cafe 為了邀請男子到她的咖啡廳

    (D) To inquire about a property 為了詢問房地產的事

2. What type of business does the woman want to open? 女子想要開什麼類型的店？

    ▶ 這是詢問行業類別的題目，要專心聆聽跟行業類別有關的單字。大部分的提示會在前半段出現。

    (A) A supermarket 超市

    (B) A restaurant 餐廳

    (C) A coffee shop 咖啡廳

    (D) A hair salon 髮廊

3. What are the workers doing today? 今天工人正在做什麼？

    ▶ 此題是詢問第三者的事，要專心聆聽提到第三者的對話。「workers」出現時請專心聆聽。

    (A) Painting the place 油漆該空間

    (B) Cleaning the windows 清理窗戶

    (C) Renovating the kitchen 翻修廚房

    (D) Removing the furniture 移除家具

聆聽對話時

Questions 1-3 refer to the following conversation. 第1-3題請參照以下的對話。

W: Hi. My name is Jessica, and **1** I'm calling to ask about the store available to rent.

    ▶ 打電話的目的會在以「I'm calling~」開頭的對話中出現。女子問的是「房地產的出租」，所以(D)為正確答案。

    2 I'm interested in opening a small cafe. ▶ 這句提到了行業類別。(C)為正確答案。

    女：嗨，我是潔西卡。我打電話來是想問店面是否能出租。我對開一間小咖啡廳很感興趣。

M: Oh, that's great news! When would you like to open the cafe? We have to sign a contract at least one week before your store opens.

    男：噢，真是好消息！您想要何時開咖啡廳？我們至少得在您開店前一週簽好合約。

W: Can I have a look at the store first?

    女：我可以先看看店面嗎？

M: **3** Some workers are repainting the space today. How about tomorrow?

    ▶ 這句是提到題目中的workers的線索句子。男子說「今天工人們正在油漆那個空間」，所以(A)為正確答案。

    男：今天工人們正在重新油漆那個空間。明天怎麼樣？

詞彙整理 **rent** 出租 **sign a contract** 簽約 **at least** 至少，最少 **repaint** 重新油漆

攻略POINT ❶ 詢問打電話目的的題目，提示會在I'm calling~後面出現。

    ❷ 作答詢問行業類別的題目時，要綜合對話中的單字，推測出行業類別。大部分關於行業類別的提示會在前半段出現。

    ❸ 此類詢問第三者的事的題目，要專心聆聽提到第三者的名字或職業的對話。

與事業規劃有關的常見表達方式

- I'm interested in opening a restaurant. 我對開餐廳感興趣。
- I'd like to sign a contract by next week. 我想在下週簽約。
- I need to renovate the restaurant. 我需要翻修餐廳。
- Which property are you interested in? 您對哪個建物感興趣？
- Our company is going to merge with the Campbell Corporation. 我們公司即將跟坎貝爾企業合併。
- We are planning to establish a new branch. 我們計劃成立新的分公司。
- It's time to start developing an updated version. 是時候開始開發新版本了。
- We'll have to concentrate on creating new products. 我們需要專注於創造新產品。
- When do you think the new office space will be ready? 你覺得新辦公空間會在何時準備好？

Voca Check - up! **think of** 覺得～ **renovation** 改造，翻修 **take a look at** 看～ **interview** 面試 **publicity** 宣傳 **be interested in** 對～有興趣 **specialty** 專業 **be familiar with** 對～感到熟悉 **confirm** 確認 **cost** 耗費 **space** 空間 **accommodate** 容納 **rent out** 出租 **make a decision** 做決定 **release** 發表，上市 **launch** 上市 **production** 生產 **negotiate** 協商 **dealership** 經銷店 **reference** 參考資料 **inspect** 檢查 **location** 地點，位置 **plan to** 計劃～ **recommend** 推薦 **current address** 現居地址 **selection** 選擇 **up-to-date** 最新的 **inquire** 詢問 **try out**（當作試驗）嘗試 **reliable** 可信賴的 **client** 客人 **special order** 特別訂單 **on display** 展示的，陳列的 **total cost** 總費用

1. What does the man request?

    (A) Information about remodeling
    (B) The contact number of the owner
    (C) The location of the restaurant
    (D) The price of the property

2. What does the woman suggest that the man do?

    (A) Change his business hours
    (B) Make an invitation card
    (C) Contact a real estate agent
    (D) Visit the agent by tomorrow

3. What is the woman worried about doing?

    (A) Finding an interior designer
    (B) Purchasing a restaurant
    (C) Removing some old furniture
    (D) Hiring a new staff member

▶ 答案與解析請參考解析本第61頁

1. Who most likely is the man?

   (A) An accountant
   (B) An architect
   (C) A bank clerk
   (D) A technician

2. What is the woman's problem?

   (A) She recently argued with one of her colleagues.
   (B) Her computer broke down.
   (C) She needs some reference material to finish her project.
   (D) She lost some documents because of the technical support team.

3. What does the woman request that the man do?

   (A) Install a new program
   (B) Invite her to an international seminar
   (C) Attend a meeting instead of her
   (D) Repair her computer by tomorrow

4. What are the speakers mainly discussing?

   (A) An annual party
   (B) A special promotion
   (C) An interview
   (D) A speech

5. What is the man's job?

   (A) Lawyer
   (B) Office worker
   (C) Salesperson
   (D) Lecturer

6. What does the woman need to bring?

   (A) A curriculum vitae
   (B) Some office supplies
   (C) A reference letter
   (D) A photo

7. What are the speakers mainly talking about?

    (A) A new publishing company

    (B) A photography award

    (C) An upcoming project

    (D) A recent industry conference

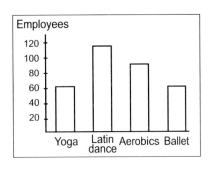

8. What is mentioned about Stargate?

    (A) It went through restructuring.

    (B) It recently received an award.

    (C) It hired some new employees.

    (D) It will attend an upcoming conference.

10. What event did the woman just attend?

    (A) A seminar

    (B) A trade fair

    (C) A meeting

    (D) An awards ceremony

9. What is Andrew asked to do?

    (A) Write an article

    (B) Contact an IT company

    (C) Buy some lunch

    (D) Take some pictures

11. Look at the graphic. Which class will be discontinued?

    (A) Yoga

    (B) Latin dance

    (C) Aerobics

    (D) Ballet

12. Why is the man concerned?

    (A) The survey is way behind schedule.

    (B) He is going to be late for an upcoming meeting.

    (C) He is not ready for a presentation.

    (D) A recent decision will let down some employees.

▶ 答案與解析請參考解析本第62頁

聽寫訓練

Questions 1-3 refer to the following conversation.

M : Hello. My name is Jason, ＿＿＿＿＿＿＿＿＿＿＿＿＿＿＿ the sales position you

＿＿＿＿＿＿＿＿＿＿＿＿＿＿.

W : Thank you for calling. As you ＿＿＿＿＿＿＿＿＿＿＿＿＿＿, we're looking for

＿＿＿＿＿＿＿＿＿＿＿ selling computers.

M : Don't worry about that. ＿＿＿＿＿＿＿＿＿＿＿＿＿＿ computer shop ＿＿＿＿

＿＿＿＿＿＿＿ for 3 years.

W : That's really good news! ＿＿＿＿＿＿＿＿＿＿＿＿＿＿＿＿＿＿＿＿＿

＿＿＿＿?

Question 1 refers to the following conversation.

W : This is Susanna from ＿＿＿＿＿＿＿＿＿＿＿＿＿＿＿. I'm calling about an idea

＿＿＿＿＿＿＿＿＿＿＿＿＿＿ your restaurant.

M : Oh, that's interesting! Because we ＿＿＿＿＿＿＿＿＿＿＿＿＿＿, I want you to see

it. Can you ＿＿＿＿＿＿＿＿＿＿＿＿＿＿ it?

W : Sure, ＿＿＿＿＿＿＿＿＿＿＿ tomorrow, and, while I'm there, we can ＿＿＿＿

＿＿＿＿＿＿＿＿＿＿＿＿＿＿＿＿.

Unit 26 設施、網絡管理 ┊ **Step 3** 實戰演練 ⊙ dictation-35.mp3

Question 1 refers to the following conversation.

M : Do you know ＿＿＿＿＿＿＿＿＿＿＿＿＿＿＿＿ will come ＿＿＿＿＿＿＿＿＿＿＿＿＿

＿＿＿＿＿ conditioner?

W : Tomorrow afternoon, I guess. ＿＿＿＿＿＿＿＿＿＿＿＿＿＿＿＿＿＿＿＿?

M : ＿＿＿＿＿＿＿＿＿＿＿＿＿＿＿＿＿＿＿＿＿. If it isn't working by today, I'll have to

＿＿＿＿＿＿＿＿＿＿＿＿＿＿＿＿. I'd rather ＿＿＿＿＿＿＿＿＿＿.

W : Don't worry about it. I can ＿＿＿＿＿＿＿＿＿＿＿＿＿ and check ＿＿＿＿＿＿＿

＿＿＿＿＿＿＿＿＿＿＿＿＿ by this afternoon or not.

Unit 27 會計、預算 ┊ **Step 3** 實戰演練 ⊙ dictation-36.mp3

Questions 1-3 refer to the following conversation.

M : Tracy, I ＿＿＿＿＿＿＿＿＿＿＿＿＿＿＿＿＿＿＿＿＿＿＿＿＿＿＿＿＿＿

＿＿＿＿＿＿＿＿＿＿＿＿ by 20 percent. How do you think we can do that?

W : Really? I ＿＿＿＿＿＿＿＿＿＿＿＿＿＿＿＿＿＿＿.

How are we going to ＿＿＿＿＿＿＿＿＿＿＿＿＿＿＿＿＿＿ for our department?

M : Hmm, I think ＿＿＿＿＿＿＿＿＿＿＿＿＿＿＿＿＿＿＿＿＿＿＿ for it again.

We have to ＿＿＿＿＿＿＿＿＿＿＿＿＿＿＿＿＿＿＿.

W : I should call the supplier ＿＿＿＿＿＿＿＿＿＿＿＿＿＿＿＿＿＿＿＿＿＿＿＿＿

them that we have to ＿＿＿＿＿＿＿＿＿＿＿＿＿＿＿＿＿.

聽寫訓練

Unit 28　事業規劃　　Step 3 實戰演練　　🎧 dictation-37.mp3

W : Did you already _____ for your

new restaurant?

M : Well, I _____ yesterday to get

some information _____. But I still _____

_____.

W : I think you should _____. Anyway, I'm worried _____

_____ is going to _____.

Review Test　　🎧 dictation-38.mp3

Questions 1-3 refer to the following conversation.

M : Hi. This is Martin _____. I got a call from

someone in your staff that _____.

W : Thanks for coming. Suddenly, _____ when I was about

to complete my project. After that, _____

_____.

M : I think _____

_____.

W : Okay. But can you fix it by tomorrow? I have to finish my work before this weekend.

Questions 4-6 refer to the following conversation.

M : Hello, Ms. Vera. I'm John from the Human Resources Department at TACC. _____

_____, and I want you to _____

_____.

W : Thank you. I was waiting for your call. Do I need to _____

_____?

M : You need to come with a _____.

Questions 7-9 refer to the following conversation.

W : Our magazine is planning _____
_____ in the state next month. _____
_____?

M1 : Yes, I am. I want to write about the IT firm Stargate. _____
_____ at last year's industry conference.

W : Okay, Ken. That sounds great. And, Andrew, _____
_____ for the article?

M2 : Sure, I'd be glad to. When are you planning to visit the company, Ken?

M1 : _____
_____ right away.

Questions 10-12 refer to the following conversation.

W : Hi, Steve. Sorry to interrupt. I just got out of a budget meeting. I heard that _____
_____ due to the recent budget
cuts.

M : I also heard that. Mr. Olson said _____
_____ to operate.

W : That doesn't make sense. According to the survey we took last month, _____
_____ with employees.

M : I know what you're saying. Many _____ to learn that we are
_____ anymore.

PART 3

Directions: You will hear some conversations between two or three people. You will be asked to answer three questions about what the speakers say in each conversation. Select the best response to each question and mark the letter (A), (B), (C), or (D) on your answer sheet. The conversations will not be printed in your test book and will be spoken only one time.

32. What are the speakers mainly discussing?

(A) Sending mail
(B) Going to Washington
(C) Sending a package
(D) Buying a present

33. What does the woman suggest?

(A) Using express delivery
(B) Sending a package by next week
(C) Packing the item in another box
(D) Asking another person for help

34. What most likely will the man decide to do?

(A) Send the package by express delivery service
(B) Choose a less expensive service
(C) Take the package back to his home
(D) Reserve other services

35. What are the speakers working on?

(A) Clothing design
(B) Creating a brochure
(C) An advertising budget
(D) A safety manual

36. What does the woman suggest?

(A) Canceling a reservation
(B) Adding some new content
(C) Conducting a customer survey
(D) Editing the entire report

37. What does the woman say she is pleased about?

(A) The high-quality service at a store
(B) Positive reviews from customers
(C) The result of a customer survey
(D) An upward trend in sales

38. What is the woman having trouble with?

   (A) Implementing a new system
   (B) Entering a password
   (C) Sending an email
   (D) Using an electronic device

39. Who has the woman been trying to contact?

   (A) Technical support
   (B) A plumber
   (C) A receptionist
   (D) The maintenance team

40. What does the man offer to do?

   (A) Help the woman the next day
   (B) Call another support team
   (C) Help the woman find her password
   (D) Find a telephone number

41. What are the speakers mainly discussing?

   (A) An electronic dictionary
   (B) A mobile phone
   (C) A laptop
   (D) An MP3 player

42. Why does the woman recommend the New Electronics Store?

   (A) The prices are reasonable.
   (B) The store is near them.
   (C) The store is having a sale.
   (D) The owner is her friend.

43. What has the man forgotten?

   (A) The location of a store
   (B) The price of a mobile phone
   (C) The place where he lost his mobile phone
   (D) The name of a store

44. What event are the speakers planning to attend?

   (A) A meeting
   (B) An art class
   (C) A car exhibit
   (D) An art exhibit

45. How did the man learn about the event?

   (A) From an art magazine
   (B) From an article
   (C) From a TV advertisement
   (D) From his friend

46. What does the man suggest?

   (A) Entering the exhibition
   (B) Giving up on seeing the exhibit
   (C) Parking in the parking lot
   (D) Finding another exhibition

47. What are they mainly talking about?

   (A) A department store
   (B) A local grocery store
   (C) A nearby restaurant
   (D) A new website

48. What is the woman concerned about?

   (A) Poor service
   (B) A long waiting time
   (C) A lack of parking areas
   (D) A high price

49. What is available this week?

   (A) Free delivery
   (B) A price discount
   (C) New menu items
   (D) A catering service

50. What are the speakers discussing?

    (A) An airport parking garage
    (B) A flight ticket
    (C) Renting a vehicle
    (D) A travel package

51. Where most likely does the man work?

    (A) At a rental car agency
    (B) At an airport
    (C) At a travel agency
    (D) At a car dealership

52. According to the man, what is the fifty dollar charge for?

    (A) Buying a return ticket
    (B) Parking in the long-term parking lot
    (C) Providing a pick-up service
    (D) Returning a car at a different city

53. What are the speakers preparing for?

    (A) An anniversary event
    (B) A training program
    (C) The launch of a new product
    (D) A board meeting

54. What does the man imply when he says, "The audience response was very positive"?

    (A) He wants the audience to give feedback.
    (B) He agrees that a meeting must be moved.
    (C) He hopes that all employees will attend an event.
    (D) He thinks Mr. Ling is well qualified for some work.

55. What will the woman most likely do next?

    (A) Report to a manager
    (B) Give a speech
    (C) Make a phone call
    (D) Have a meeting

56. What most likely is the woman's occupation?

    (A) Salesperson
    (B) Accountant
    (C) Designer
    (D) Artist

57. What are the speakers mainly discussing?

    (A) An award
    (B) A job opening
    (C) A business
    (D) A news story

58. What does the woman want Kenny to send her?

    (A) A prize
    (B) An application form
    (C) A curriculum vitae
    (D) A letter

59. Where does the man most likely work?

    (A) At a stationery store
    (B) At a catering company
    (C) At a grocery store
    (D) At a moving company

60. What problem does the woman mention?

    (A) An item arrived damaged.
    (B) Items in a store are too expensive.
    (C) A delivery is late.
    (D) A discount was not applied.

61. What does the woman imply when she says, "I'm a bit worried because I have to prepare some materials for tomorrow's meeting"?

    (A) She will be on sick leave for a few days.
    (B) She has to use the copier soon.
    (C) A reservation has been lost.
    (D) Some materials have not been delivered.

Room Type	Seats
Agora	180
Gold	100
Silver	70
Business	30

62. What kind of event is going to be held?

(A) A shareholders' meeting
(B) A press conference
(C) A seminar for new recruits
(D) An awards ceremony

63. What does the woman request?

(A) Directions to the hotel
(B) Presentation equipment
(C) A sample of a product
(D) A tour of a facility

64. Look at the graphic. Which conference room will the woman most likely choose?

(A) Agora
(B) Gold
(C) Silver
(D) Business

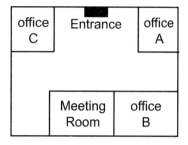

65. Who is the man?

(A) A sales representative
(B) An office worker
(C) A delivery person
(D) A janitor

66. What will the woman do this afternoon?

(A) Attend a meeting
(B) Train new employees
(C) Make copies
(D) Conduct a survey

67. Look at the graphic. Which room will the man most likely drop by?

(A) Meeting Room
(B) Office A
(C) Office B
(D) Office C

Time	Topic
9:00 A.M.-9:50 A.M.	Patient Safety
10:00 A.M.-10:50 A.M.	Patient Care
11:00 A.M.-11:50 A.M.	Mental Health
1:00 P.M.-1:50 P.M.	Diet & Nutrition

68. Look at the graphic. Which topic will the woman discuss?

(A) Patient Safety
(B) Patient Care
(C) Mental Health
(D) Diet & Nutrition

69. What problem does the woman mention?

(A) Some staff members are unavailable.
(B) An item is out of stock.
(C) A device is not working properly.
(D) A customer was not satisfied.

70. What does the man say he will do next?

(A) Visit a website
(B) Report to a manager
(C) Submit a document
(D) Go downstairs

▶ 答案與解析請參考解析本第65頁

PART 3

Directions: You will hear some conversations between two or three people. You will be asked to answer three questions about what the speakers say in each conversation. Select the best response to each question and mark the letter (A), (B), (C), or (D) on your answer sheet. The conversations will not be printed in your test book and will be spoken only one time.

32. Who is Mary?

(A) A sales manager
(B) A sales representative
(C) A human resources manager
(D) A secretary

33. According to the speakers, why will Mary be missed?

(A) She is highly respected by customers.
(B) She is the top salesperson.
(C) She has been with the company for a long time.
(D) She does her job efficiently.

34. What does the woman ask the man to do?

(A) Conduct a job interview
(B) Look for a candidate for a job
(C) Assume the position of manager
(D) Interview a job applicant

35. Who most likely is the woman?

(A) A caterer
(B) An architect
(C) A reporter
(D) A salesperson

36. What is said about the park?

(A) It has closed.
(B) It has been renovated.
(C) It has opened.
(D) It has been moved.

37. What impresses the man about the park?

(A) The restroom
(B) The playground
(C) The swimming pool
(D) The pond

38. Where does the woman want to go?

    (A) To the airport
    (B) To the bus station
    (C) To the train station
    (D) To the ticket booth

39. Why does the woman have to cross the road?

    (A) To attend a meeting
    (B) To visit a store
    (C) To meet someone
    (D) To go to a bus station

40. Who sells tickets?

    (A) A salesperson
    (B) A flight attendant
    (C) A bus driver
    (D) A technician

41. What is the purpose of the contest?

    (A) To create a campaign theme
    (B) To reduce expenditures
    (C) To increase the customer base
    (D) To recruit additional employees

42. Why is the woman unsure about participating?

    (A) She is going on a vacation.
    (B) She will be changing jobs.
    (C) She does not have any experience.
    (D) She has a work deadline.

43. What do the men imply about the woman?

    (A) She is the only marketing specialist at the company.
    (B) She has won a prize before.
    (C) She has come up with many innovative ideas.
    (D) She wants to travel to Europe.

44. What is the purpose of the call?

    (A) To make a payment
    (B) To speak with a doctor
    (C) To make an appointment
    (D) To reschedule an appointment

45. Who most likely is the man talking to?

    (A) A secretary
    (B) A salesperson
    (C) A receptionist
    (D) A patient

46. When does the man plan to see Dr. Smith?

    (A) On Tuesday
    (B) On Wednesday
    (C) On Thursday
    (D) On Friday

47. Why is the man calling?

    (A) To ask about a price
    (B) To make a hotel reservation
    (C) To sign up for a membership
    (D) To arrange an appointment

48. When will the man probably come in?

    (A) Next Monday
    (B) Next Tuesday
    (C) Next Thursday
    (D) Next Friday

49. What does the man mean when he says, "I have an emergency meeting soon"?

    (A) He wants to see a doctor right away.
    (B) He would like to hear more information.
    (C) He can't talk any longer.
    (D) He thinks changing a date will be difficult.

50. Where does this conversation take place?

 (A) At an electronics store
 (B) At a clothing store
 (C) At a supermarket
 (D) At an office

51. What did the woman do yesterday?

 (A) She visited her friend.
 (B) She spoke with another staff member.
 (C) She went to a museum.
 (D) She bought a shirt.

52. According to the conversation, what does the man suggest that the woman do?

 (A) Call the company's headquarters
 (B) Come back another day
 (C) Visit an online store
 (D) Go to another shop

53. Why is the man at the business?

 (A) To reschedule a meeting
 (B) To talk to a repairperson
 (C) To have a job interview
 (D) To arrange transportation

54. Why does the woman say, "You will have your turn in a few minutes"?

 (A) Some products seem to be out of stock.
 (B) The man's interview will start soon.
 (C) A celebration will be held in a minute.
 (D) An important client is waiting for the man.

55. What does the woman say about Ms. Packer?

 (A) She is in a meeting at the moment.
 (B) She has been transferred to another office.
 (C) She is on sick leave for a while.
 (D) She is currently away on business.

56. Why is the man calling?

 (A) To inquire about the store's business hours
 (B) To ask about a missing item
 (C) To speak with the manager
 (D) To ask for a refund

57. What is indicated about the mobile phone?

 (A) It is black in color.
 (B) It has a scratch.
 (C) It is on the table.
 (D) It is white in color.

58. Why does the woman ask the man to come tomorrow?

 (A) The employees are on vacation.
 (B) The restaurant is under construction.
 (C) Dinner is not ready yet.
 (D) The restaurant is about to close.

59. What are the speakers mainly talking about?

 (A) A training session
 (B) A grand opening sale
 (C) An exhibition
 (D) An international seminar

60. Why is the woman not available to go this Saturday?

 (A) She will be on a business trip.
 (B) She will move to another office.
 (C) She has to finish a project.
 (D) She has another appointment.

61. What does the man say he will do?

 (A) Book a seat for the woman
 (B) Buy a ticket for the woman
 (C) Get some brochures from the gallery
 (D) Wait until next week to go with the woman

Alteration Type	Price
Alter Length – Pants	$15
Alter Length – Skirt	$18
Alter Sleeves – Jacket	$20
New Zipper – Pants/Skirt	$16

Movie Title	Available Seats
Blue Moon	3
The Hunters	4
In Paris	6
The Queens	5

62. Look at the graphic. How much will the man most likely pay?

(A) $15
(B) $16
(C) $18
(D) $20

63. What does the man say he will do the day after tomorrow?

(A) Apply for a job
(B) Attend a conference
(C) Go to an interview
(D) Have a meeting with a client

64. What does the man inquire about?

(A) A laundry price
(B) A closing time
(C) A discount
(D) A cleaning product

65. Who most likely is the woman?

(A) An actress
(B) A box office employee
(C) A movie director
(D) A film critic

66. What does the man ask the woman about?

(A) A popular movie
(B) The film schedule for next week
(C) A television program
(D) A movie star

67. Look at the graphic. Which movie will the man most likely see?

(A) Blue Moon
(B) The Hunters
(C) In Paris
(D) The Queens

▶ 答案與解析請參考解析本第73頁

PART 4

簡短獨白

第四大題是聽完獨白後作答三道題目的類型，總共10則獨白（30題）。
（共 30 題）

Voca Preview

請勾選不認識的單字，學習完類型分析後再重新確認勾選的單字。

☐ **announcement** 公布

☐ **employee benefit** 員工福利

☐ **timecard** 工作時間記錄卡

☐ **time sheet** 工作時間表

☐ **survey** 調查報告

☐ **office equipment** 辦公設備

☐ **replacement** 替代者，替代品

☐ **payroll division** 薪資部門

☐ **customer information** 顧客資訊

☐ **workstation** 工作地點，工作站

☐ **make a complaint** 抱怨

☐ **sign up** 註冊

☐ **complicated** 複雜的

☐ **gallery** 畫廊

☐ **upcoming** 即將到來的

☐ **pleasant environment** 愉快的環境

☐ **opportunity** 機會

☐ **annual** 年度的

☐ **direction** 方向

☐ **audit** 查帳

☐ **statistics** 統計

☐ **income** 收入

☐ **revenue** 收入，收益

☐ **loss** 損失

☐ **feedback** 回饋

☐ **advice** 忠告

☐ **reduce costs** 減少費用

☐ **increase sales** 增加銷售

☐ **boost sales** 提高銷售

☐ **fully equipped** 裝備完整的

☐ **inclement weather** 惡劣的天氣

☐ **runway** 跑道

☐ **step out** （暫時）出去

☐ **expect to** 預期～

☐ **clear away** 清除，打掃

☐ **arrange** 整理

☐ **originally** 原本

☐ **departure** 出發

☐ **delay** 延誤，延遲

☐ **meal coupon** 餐券

類型分析

11

公告

WARMING UP

診斷評估　閱讀題目後，在兩秒內掌握題目重點。

1. Who is the speaker addressing? ....
2. What kind of work will be conducted? ....
3. How long will the renovations take? ....

尋找線索　觀察獨白，找出上述題目的線索後，掌握內容。

Good morning. I want to make an announcement for a few moments. Our office will start being renovated from today. So we will move to another office for a month. Please make sure your computers are turned off before you leave the office and remove all your personal belongings from the office. If you have any questions, please call Andy at 4531-4789.

確認解答＆要點　確認正確答案，了解與公告有關的獨白的特徵。

診斷評估：掌握題目的重點

1. Who is the speaker addressing? 說話者正在跟誰說話？　▶詢問對象

2. What kind of work will be conducted? 會進行什麼種類的作業？　▶詢問作業種類

3. How long will the renovations take? 翻修會花多久的時間？　▶詢問翻修期間

尋找線索：分析測驗內容

Good morning. I want to make an announcement for a few moments.

Our office will start being renovated from today.

▶ 1. 公告主旨的答題依據／2. 作業種類的答題依據

早安，我想花些時間公布一件事。我們的辦公室將從今天開始翻修。

> 公告前半段會出現公告對象和目的。

So we will move to another office for a month.

▶ 3. 翻修期間的答題依據

所以，我們會搬到另一間辦公室一個月。

> 日程或變更事項會在前半段或中間出現。

Please make sure your computers are turned off before you leave the office and remove all your personal belongings from the office.

離開辦公室前請確定電腦已關閉，並清空辦公室的個人物品。

> 中間或後半段會出現詳細的叮嚀和要求事項。

If you have any questions, please call Andy at 4531-4789.

如果有任何問題，請撥打4351-4789聯絡安迪。

> 公告後半段會提出要求或提供聯絡方式。

詞彙整理 **make an announcement** 公布，宣布 **renovate** 改造，翻修 **turn off** 關閉 **remove** 去掉，消除 **personal belongings** 個人物品

聆聽在公司的工作坊、聚會上向員工傳達的公告時，須仔細聽第一句問候語之後的句子，以及在後半段以You can、You should作為開頭的建議句。

 代表題型　先在十秒內讀完三道題目，聆聽獨白後選出正確答案。　 🎧 73.mp3

4. What is the announcement about?

    (A) A new system
    (B) A new policy
    (C) A promotional campaign
    (D) An employee benefit

5. What will happen next Monday?

    (A) An international seminar
    (B) An employee meeting
    (C) A staff workshop
    (D) The launching of a new product

6. What are the listeners asked to do?

    (A) Be present at the training session
    (B) Bring some documents
    (C) Prepare for a presentation
    (D) Attend an international seminar

攻略解題法 了解該如何作答與公司內部公告有關的題目。

4. What is the announcement about? 公告跟什麼有關？

▶ 公告目的會在前半段出現，所以要仔細聽前半段。

(A) A new system 新系統
(B) A new policy 新政策
(C) A promotional campaign 宣傳活動
(D) An employee benefit 員工福利

5. What will happen next Monday? 下個星期一會發生什麼事？

▶ 日程或變更事項會在中間出現，所以聽完公告目的後，要專心聆聽跟日程有關的部分。

(A) An international seminar 國際研討會
(B) An employee meeting 員工會議
(C) A staff workshop 員工工作坊
(D) The launching of a new product 新產品上市

6. What are the listeners asked to do? 聽者被要求做什麼？

▶ 叮嚀和要求事項會在後半段出現。

(A) Be present at the training session 參加培訓課程
(B) Bring some documents 帶某些文件
(C) Prepare for a presentation 準備簡報
(D) Attend an international seminar 參加國際研討會

 聽聽對話時

Good afternoon. ⁴ I just want to let you know that the new customer reporting system will be installed on the Customer Service Department's computers next week. This

▶ 公告目的會在前半段出現。內容與「新的顧客回報系統」有關，所以(A)為正確答案。

system will help us by making it easier to enter customers' information.
午安。我只是想讓大家知道，下個禮拜客服部門的電腦會安裝新的顧客回報系統。這個系統將協助我們更輕鬆地輸入顧客的資訊。

⁵ There will be a training session for two hours next Monday starting at 9 a.m.

▶ next Monday前面說了「培訓課程」，所以(C)為正確答案。題目中的表達方式是staff workshop。

下星期一早上九點開始將有兩小時的培訓課程。

The technical support team will train us to use the software. ⁶ Please make sure all of you attend the training session. If you have any questions, please let me know.

▶ 詢問要求內容的題目，相關線索會在後半段的命令句中出現。說話者要求員工「參加培訓課程」，所以(A)為正確答案。

技術支援組會訓練我們使用這個軟體。請各位務必參加這個培訓課程。如果有任何問題，請跟我說。

詞彙整理 **install** 安裝 **enter** 輸入 **training session** 培訓課程 **technical support team** 技術支援組

攻略POINT ❶ 作答詢問具體事項的「What will happen＋時間點？」題目時，要專心聆聽出現時間點的前後內容。
❷ 音檔中的表達方式常常會在改述後，再出現在選項中。例如：training session 培訓課程 → staff workshop 員工工作坊

公司內部公告的結構

公司內部公告的鋪陳	公司內部公告相關句型
公告目的與地點	• I'd like to let everyone know ~. 我想讓各位知道～。 • I'm happy to announce that ~. 很高興宣布～。 • Thank you all again for ~. 再次感謝各位～。 • Welcome to ~. 歡迎來到～。
日程與變更事項	• next Tuesday morning 下星期二早上 • It will take several hours to ~. 將花幾個小時～。 • They will repair ~. 他們會修理～。 • I'd like to announce ~. 我想宣布～。
叮嚀與要求事項	• Please make sure that ~. 請務必～。 • You should ~. 各位應該～。 • Can I ask for ~? 可以請各位～嗎？
諮詢與聯絡方式	• If you have any questions, ~. 如果有任何問題～。 • Please let me know ~. 請讓我知道～。

Voca Check - up! 公司內部公告相關詞彙

expense 經費，費用 **reimbursement** 報帳 **receipt** 收據 **timecard** 工作時間記錄卡 **time sheet** 工作時間表 **survey** 調查報告 **office equipment** 辦公設備 **office supply** 辦公用品 **application** 申請書 **replace** 代替 **replacement** 代替者，替代品 **employee training** 員工培訓 **workshop** 工作坊 **payroll division** 薪資部門 **Accounting Department** 會計部 **Marketing Department** 行銷部 **Human Resources Department** 人事部 **sales figure** 銷售額 **install** 安裝 **customer information** 顧客資訊 **let me know** 告知我 **workstation** 工作地點，工作站

4. Where are the listeners?

(A) At an office

(B) At an airport

(C) At a supermarket

(D) At a museum

5. Who is the announcement for?

(A) Technicians

(B) Customers

(C) Office workers

(D) Store managers

6. According to the announcement, what will begin this afternoon?

(A) Renovations

(B) The replacement of some equipment

(C) An inspection

(D) Repairs

▶ 答案與解析請參考解析本第81頁

Unit 30　公共場所公告

在電影院、機場、購物中心等地方播放的公告內容，主要為注意事項或表演時間等。尤其是購物中心會提到營業時間、折扣、打烊等。Welcome to後面的內容會出現廣播的原因，所以要專心聆聽這個部分。請記住，注意事項通常會在最後面提到。

 代表題型　先在十秒內讀完三道題目，聆聽獨白後選出正確答案。　 75.mp3

4. Where is the announcement taking place?

   (A) At a clothing store

   (B) At an office

   (C) At a gallery

   (D) At a cinema

5. What is being offered today only?

   (A) A gift voucher

   (B) A discount on certain items

   (C) A free gift with any purchase

   (D) Delivery service

6. According to the speaker, why should the listeners visit the information desk?

   (A) To make a complaint

   (B) To get information

   (C) To speak with a staff member

   (D) To complete a form

攻略解題法 了解該如何作答與公共場所公告有關的題目。

4. Where is the announcement taking place? 公告是在哪裡宣布的？

▶ 這是詢問公告地點的題目，所以要專心聆聽前半段。

(A) At a clothing store 服飾店
(B) At an office 辦公室
(C) At a gallery 畫廊
(D) At a cinema 電影院

5. What is being offered today only? 只在今天提供的東西是什麼？

▶ 作答詢問具體資訊的題目時，要專心聆聽位於中間的相關資訊。

(A) A gift voucher 禮品券
(B) A discount on certain items 特定商品的折扣
(C) A free gift with any purchase 任一筆消費贈送的免費禮物
(D) Delivery service 寄送服務

6. According to the speaker, why should the listeners visit the information desk?
根據說話者，聽者為什麼應該去服務台？

▶ 尋找叮嚀、要求事項時，要仔細聆聽後半段提到命令句的部分。

(A) To make a complaint 為了抱怨
(B) To get information 為了取得資訊
(C) To speak with a staff member 為了跟員工談話
(D) To complete a form 為了填寫表格

Welcome to Paris Design. Attention, all shoppers! [4] Our boutique is having a sale right now!

▶ 公告地點會在問候語的後面出現。這題問的是公告地點，所以聽到「boutique」後就能知道(A)為正確答案。

歡迎來到巴黎設計。請各位購物者注意！我們的精品正在打折！

[5] For the next two hours, we are offering a 15% discount on some items. But before

▶ 若有聽到題目中的特定時間點（next two hours算為today之內），就能知道(B)為正確答案。

you can get the discount, you need to sign up to become a member of Paris Design.
在接下來的兩個小時內，我們會提供某些商品十五％的折扣。但是在享有折扣前，您需要註冊成為巴黎設計的會員。

It's not as complicated to join as you may think. [6] Just visit the information counter
and fill out an application form.

▶ 叮嚀、要求事項的相關線索會在後半段出現。廣播提到「到服務櫃檯填寫申請表格」，所以(D)為正確答案。

加入方式沒有您想像中的複雜。只要到服務台填寫申請表格即可。

Thank you for coming and enjoy shopping here.
感謝您的范臨，祝您購物愉快。

詞彙整理 **offer** 提供 **sign up** 註冊 **complicated** 複雜的 **application form** 申請書，申請表

攻略POINT ❶ 公告地點的相關線索會在前一、兩句出現。
❷ 作答詢問具體資訊的題目時，要注意聽中間部分。
❸ 作答跟叮嚀、要求事項有關的題目時，要仔細聆聽後半段提到命令句的部分。

公共場所公告的結構

公共場所公告的鋪陳	公共場所公告相關句型
問候語、地點、介紹	• Attention, all shoppers.　請各位購物者注意。 • Welcome to ~.　歡迎蒞臨~。
公告目的	• Our store will be closing＋時間.　本店將於~打烊。 • I'm sorry to announce that ~.　很抱歉地在此宣布~。
公告內容	• We kindly ask that ~.　我們希望您~。 • starting next week　從下個禮拜開始
福利、建議、叮嚀事項	• We'd like to remind you that ~.　提醒各位~。 • Remember to ~.　請記得~。
結語	• We appreciate ~.　我們感謝~。 • Thank you for ~.　感謝您~。

Voca Check - up! 公共場所公告相關詞彙

gallery 畫廊 **gift voucher** 禮品券 **move** 移動，搬動 **convenience** 方便，便利 **upcoming** 即將到來的 **pleasant environment** 愉快的環境 **opportunity** 機會 **mover** 搬東西的人 **make an announcement** 宣布，公布 **annual** 年度的 **reservation** 預約 **direction** 方向 **loss** 損失 **feedback** 回饋 **purchase** 購買 **delivery service** 寄送服務 **complaint** 抱怨 **appreciate** 感謝 **information desk** 服務台

Step 3 | 實戰演練　　　　　🎧 76.mp3

4. When will the gallery close?

   (A) In ten minutes

   (B) In thirty minutes

   (C) In one hour

   (D) In two hours

5. Who is being addressed?

   (A) A guest

   (B) A staff member

   (C) A librarian

   (D) An artist

6. What are the listeners asked to do?

   (A) Go out of the lobby

   (B) Move to the cafe

   (C) Leave the restaurant

   (D) Buy a gift at the store

▶ 答案與解析請參考解析本第81頁

1. According to the speaker, what is the new office like?

   (A) It has a fully equipped meeting space.
   (B) It has a pleasant environment.
   (C) It has a beautiful view.
   (D) It has a spacious conference room.

2. When will the company move to the new building?

   (A) On Friday
   (B) On Saturday
   (C) On Sunday
   (D) On Monday

3. What are the listeners asked to do?

   (A) Order some office supplies
   (B) Remove the old furniture
   (C) Arrange the office supplies
   (D) Move their own documents

4. Where does this announcement most likely take place?

   (A) On a plane
   (B) At a bus station
   (C) On a cruise ship
   (D) At an airport

5. What is the cause of the problem?

   (A) Inclement weather conditions
   (B) Mechanical problems
   (C) The delay of a previous flight
   (D) The repairing of the runway

6. According to the announcement, what has been changed?

   (A) The arrival time
   (B) The departure time
   (C) The schedule for a trip
   (D) The meal coupons

7. What has changed about the annual party?

   (A) The guests
   (B) The date
   (C) The price
   (D) The location

8. When will the party begin?

   (A) At 6 p.m.
   (B) At 7 p.m.
   (C) At 8 p.m.
   (D) At 9 p.m.

9. Why should employees contact Jeremy?

   (A) To arrange transportation
   (B) To get directions
   (C) To purchase tickets
   (D) To reserve seats

10. What is being announced?

   (A) A rescheduled meeting
   (B) A new working arrangement
   (C) An office relocation
   (D) An increase in salaries

11. What does the woman mean when she says, "Here's the deal"?

   (A) She is trying to make a suggestion.
   (B) She wants to distribute something to the listeners.
   (C) She disagrees with some employees' opinions.
   (D) She is expressing her appreciation to the listeners.

12. When does the speaker say the change will take effect?

   (A) Imminently
   (B) The following day
   (C) Next month
   (D) Next week

▶ 答案與解析請參考解析本第82頁

聽寫訓練

Questions 4-6 refer to the following announcement.

Attention, _____. I'd like to _____ some of the printers in our department _____ this afternoon. A maintenance man will _____ this afternoon. All employees should _____ while the replacement work _____. If you _____, please call the Maintenance Department.

Questions 4-6 refer to the following announcement.

Attention, visitors. Our gallery _____. The coffee shop and restaurant will _____ p.m. for _____. _____, since the gallery will be closing in 1 hour, all visitors _____ main lobby. If you _____ at the information counter, do not _____. We hope to see _____ soon.

聽寫訓練

Review Test   🎧 dictation-41.mp3

Questions 1-3 refer to the following conversation.

Good morning, employees. I'd like to announce that we're going to _____ _____ _____ _____ _____ _____ next Monday. I'm sure that everyone is expecting to see a _____ to work in. The movers will be _____. It's a good opportunity for us to _____ _____. Please make sure you have done this _____.

Question 4-6 refer to the following notice.

Attention, all passengers on Sky Airline's _____ _____. Due to _____ _____, all flights have been _____. This flight was originally _____ _____, but it has been rescheduled and will now _____ _____, so it will be delayed _____ _____.Thank you for your _____. We _____ for this inconvenience. We will provide _____ which you can use at any of the _____.

Question 7-9 refer to the following notice.

Good morning. I want to _____ before we start. As you all know, our annual party is tomorrow, but _____ to the Upper Star Resort. We did that due to a _____. However, it will be at the _____ You can check out a rough map of how to get to the new _____ _____. I believe many of you have already seen it on the notice board in the lobby. If you have _____ or need transportation, _____ at 234-4257.

Questions 10-12 refer to the following announcement.

I want to inform you all about _____

_____. You recently completed a questionnaire on efficient practices in the

office, and the consensus is that you would be _____

_____ in the day. So,

umm… _____. We will try out this suggestion starting next week,

when your _____

. Employees will then be able to _____

_____ than previously. Please note that these adjustments will _____

_____.

Voca Preview

請勾選不認識的單字，學習完類型分析後再重新確認勾選的單字。

- discuss 討論
- be supposed to 預計應該～
- ordered product 訂購的商品
- manufacture 製造
- recommend 推薦
- purchase 購買
- details 細節
- arrange 安排
- explain 說明
- look forward to -ing 期待～
- patient 患者
- service representative 服務專員
- currently 目前
- instruction 指示
- account 帳戶，帳號
- public holiday 公休日，國定假日
- regarding 關於
- business hours 營業時間
- operator 接線生
- delicious 美味的

- insect 昆蟲
- request 請求
- tenant 承租人
- landlord 房東
- notify 通知
- advertise 廣告
- stationery store 文具店
- give away 發放
- membership fee 會員費
- renew 更新
- available 可利用的
- get in touch with 跟～聯絡
- owner 所有人，主人
- known for 以～聞名
- provide 提供
- unique 獨特的
- inquiry 詢問，問題
- regard 注意
- make haste 趕緊，快速
- questionnaire 問卷

類型分析 12

各大主題攻略—訊息

WARMING UP

1. What is the main purpose of the message? ....

2. What problem is mentioned? ....

3. What will the listeners probably do next? ....

尋找線索　觀察獨白，找出上述題目的線索後，掌握內容。

Hi. This is Sam from the Beautiful Paint Company. I'm calling to confirm your order of the paints for your new house. As we discussed on Monday, we are actually supposed to send your ordered product tomorrow, but the brand MM7 which you requested is no longer manufactured. So we recommend that you purchase another brand, called Tott. Please call us to make sure which brand you want us to send.

確認解答＆要點 確認正確答案，了解訊息的特徵。

診斷評估：掌握題目的重點

1. What is the main purpose of the message? 這則訊息的主旨是什麼？ ▶ 詢問目的

2. What problem is mentioned? 提到了什麼問題？ ▶ 詢問提到的問題

3. What will the listeners probably do next? 聽者接下來可能會做什麼？
   ▶ 詢問接下來會做的事

尋找線索：分析測驗內容

Hi. This is Sam from the Beautiful Paint Company.

I'm calling to confirm your order of the paints for your new house.

▶ 1. 打電話的目的的答題依據

您好。我是美漆公司的山姆。來電是想跟您確認您替新家訂購的油漆。

> 須記住在訊息前半段出現的發訊者、收訊者、職業、行業類別、公司等，並專
> 心聆聽前半段跟題目有關的內容。

As we discussed on Monday, we are actually supposed to send your ordered product

tomorrow, but the brand MM7 which you requested is no longer manufactured.

▶ 2. 訂購問題的答題依據。獨白中提到的問題是客人想使用的品牌停產了。

正如我們星期一所討論的，我們本來預計應該在明天寄出您訂購的產品，但是您要求的MM7品牌不再生產了。

> 問題會在簡短問候之後開始提起。

So we recommend that you purchase another brand, called Tott.

所以我們建議您購買另一個叫做陶德的牌子。

Please call us to make sure which brand you want us to send.

▶ 3. 接下來會做的事的答題依據。作答next題型時要專心聆聽後半段。

為了確認您希望我們寄哪個牌子給您，請打電話給我們。

> 接下來（next）會做的事、要求、建議和未來日程會在後半段出現。

詞彙整理 **be supposed to** 預計應該～ **manufacture** 製造，生產 **purchase** 購買

語音訊息

Step 1 實戰重點

語音訊息是打電話的人留下的訊息，只要準確地理解訊息的鋪陳順序就能輕鬆解題，所以請事先熟悉訊息的鋪陳順序。

🎓 **代表題型** 先在十秒內讀完三道題目，聆聽獨白後選出正確答案。 78.mp3

4. What is the purpose of the message?

   (A) To reserve a tour

   (B) To schedule an appointment

   (C) To confirm an appointment

   (D) To change a schedule

5. Who will be interviewing Sarah?

   (A) A manager

   (B) A supervisor

   (C) A director

   (D) A president

6. What does William Pitt ask Sarah to do?

   (A) Apply for a position

   (B) Call him to confirm an interview

   (C) Send him more details

   (D) Call him to arrange a meeting

攻略解題法 了解該如何作答與語音訊息有關的題目。

4. What is the purpose of the message? 這則訊息的主旨是什麼？
   ▶ 發訊者和收訊者在訊息的前半段出現之後，目的會在以I'm calling to開始的句子中出現。

   (A) To reserve a tour　為了預訂旅行
   (B) To schedule an appointment　為了安排會面時間
   (C) To confirm an appointment　為了確認預定
   (D) To change a schedule　為了改變行程

5. Who will be interviewing Sarah? 誰會面試莎拉？
   ▶ 具體資訊會在目的、問題的後面出現。這句問的是面試官的具體資訊，所以要仔細聆聽出現特定人物的名字或職責的句子。

   (A) A manager　經理
   (B) A supervisor　上司
   (C) A director　主任
   (D) A president　總裁

6. What does William Pitt ask Sarah to do? 威廉‧皮特要求莎拉做什麼？
   ▶ 這是詢問要求事項的題目，所以要專心聆聽後半段中的命令句。

   (A) Apply for a position　應徵一個職位
   (B) Call him to confirm an interview　打電話給他確認面試
   (C) Send him more details　寄更多的細節給他
   (D) Call him to arrange a meeting　打電話給他安排會議

Hi, Sarah. This is William Pitt from the Beautiful Travel Agency. [4] I'm calling to schedule an interview with you. We received your application last week.
▶ 電話訊息中以「I'm calling~」開頭的部分會出現打電話的目的。來電者是因為「面試」才打電話的，所以(B)為正確答案。

嗨，莎拉。我是美麗旅遊社的威廉‧皮特。我打電話是想跟您安排面試時間。我們上週收到了您的應徵信。

You are someone who has the work experience that we are looking for. [5] You're going to interview with my supervisor Miranda.
▶ 具體資訊會在來電目的之後出現。這裡出現了關於面試者的資訊，被面試的人是莎拉，而來電者的上司會進行面試。

您是具備我們正在找的工作經驗的人。您將會跟我的上司米蘭達面試。

I will explain our staff policy to you after your interview. [6] Please let me know if you are available next Monday from 3 to 4 p.m. You can reach me at 333-1928.
▶ 這句是命令句，出現了跟要求有關的線索。(B)為正確答案。

面試之後，我會跟您說明我們的員工政策。請告訴我您下週一下午三到四點是否有空。您可以撥打333-1928與我聯繫。

I look forward to hearing from you soon. Thank you.　期待很快就能收到您的消息，謝謝。

詞彙整理 **schedule** 安排日程 **application** 申請書，應徵信 **available** 可利用的 **look forward to-ing** 期待

攻略POINT ❶ 發訊者和收訊者在電話訊息的前半段出現之後，目的通常會在以I'm calling to開始的句子中出現。
　　　　 ❷ 此類詢問要求內容的題目，要專心聆聽後半段中的命令句。

語音訊息的結構

語音訊息的鋪陳	語音訊息相關句型
問候、發訊者或收訊者的資訊、職業、行業類別、公司	• Hi, Mr, Brown ~.　嗨，布朗先生～。 • This is 名字 from 公司 ~.　我是～公司的～（名字）。 • This is Mary Johnson, the sales manager at the Star Dress Boutique.　我是星點洋裝精品的銷售經理瑪莉‧瓊森。
目的、問題	• I'm calling about ~.　我打電話是想談～。 • I'm calling to ~.　我打電話是為了～。 • I'd like to inform ~.　我想通知您～。 • You sent us a message with your concerns about ~.　您發了擔心～的訊息給我們。。
跟時間點有關的具體資訊	• On Monday　在星期一 • On August 5　在八月五日
要求與建議	• Please call me back at ＋聯絡方式.　請回撥～給我。 • We ask that ~.　我們要求～ • I want to ~.　我希望～
日後的行程	• We'll be posting answers.　我們會公告答覆。
聯絡資訊	• You can visit our website.　您可以拜訪我們的網站。 • I can be reached at 聯絡方式.　請透過～與我聯繫。

Step **3** | 實戰演練　🔊 79.mp3

4. Who most likely is the caller?

(A A sales staff member
(B) An engineer
(C) A real estate agent
(D) A supplier

5. Where does the speaker most likely work?

(A) In a post office

(B) In a clothing store

(C) In a bank

(D) In a restaurant

6. When will the promotion begin?

(A) This weekend

(B) Next week

(C) Next weekend

(D) Next Monday

▶ 答案與解析請參考解析本第85頁

自動回覆系統

自動回覆系統可以分成告知收訊者不在的訊息，以及自動介紹公司的訊息。告知收訊者不在的錄音內容通常跟個人、商店或辦公室有關。自動介紹或說明性的訊息主要跟銀行或公司有關。為了輕鬆解題，須事先熟知錄音訊息的鋪陳順序。

 代表題型 先在十秒內讀完三道題目，聆聽獨白後選出正確答案。 80.mp3

4. Who is the message intended for?

(A) Hospital patients

(B) Tourists

(C) Bank customers

(D) Bank employees

5 What is suggested about the customer service representatives?

(A) They work in another office.

(B) They are not currently working.

(C) They are on other lines.

(D) They haven't arrived yet.

6. What will the listener hear by pressing 3?

(A) Instructions in Chinese

(B) Information about an account

(C) The bank's working hours

(D) The bank's location

攻略解題法 了解該如何作答與自動回覆系統有關的題目。

4. Who is the message intended for? 這則訊息的對象是誰？

▶ 關於來電者（發訊者）的線索會在前半段問候後面的「Thank you for calling~、You have reached~」句子中出現。

(A) Hospital patients　醫院患者
(B) Tourists　觀光客
(C) Bank customers　銀行客戶
(D) Bank employees　銀行員工

5. What is suggested about the customer service representatives?
暗示了關於客服專員的什麼？

▶ 前半段會介紹公司或收訊者的身分，或是提到沒接電話的原因。

(A) They work in another office.　他們在另一間辦公室工作。
(B) They are not currently working.　他們目前非上班時間。
(C) They are on other lines.　他們正在接其他電話。
(D) They haven't arrived yet.　他們還沒抵達。

6. What will the listener hear by pressing 3?　聽者按3之後會聽到什麼？

▶ 服務導引號碼會在後半段出現，所以要仔細聆聽提到「Please press＋號碼 (to find~)、Press＋號碼 (to check~)」的部分。

(A) Instructions in Chinese 中文說明
(B) Information about an account　關於帳戶的資訊
(C) The bank's working hours　銀行營業時間
(D) The bank's location　銀行的位置

Hello. ⁴ You have reached Brown Bank.

　　　　▶ 前半段提到這裡是銀行，所以這則訊息的對象是(C)。　您好，這裡是布朗銀行。

⁵ We are currently closed because of the public holiday.　▶ 訊息前半段是介紹公司或收訊者的身分，或是提到沒接電話的原因。訊息前半段一定會出現一個以上的答題線索，所以務必專心聆聽此部分。
由於是國定假日，我們目前未營業。

Our regular working hours are from 9 a.m. to 4 p.m. from Monday to Friday, and we are closed on all public holidays. For instructions in Chinese, press 2.　我們的正規上班時間為週一至週五，早上九點至下午四點。所有國定假日皆休息。聆聽中文說明請按2。

⁶ To check on information regarding new accounts, press 3.　▶ 服務導引號碼會在後半段出現。此處提到「press＋號碼」，是第六題的線索。(B)是正確答案。　想確認關於新帳戶的資訊，請按3。

If you need to speak with a customer service representative, please call back during our regular business hours. Thank you for calling and have a nice day.
若您需要跟客服專員通話，請在我們的正常上班時間回撥。謝謝您的來電，祝您有愉快的一天。

詞彙整理 currently 現在，目前 **public holiday** 國定假日，公休日 **regular working hours** 正常上班時間 **instruction** 說明，指示 **regarding** 關於～ **account** 帳戶 **customer service representative** 客服專員

攻略POINT ❶ 訊息前半段的問候後面的「Thank you for calling~、You have reached~」會出現關於來電者的線索。
　　　　❷ 此類跟服務導引號碼有關的題目，在中、後半段提到「Please press＋號碼 (to find~)、Press＋號碼 (to check~)」的部分會出現正確答案的線索。

自動回覆系統的結構

自動回覆系統的鋪陳	自動回覆系統相關句型
問候 （公司與收訊者的介紹）	• Hello. You've reached＋公司／部門. 您好，這裡是～。 • Thanks for calling ~. 感謝來電～。 • Thank you for calling ~. 感謝您來電～。
公司介紹、不在的理由、 營業時間	• Our company is known for ~. 敝公司以～聞名。 • The office is currently closed ~. 辦公室目前休息中。 • Our business hours are ~. 我們的營業時間是～。
服務介紹與聯絡方式	• Please press 3 to find ~. 若想找～，請按3。 • Press 1 to check ~. 若想確認～，請按1。 • Please call back ~. 請回撥至～。
建議、要求與叮囑	• For more information 欲知更多資訊 • Please call again. 請再打一次。

Voca Check - up! 自動回覆系統相關詞彙

pound key 井字鍵 **star key** 米字鍵 **page** 廣播叫（人） **stay on the line** 不要掛斷 **hold** 稍等 **press number**＋號碼 請按 ~ **operator** 接線生 **talk to** 跟～通話 **Our store is at ~.** 我們商店位於～。 **We are open from ~.** 我們的營業時間是～。 **business hours** 營業時間

Step 3   實戰演練   🎧 81.mp3

4. According to the message, what is the Victory Zoo known for?

   (A) Its delicious food

   (B) Having a diverse number of animals

   (C) A wide range of insects

   (D) Its unusual plants

5. Why should the listeners press 1?

   (A) To book a ticket

   (B) To buy a ticket

   (C) To cancel a reservation

   (D) To ask for information

6. How can the listeners get more information?

   (A) By pressing the number 1

   (B) By visiting a website

   (C) By calling the given number

   (D) By requesting a pamphlet

▶ 答案與解析請參考解析本第85頁

1. Who would most likely be the caller?

(A) An office tenant
(B) A maintenance man
(C) A real estate agent
(D) A landlord

2. What is the purpose of the message?

(A) To give the location of an office
(B) To notify the man that an office is available to rent
(C) To announce some construction work
(D) To advertise a new building

3. What will the listener do next?

(A) Sign a contract
(B) Move to a new office
(C) Contact Linda Rey
(D) Call the owner of a building

4. What sort of business has the listener called?

(A) A furniture store
(B) A clothing store
(C) A computer store
(D) A stationery store

5. What is the online store known for?

(A) Sturdy furniture
(B) Unusual clothes
(C) Modern designs
(D) A system that makes paying easy

6. Why should the listeners press 1?

(A) To check on a delivery
(B) To find out a location
(C) To order a product
(D) To speak with a staff member

7. What does the store sell?

    (A) Electronic devices
    (B) Furniture
    (C) Stationery
    (D) Books

8. Why is Joy calling?

    (A) To ask about a survey
    (B) To give away a free gift
    (C) To discuss a membership fee
    (D) To offer the listener a position

9. What is the listener asked to do?

    (A) Send an application
    (B) Visit the store within 2 days
    (C) Renew a membership
    (D) Call the store

10. Who most likely is this message for?

    (A) An architect
    (B) A personnel manager
    (C) A building manager
    (D) A moving crew member

11. What does the woman mean when she says, "Here's the thing"?

    (A) She feels sorry about canceling the agreement.
    (B) She found something she was looking for.
    (C) She wants to give something to the man.
    (D) She wants to explain a problem.

12. What does the speaker ask the listener to do?

    (A) Reimburse her for the money she spent
    (B) Give her some information
    (C) Help her clean an apartment
    (D) Write a new contract

▶ 答案與解析請參考解析本第86頁

聽寫訓練

Unit 31 語音訊息 ┊ **Step 3** 實戰演練   🎧 dictation-42.mp3

Questions 4-6 refer to the following telephone message.

Hello. This is Mary Johnson, _____ at the Star Dress Boutique. I'm

calling _____ the wrong products _____

_____. The shipment you sent me _____, not skirts.

I'd _____ send the correct order _____

_____, and I don't want you to _____

_____. We're having a special promotion next weekend. _____

_____, I will _____ by this weekend.

Unit 32 自動回覆系統 ┊ **Step 3** 實戰演練   🎧 dictation-43.mp3

Questions 4-6 refer to the following recorded message.

Thank you for calling the Victory Zoo. Our zoo is _____ for our _____

_____. We're open every day _____

_____. Entrance tickets can _____ by

phone. If you want to _____, press 1. Cash and credit cards

_____, and you can pay at the ticket booth _____.

For more information, please call _____

representatives at 999-6738.

Review Test   🎧 dictation-44.mp3

Question 1-3 refer to the following telephone message.

Good morning. This is Linda Rey from Star Realty. I'm calling to let you know that _____

_____ which you might be interested in has _____. It's near the bus station,

bank, and post office. _____. I'm sure

you must be interested in seeing the office. Please get in touch with me as soon as possible,

and I'll ask the owner of the building _____ you can have a _____

_____. You can _____

_____. Thanks, Mr. Anderson. I hope to hear from you soon.

Question 4-6 refer to the following recorded message.

Thank you for calling the Blackberry Online Store, the _____

_____ in the U.K. Blackberry is known for _____

_____ and accessories. Please listen carefully to the following options. Please _____

_____ to check the current _____. _____

_____ to check the _____. For all _____

_____, please _____, and one of our customer service _____

_____ you soon.

Question 7-9 refer to the following telephone message.

Hello. This is Joy from Joy's Computer Store. I'm calling to see if you mind answering some

_____ _____ _____ _____. If you answer this

questionnaire, we'll _____ which will give

you _____ at our store. But you should make

haste as you must _____ to receive the

discount coupon. Just call us at 695-4215 so that we can send you a questionnaire.

Questions 10-12 refer to the following telephone message.

Hello, Mr. Conner. I'm Karen Riley from Apartment B6. I'm calling to let you know that I will be

managing the Boston branch starting next month. _____

_____ of this place a _____.

I've arranged for a moving company to _____

_____, and I'll be sure to have the apartment cleaned afterward. _____

_____. Um... When I signed the contract two years ago, I think

there was a clause about _____

_____ of the security deposit. I don't remember the exact terms, so can you _____

_____ and explain them to me? Thanks a lot.

Voca Preview

請勾選不認識的單字，學習完類型分析後再重新確認勾選的單字。

- [ ] **celebrate** 慶祝
- [ ] **anniversary** 紀念日
- [ ] **free admission** 免費入場
- [ ] **resident** 居民
- [ ] **state** 提及
- [ ] **world-renowned** 舉世聞名的
- [ ] **weather condition** 天氣狀況
- [ ] **politician** 政治人物
- [ ] **humid** 潮濕的
- [ ] **unseasonably** 不合時宜地
- [ ] **temperature** 溫度
- [ ] **rise** 上升
- [ ] **shower** 陣雨
- [ ] **drizzle** 毛毛雨
- [ ] **flood** 洪水
- [ ] **downpour** 暴雨
- [ ] **foggy** 有霧的
- [ ] **cloudy** 多雲的
- [ ] **dry** 乾燥的
- [ ] **drought** 乾旱

- [ ] **Celsius** 攝氏
- [ ] **Fahrenheit** 華氏
- [ ] **car accident** 車禍
- [ ] **damaged** 受損的
- [ ] **head** （往特定方向）出發
- [ ] **ongoing** 持續的
- [ ] **avoid** 避免
- [ ] **stall** 拋錨
- [ ] **alternate route** 替代道路
- [ ] **be held up** 被堵住的
- [ ] **architect** 建築師
- [ ] **specialized** 專業的
- [ ] **local** 當地的，地區的
- [ ] **charity event** 慈善活動
- [ ] **organization** 團體，組織
- [ ] **electricity shortage** 缺電
- [ ] **consumption** 消費
- [ ] **rapidly** 急速地
- [ ] **scorching** 激烈的
- [ ] **outer road** 銜接道路

類型分析

13

各大主題攻略—廣播

WARMING UP

診斷評估　閱讀題目後，在兩秒內掌握題目重點。

1. Who most likely is the speaker? ....

2. What will happen on September 12? ....

3. What will the listeners likely hear next? ....

尋找線索　觀察獨白，找出上述題目的線索後，掌握內容。

Good morning. This is Alex Johnson with the local news. The Wilton City Museum's 20th anniversary is coming next week on September 12. To celebrate its 20th anniversary, the city council will provide free admission for all residents of Wilton. Free drinks will also be provided by the city council. The city council stated that this is a perfect chance to see a world-renowned museum without having to pay anything. And now for an update on the weather forecast.

確認解答＆要點　確認正確答案，了解跟廣播獨白有關的特徵。

診斷評估：掌握題目的重點

1. Who most likely is the speaker?　說話者最有可能是誰？ ▶ 詢問對象

2. What will happen on September 12?　9月12日會發生什麼事？ ▶ 詢問將在9月12日發生的事

3. What will the listeners likely hear next?　聽者接下來有可能會聽到什麼？

　　▶ 詢問接下來會聽到的內容

尋找線索：分析測驗內容

Good morning. This is Alex Johnson with the local news.

▶ 1. 藉由開頭的問候語，可以知道說話者是新聞主播，聽者是聽眾。

早安。我是當地新聞的亞力克斯・強森。

　　新聞的前半段會出現問候語、說話者、目前的時間和新聞種類等。

The Wilton City Museum's 20th anniversary is coming next week on September 12.

▶ 1. 可以知道9月12日是二十週年紀念日的依據。

下週的九月十二日是威爾頓市立博物館的二十週年紀念日。

　　問候語之後會出現報導的主題、細節。

To celebrate its 20th anniversary, the city council will provide free admission for all residents of Wilton. Free drinks will also be provided by the city council. The city council stated that this is a perfect chance to see a world-renowned museum without having to pay anything.　為了慶祝二十週年紀念日，市議會將提供所有威爾頓居民免費入場，還有提供免費的飲料。市議會表示這是免費欣賞舉世聞名的博物館的絕佳機會。

And now for an update on the weather forecast.

▶ 3. 下一個廣播通常會在最後面提到。這裡的下個廣播是天氣預報。　接下來是最新的天氣預報。

　　叮嚀和下個廣播的介紹會在結尾出現。

詞彙整理 **celebrate** 慶祝　**admission** 入場　**resident** 居民，住民　**state** 提及　**world-renowned** 舉世聞名的

請務必熟記跟天氣有關的表達方式。接在轉折（however、but）、結論（so）等詞彙後面的句子一定會出現答題線索，所以聆聽時請不要錯過這個部分。

 代表題型　先在十秒內讀完三道題目，聆聽獨白後選出正確答案。 83.mp3

4. What is this report for?

   (A) To advertise public transportation

   (B) To report the weather conditions

   (C) To interview some politicians

   (D) To announce some construction work

5. What does the announcer suggest the listeners do today?

   (A) Take their umbrellas

   (B) Wear raincoats

   (C) Use public transportation

   (D) Drink a lot of water

6. How will the weather be on the weekend?

   (A) Partly cloudy

   (B) Rainy

   (C) Hot and humid

   (D) Sunny

攻略解題法 了解該如何作答與天氣預報有關的題目。

4. What is this report for? 這則報導的目的是什麼？ ▶ 廣播節目的介紹會在前半段出現。

(A) To advertise public transportation 為了宣傳大眾交通工具

(B) To report the weather conditions 為了報導天氣狀況

(C) To interview some politicians 為了採訪某些政治人物

(D) To announce some construction work 為了公布建築工程

5. What does the announcer suggest the listeners do today?

播音員建議聽者今天做什麼？ ▶ 節目介紹的後面會馬上出現關於天氣的建議。

(A) Take their umbrellas 帶雨傘

(B) Wear raincoats 穿雨衣

(C) Use public transportation 使用大眾交通工具

(D) Drink a lot of water 多喝水

6. How will the weather be on the weekend? 週末的天氣怎麼樣？

▶ 關於未來天氣的答題線索會在後半段出現。

(A) Partly cloudy 部分多雲

(B) Rainy 下雨

(C) Hot and humid 炎熱和潮濕

(D) Sunny 晴朗

 聆聽對話時

[4] This is Stacy Howard with your weather update.

▶ 前半段會介紹廣播的種類。播音員說要更新天氣預報，所以(B)為正確答案。

我是史黛西·霍華德，為各位報導最新天氣。

Today's weather is going to be rainy. If you are going to leave your house, [5] don't forget to bring your umbrella with you.

▶ 提到節目種類之後，下一句立刻出現跟天氣有關的建議。(A)為正確答案。

今天將是雨天。如果各位現在要外出，別忘記帶上雨傘。

Tomorrow will be sunny, and the weather will be nice. However,[6] on the weekend, we will see some unseasonably hot and humid weather throughout the country.

▶ 後半段也是報導未來天氣狀況的部分，尤其是接在However後面的句子一定會出現答題線索。(C)為正確答案。

明天晴朗，天氣佳。不過，全國週末的天氣會異常地炎熱和潮濕。

The temperature is expected to continue rising on the weekend. That is all for the morning weather report.

預期溫度會在週末時持續上升。以上是晨間天氣報導。

詞彙整理 **unseasonably** 不合時宜地，不適時地 **humid** 潮濕的 **temperature** 溫度，氣溫 **be expected to** 預期～

攻略POINT ❶ 前半段會提到廣播的種類。

❷ 介紹完節目並說明天氣狀況後，會出現關於天氣的衣服穿搭或攜帶物品等建議。

❸ 未來的天氣狀況會在後半段跟具體的時間點（tomorrow、on the weekend）一起出現。

❹ 在表示轉折的詞彙（however、but）後面出現的句子很有可能是答題線索，所以務必專心聆聽。

天氣預報的結構

天氣預報的鋪陳	天氣預報相關題型
問候、節目介紹	• Good evening. You're listening to ~.　晚安。您正在收聽的是～。 • This is for the morning weather forecast.　現在是晨間天氣預報。
目前的天氣、建議	• The current temperature is ~.　目前的溫度為～。 • Don't forget to take ~.　別忘記帶～。
未來的天氣	• However, the sky ~.　不過，天空～。 • Tomorrow will ~.　明天會～。
下個廣播介紹	• I'll have the next weather report in＋時間. 　我將在～後播報下一則天氣預報。

Voca Check - up!　天氣預報相關詞彙

rain 雨　**shower** 陣雨　**drizzle** 毛毛雨　**windy** 多風的　**flood** 洪水　**downpour** 暴雨　**foggy / misty** 有霧的　**cloudy / overcast** 多雲的　**humid** 潮濕的　**dry** 乾燥的　**drought** 乾旱　**sunny / clear / blue sky** 晴朗的　**temperature** 溫度　**degree** ～度　**Celsius** 攝氏　**Fahrenheit** 華氏　**weather report** 天氣預報

4. How will the weather change today?

(A) It will snow.

(B) It will be colder.

(C) It will get hotter.

(D) It will become foggy.

5. What will happen on Sunday?

(A) The temperature will increase.

(B) Fierce winds will blow.

(C) Snow is expected.

(D) The temperature will remain the same.

6. What will the listeners probably hear next?

(A) A traffic report

(B) An advertisement

(C) A sports report

(D) Business news

▶ 答案與解析請參考解析本第89頁

Unit 34　交通廣播

Step 1　實戰重點

造成交通堵塞的原因有道路施工、天氣惡劣等。這種時候的交通廣播內容，通常都是要聽眾改道或使用大眾交通工具。廣播時間、聽者要做的事或建議事項等都是常見的題目。

代表題型　先在十秒內讀完三道題目，聆聽獨白後選出正確答案。　 85.mp3

4. According to the report, what caused the traffic delay this morning?

   (A) Poor weather conditions

   (B) A car accident

   (C) A damaged road

   (D) Road repairs

5. What advice does the speaker give?

   (A) Wait until the afternoon

   (B) Take an alternate route

   (C) Call an ambulance

   (D) Use public transportation

6. Who is this talk for?

   (A) Police

   (B) Motorists

   (C) Customers

   (D) Tourists

攻略解題法 了解該如何作答與交通廣播有關的題目。

4. According to the report, what caused the traffic delay this morning?
根據這則報導，是什麼造成今早的交通堵塞？
▶ 交通堵塞的理由會在前半段出現，所以從一開始就要仔細聆聽。

(A) Poor weather conditions　天候不佳
(B) A car accident　車禍
(C) A damaged road　毀損的道路
(D) Road repairs　道路維修

5. What advice does the speaker give?　說話者給了什麼建議？
▶ 此類詢問建議內容的題目，要專心聽recommend後面的句子。

(A) Wait until the afternoon　等到下午
(B) Take an alternate route　走替代道路
(C) Call an ambulance　叫救護車
(D) Use public transportation　使用大眾交通工具

6. Who is this talk for?　這則廣播的對象是誰？
▶ 有關聽眾的線索，在一開始就可以聽到。

(A) Police　警察
(B) Motorists　駕駛人
(C) Customers　顧客
(D) Tourists　觀光客

聽聽對話時

4/6 This is Gary Turk with a special traffic report. There is terrible traffic congestion on Highway 7 due to a traffic accident, so expect long delays in traffic for the entire morning.　▶ 交通廣播的前半段會先問候聽眾，然後提到塞車的原因，所以要仔細聆聽這個部分。第四題的正確答案為(B)。交通廣播的聆聽對象會在前半段出現，這裡報導的是塞車情況，所以對象是駕駛人。第六題的正確答案為(B)。
我是蓋瑞・特克，在此播報一則特別路況報導。由於一起交通意外，七號高速公路目前嚴重堵車，所以預計整個早上都會出現長時間的交通延滯。

If you are heading northbound on Main Street, **5** we recommend taking Route 13 to get downtown.　▶ 尋找關於替代方案的提示時，要仔細聆聽 recommend V-ing 的句子。廣播建議改道，所以 (B) 為正確答案。
若您正從主街往北邊開，我們建議您改走十三號道路前往市中心。

Police and ambulances are now trying to get control of the situation. Keep listening for a full traffic report in twenty minutes.　警方和救護車正試著控制情況。請繼續收聽二十分鐘後的完整路況報導。

詞彙整理 **special traffic report** 特別路況報導　**traffic congestion** 交通堵塞　**highway** 高速公路　**traffic accident** 交通意外　**delay** 延滯，耽擱　**head**（前往～）出發　**downtown** 在市內，往市內

攻略POINT ❶ 交通廣播的題型，一定會出現詢問交通堵塞理由的題目。前半段問候完聽眾之後，會提到塞車原因，所以要仔細聆聽這個部分。
❷ 尋找關於替代方案的提示時，要仔細聆聽recommend V-ing的句子。

交通廣播的結構

交通廣播的鋪陳	交通廣播相關句型
問候	• Good morning, commuters. 早安，各位通勤者。 • This is the 8:00 A.M. traffic report. 現在是早上八點的路況報導。
交通狀況與塞車原因	• because of the ongoing thunderstorm 由於持續的大雷雨 • There was repair work. 進行過維修工程。
替代方案	• We recommend avoiding ~. 我們建議您避開～。 • Drivers should consider using ~. 駕駛人可以考慮使用～。 • We advise you to take Route 15. 我們建議您走十五號道路。
下個廣播時間的說明	• Coming up at 7:00. 七點見。

Voca Check - up! 交通廣播相關詞彙

traffic report 路況報導 **commuter** 通勤者 **motorist** 駕車者 **driver** 駕駛員 **stall** 拋錨 **construction** 施工 **lane** 車道 **road / route** 道路 **accident** 意外 **avenue** 大道 **street** 街道 **path** 小徑 **alternate route** 替代道路 **be closed down** 被封路的 **traffic jam** 交通堵塞 **be held up** 被堵住的

4. Where should the listeners expect delays?

(A) On the outer road

(B) On Highway 22

(C) Near the train station

(D) In the suburbs

5. What caused the delay?

(A) A traffic accident

(B) The celebrating of Christmas Eve

(C) Heavy traffic

(D) A closed exit

6. What does the speaker recommend?

(A) Driving at reduced speeds

(B) Listening for news updates

(C) Taking another road

(D) Calling the police

▶ 答案與解析請參考解析本第89頁

Step 1 　實戰重點

新聞報導前半段中出現的announce that~是提及新聞主題的部分，所以要仔細聆聽，別錯過了。還要區分出現的人物是播音員、受邀嘉賓還是第三者。

 代表題型 先在十秒內讀完三道題目，聆聽獨白後選出正確答案。　 87.mp3

---

4. What is the report mainly about?

   (A) A computer room

   (B) A public library

   (C) A city park

   (D) A shopping mall

5. Who is Bob Jackson?

   (A) A news reporter

   (B) A city official

   (C) A librarian

   (D) An architect

6. When will the work on the project begin?

   (A) In August

   (B) In September

   (C) In October

   (D) In December

攻略解題法 了解該如何作答與新聞有關的題目。

聆聽對話前閱讀題目時

4. What is the report mainly about? 報導主要與什麼有關？
   ▶ 此類詢問報導主題的題目，要仔細聆聽前半段。
   (A) A computer room 電腦室
   (B) A public library 公共圖書館
   (C) A city park 市立公園
   (D) A shopping mall 購物中心

5. Who is Bob Jackson? 鮑勃‧傑克森是誰？
   ▶ 要掌握到提及的人物是播音員、受邀嘉賓還是第三者，再推測對方的職業。
   (A) A news reporter 新聞記者
   (B) A city official 市政府官員
   (C) A librarian 圖書館員
   (D) An architect 建築師

6. When will the work on the project begin? 施工項目何時開始？
   ▶ 這題要推測未來的事。關於未來的推測線索會在後半段出現。
   (A) In August 8月
   (B) In September 9月
   (C) In October 10月
   (D) In December 12月

聆聽對話時

Good evening. In local news, **4** the city of Manchester has decided to build a new public library. ▶ 新聞報導需要引起聽眾的注意，所以會先提到主題再報導詳細的事實。這裡提到要蓋一棟新的公共圖書館，所以(B)為正確答案。 晚安。當地新聞指出曼徹斯特市已決定建造一棟新的公共圖書館。

The library will be located beside Manchester Park. The city council plans for the library to include a room for children and a specialized computer room for e-book users as well. 圖書館將位於曼徹斯特公園隔壁。市議會計劃讓這座圖書館包含一個兒童用空間和一間電子書使用者的專業電腦室。

5 City mayor Bob Jackson said that the public library will be a place that will appeal to families. ▶ 職責和人名一起出現。獨白中的city mayor被改述成選項中的city official。
市長鮑勃‧傑克森表示公共圖書館將會是個吸引家庭前往的地方。

6 Construction will begin on August 1, and the opening day celebration is scheduled for December. ▶ 猜測未來會發生什麼事的句子會在後半段出現。
工程將從八月一日開始，開幕式預定在十二月舉行。

詞彙整理 **local** 地區的，當地的 **city council** 市議會 **plan** 計劃 **specialized** 專業的 **e-book** 電子書 **city councilman** 市議會議員 **construction** 建設，工程 **celebration** 慶祝活動，紀念

攻略POINT ❶ 確認提及的人物是播音員、受邀嘉賓還是第三者，再推測對方的職業。
　　　　　 ❷ 關於未來的推測線索會在後半段出現。

新聞的結構

新聞的鋪陳	新聞相關句型
問候語、新聞種類	• This is Tony White.　我是東尼‧懷特。 • In today's local news　今天的當地新聞
主題、細節、預測未來	• We announced that ~.　我們宣布～ • A spokesperson announced ~.　發言人宣布～ • The Lancaster reported that ~.　蘭卡斯特報導指出～
叮嚀與說明下個廣播順序	• Tune in ~.　收聽～頻道（～節目）。 • I'll be back again.　稍後回來。

Voca Check - up! 新聞相關詞彙

station 廣播電臺　**stay tuned** 繼續收聽　**Thank you for listening.** 謝謝各位的收聽。　**We'll be right back after~.** ～之後立刻回來。　**spokesperson** 發言人　**tune in** 收聽～頻道

Step 3 | 實戰演練　 88.mp3

4. What is the news report mainly about?

(A) The opening of a new business

(B) The holding of a charity event

(C) The introduction of a new product

(D) A merger between two companies

5. What does Ms. Nelson mention?

(A) Various kinds of dresses will be displayed.

(B) Everyone can buy a dress for a cheap price.

(C) The dresses are limited in number.

(D) The dresses are only for the upper class.

6. According to Ms. Nelson, what will most likely happen by the end of the year?

(A) The company will open some new branches.

(B) The company will give away some money to charity organization.

(C) Sales of dresses will increase.

(D) Additional employees will be hired.

▶ 答案與解析請參考解析本第90頁

1. What is the main purpose of the report?

   (A) To advertise a new product
   (B) To look for an employee
   (C) To ask people to conserve water
   (D) To introduce a new business

2. According to the report, what will happen soon?

   (A) A lack of water
   (B) Flood damage
   (C) An electricity shortage
   (D) Financial difficulties

3. What will the listeners likely do next?

   (A) Visit the company
   (B) Report service problems
   (C) Contact the corporation
   (D) Reduce their water consumption

4. What is the purpose of the broadcast?

   (A) To introduce an actor
   (B) To report the weather conditions
   (C) To announce some construction work
   (D) To advertise a hospital

5. What does the speaker suggest that the listeners do?

   (A) Drink a cup of hot tea
   (B) Wear a warm jacket
   (C) Take an umbrella
   (D) Wait for the next weather update

6. According to the speaker, what can listeners find on the website?

   (A) Local news articles
   (B) The weather conditions
   (C) Health information
   (D) A traffic report

7. What is the main purpose of the report?

   (A) To provide a weather report
   (B) To announce the city festival
   (C) To provide construction information
   (D) To advertise a new car

8. What does the speaker recommend?

   (A) Listening for news updates
   (B) Driving carefully
   (C) Taking public transportation
   (D) Taking another route

9. How can the listeners get updated information?

   (A) By listening to the radio
   (B) By watching TV
   (C) By visiting a website
   (D) By calling a number

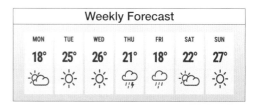

10. What's the purpose of the announcement?

    (A) To warn people about tornadoes
    (B) To advise residents not to go out in the snow
    (C) To caution people about flash floods
    (D) To report the weather for the weekend

11. Look at the graphic. What day is the announcement made on?

    (A) Monday
    (B) Tuesday
    (C) Wednesday
    (D) Thursday

12. What are people in the affected areas advised NOT to do?

    (A) Stay indoors
    (B) Call 911
    (C) Put vehicles under cover
    (D) Drive through floodwaters

▶ 答案與解析請參考解析本第90頁

聽寫訓練

Unit 33　天氣預報 ┆ **Step 3** 實戰演練　　　　　　　　　　　　🎧 dictation-45.mp3

Questions 4-6 refer to the following radio broadcast.

Good morning. There will be _____.
Through the morning, the temperature _____, there will be scorching
_____. However, I have some good
news for you. The wind will _____ Saturday, and it will be _____
_____.
But it looks like _____ is coming our way on Sunday. We'll _____
_____. Now, let's go to Jane Watson _____
today's top sports news.

Unit 34　交通廣播 ┆ **Step 3** 實戰演練　　　　　　　　　　　　🎧 dictation-46.mp3

Questions 4-6 refer to the following radio broadcast.

Good evening. This is Mary Cooper _____.
Many cars are _____ around the shopping mall
and in the downtown area. Even _____ is full of _____
_____ celebrating Christmas Eve. Drivers may _____
_____ from the outer road to the downtown area. We _____
_____ and taking Highway 22 _____
_____ on this road. _____ Minn's international business news
today.

聽寫訓練

Questions 4-6 refer to the following news report.

Thanks for _____ VNC's morning business report. Early this morning, Vivian Nelson, _____ Design Boutique, _____ her company has _____ _____ with a simple design. Nelson said that the public _____ this dress _____. The dress _____ at many boutiques soon. Ms. Nelson also announced that _____, 20% of the company's total sales _____. And now _____ the morning weather forecast.

Questions 1-3 refer to the following news report.

In local news, the North American Water Resources Corporation is _____ _____. The corporation said that our state may have _____. Therefore, the corporation is requesting that people take some _____ like _____ and _____ while brushing their teeth. More information can be found on the North American Water Resources Corporation's website.

Questions 4-6 refer to the following broadcast.

_____ will continue through _____ _____. So let us make _____. The most important thing is to keep your body warm by _____. That is especially _____ like we are having this weekend. For more information on _____, check

out _____ at www.weatherforecast.com.

Questions 7-9 refer to the following broadcast.

Good morning. This is Caroline Mack at WABC. Starting next Monday, _____

_____ due to _____. _____ around

the airport area will _____ when the roadwork starts. It is recommended that

_____ until the roadwork is completed _____

_____. Please visit our website at www.abcstation.com to check out the _____

_____.

Questions 10-12 refer to the following broadcast and chart.

For people living in and _____, _____

_____ to form in the region. Some of them are expected to be _____

_____, bringing very _____ that may _____

_____. The State Emergency Service advises that people in the

areas should _____, preferably indoors and _____.

Try to _____ in the thunderstorm. Beware of fallen trees

and power lines, and _____, _____, _____

_____. For more updated weather forecasts, please continue to _____

_____.

Voca Preview

請勾選不認識的單字，學習完類型分析後再重新確認勾選的單字。

- [ ] **supervise** 監督，管理
- [ ] **hold a party** 舉辦派對
- [ ] **recently** 最近
- [ ] **assign** 分配，分派
- [ ] **employee** 員工
- [ ] **particular** 特別的
- [ ] **subdivide into** 再分成～，細分
- [ ] **executive director** 執行董事
- [ ] **come forward** 站出來
- [ ] **propose** 提議
- [ ] **recognize** 認可
- [ ] **give an award** 頒獎
- [ ] **historian** 歷史學家
- [ ] **official** 官員
- [ ] **parking lot** 停車場
- [ ] **take part in** 參與
- [ ] **trash can** 垃圾桶
- [ ] **famous** 有名的
- [ ] **preserve** 保護
- [ ] **entrance** 入口

- [ ] **job fair** 就業博覽會
- [ ] **function** 盛大集會
- [ ] **sign up** 申請，註冊
- [ ] **itinerary** 日程
- [ ] **enroll** 報名
- [ ] **go over** 檢閱
- [ ] **take place** 發生
- [ ] **be located in** 位於
- [ ] **cathedral** 大教堂
- [ ] **broadcasting station** 廣播電臺
- [ ] **mosque** 清真寺
- [ ] **give a hand** 鼓掌
- [ ] **tirelessly** 孜孜不倦地
- [ ] **attractive** 有魅力的，有吸引力的
- [ ] **century ago** 一個世紀以前
- [ ] **well-known** 著名的
- [ ] **reputation** 名聲，名譽
- [ ] **hospitality industry** 服務業（飯店、餐飲、休閒娛樂業等）
- [ ] **structure** 結構物，建築物
- [ ] **compared to** 跟～相比

類型分析 **14**

各大主題攻略—介紹、導覽

WARMING UP

Unit 36　人物介紹

Unit 37　導覽

REVIEW TEST

聽寫訓練

WARMING UP

診斷評估　閱讀題目後，在兩秒內掌握題目重點。

1. Who is David? ....
2. How long did David work at the Bright Corporation? ....
3. What are the listeners asked to do? ....

尋找線索　觀察獨白，找出上述題目的線索後，掌握內容。

Good morning, everyone. I'd like to introduce David, the new manager of the Marketing Department. He spent ten years in the Marketing Department at the Bright Corporation. David also has a lot of experience with marketing campaigns for restaurants, hotels, and many other types of businesses. I believe all of you can learn many things from him, and he will supervise you as well. We will be holding a welcoming party for him this evening. Everyone is required to attend.

確認解答＆要點　確認正確答案，了解跟介紹、導覽有關的特徵。

診斷評估：掌握題目的重點

1. Who is David? 大衛是誰？ ▶ 詢問對象

2. How long did David work at the Bright Corporation?
大衛在布萊特公司工作多久了？ ▶ 詢問工作經歷

3. What are the listeners asked to do? 聽者被要求做什麼？ ▶ 詢問要求事項

尋找線索：分析測驗內容

Good morning, everyone. I'd like to introduce David, the new manager of the Marketing Department. ▶ 1.可知道大衛的職業、職責的依據
各位早安。我想介紹一下行銷部的新經理大衛。

　　問候、人物介紹等會在前半段出現。

He spent ten years in the Marketing Department at the Bright Corporation.
▶ 2. 可以知道大衛是擁有十年資歷的有經驗人士的依據　他在布萊特公司的行銷部待了十年。

　　人物的經歷會在介紹後出現。

David also has a lot of experience with marketing campaigns for restaurants, hotels, and many other types of businesses. I believe all of you can learn many things from him, and he will supervise you as well. We will be holding a welcoming party for him this evening.　大衛也有很多替餐廳、飯店和其他各行各業舉辦行銷活動的經驗。我相信你們所有人都可以從他身上學到很多，而他也會帶領你們。我們今晚會替他舉辦一個歡迎派對。

　　與人物相關的未來日程和計畫會在中間或後半段出現。

Everyone is required to attend. ▶ 3. 要求所有聽者出席歡迎會之後做結尾　每個人都要出席。

　　後半段會出現請求、要求或叮嚀事項，最後被介紹的人物會開始發表演說。

詞彙整理 **introduce** 介紹 **supervise** 管理 **hold a party** 舉辦派對 **be required to** 被要求～

必須仔細聆聽前半段出現的人物名稱，不要錯過人名前後提到的職業或職位。

 代表題型 先在十秒內讀完三道題目，聆聽獨白後選出正確答案。 90.mp3

---

4. What is the purpose of the speech?

(A) To introduce a new staff member

(B) To announce a new policy

(C) To explain a new training program

(D) To notify employees of a meeting

5. Where is this speech probably taking place?

(A) At a museum

(B) At a hotel

(C) At a hospital

(D) At a library

6. What will the listeners do next?

(A) They will tell Steve about the sections.

(B) They will ask Steve for a day off.

(C) They will leave for a business trip.

(D) They will move to another department.

攻略解題法 了解該如何作答與人物介紹有關的題目。

聆聽對話前閱讀題目時

4. What is the purpose of the speech? 演講目的是什麼？

   ▶ 這題詢問的是演講目的，所以要仔細聆聽前半段。

   (A) To introduce a new staff member 為了介紹新員工
   (B) To announce a new policy 為了宣布新政策
   (C) To explain a new training program 為了說明新的培訓課程
   (D) To notify employees of a meeting 為了通知員工開會

5. Where is this speech probably taking place? 演講可能在哪裡發生？

   ▶ 這題詢問的是地點，答題線索會在前半段出現。

   (A) At a museum 博物館
   (B) At a hotel 飯店
   (C) At a hospital 醫院
   (D) At a library 圖書館

6. What will the listeners do next? 聽者接下來會做什麼？

   ▶ 這題詢問的是接下來會做的事，必須專心聆聽後半段。

   (A) They will tell Steve about the sections. 他們會跟史蒂夫說區域的事。
   (B) They will ask Steve for a day off. 他們會向史蒂夫請假。
   (C) They will leave for a business trip. 他們將要出差。
   (D) They will move to another department. 他們將會換到另一個部門。

 聆聽對話時

4 I'm very pleased to introduce Steve Hilton, the new manager of the Housekeeping Department. ▶ 前半段以「I'm pleased to introduce~」開頭的部分，包含了被介紹的人物名稱和介紹原因。(A) 為正確答案。

我很開心能向各位介紹房務部的新經理史蒂夫‧希爾頓。

5 Steve will manage all of the housekeeping operations at our hotel.

▶ 地點、職業、行業類別等會在前半段出現。(B)為正確答案。

史蒂夫會管理我們飯店的所有房務運作。

Since we recently changed our housekeeping system, he will assign tasks to employees in several different sections.

由於我們最近改變了我們的房務系統，他會分派任務給多個不同區域的員工。

6 So, if you want to be in a particular section, you should tell Steve by the end of the day. ▶ 跟接下來會做的事相關的答題線索會在後半段出現，所以要仔細聆聽。說話者建議聽者跟史蒂夫說自己想要的區域。(A)為正確答案。

所以，如果你們有想要的特定區域，請在今天結束前告訴史蒂夫。

詞彙整理 manage 管理，監督 **operation** 運作 **assign** 分派 **particular** 特別的 **by the end of** 在～結束前

攻略POINT ❶ 要仔細聆聽前半段的演講、介紹目的。
　　　　　❷ 此類詢問地點、行業類別、職業的題目，要仔細聆聽前半段。
　　　　　❸ 跟接下來會做的事相關的答題線索會在後半段出現。

人物介紹的結構

人物介紹的鋪陳	人物介紹相關句型
問候、介紹活動 **與人物、目的**	• Hi, everyone. Welcome to ~　大家好。歡迎來到～。 • I'm Lauren, your instructor.　我是各位的講師蘿倫。 • Thank you for coming ~.　謝謝各位來到～。 • Good evening. You're listening to ~.　晚安。您正在收聽的是～。
介紹本日嘉賓與主角	• Our special guest is ~.　我們的特別嘉賓是～。 • I proudly present ~.　很榮幸能介紹～ • We're delighted to ~.　我們很開心能～ • We welcome journalist Victor.　我們來歡迎新聞記者維克多。
嘉賓的資訊 **（職位、過去經歷）**	• Ms. Lee was our executive director.　李女士曾是我們的執行董事。 • After she retired, Ms. Lee started the Edge. 　李女士退休後開創了艾吉公司。 • Mr. Hern has worked in the financial sector. 　赫恩先生在金融界工作。
開始採訪、 **誘導聽者參與、** **頒獎與演講、** **叮嚀與要求**	• Tonight　今晚 • On today's show　今天的表演 • Please come forward.　請站出來。 • And now let's welcome Mr. Hern.　現在讓我們來歡迎赫恩先生。

4. What is the main purpose of the speech?

(A) To propose a project

(B) To notify employees of a meeting

(C) To recognize an employee

(D) To give a bonus

5. How long has Jinny been working in the Sales Department?

(A) Half a year

(B) 1 year

(C) 2 years

(D) 3 years

6. According to the speaker, what did Jinny do?

(A) She visited many countries.

(B) She completed many projects.

(C) She sold a lot of products.

(D) She signed a contract.

Step 1 實戰重點

在觀光導覽的題目中，導覽地點及順序很重要。須特別注意聆聽表示地點的here、this後面出現的詞彙，以及出現表示順序或程序的first、after that、and then等部分。

 代表題型 先在十秒內讀完三道題目，聆聽獨白後選出正確答案。 92.mp3

4. Who is the speaker?

(A) A tour guide

(B) A historian

(C) An official

(D) An accountant

5. According to the announcement, where will the listeners take a break?

(A) At the cave

(B) At the beach

(C) At the restaurant

(D) In the parking lot

6. What are the listeners asked to do?

(A) Enjoy doing water sports

(B) Take part in the activities

(C) Throw their garbage in trash cans

(D) Look around the beach

攻略解題法 了解該如何作答與導覽有關的題目。

聆聽對話前閱讀題目時

4. Who is the speaker? 說話者是誰？

▶ 這題詢問的是說話者是誰，所以要仔細聆聽前半段。

(A) A tour guide　觀光導遊

(B) A historian　歷史學家

(C) An official　官員

(D) An accountant　會計師

5. According to the announcement, where will the listeners take a break?

根據此通知，聽者會在哪裡短暫休息？

▶ 這題詢問的是休息地點，所以要仔細聆聽前半段。

(A) At the cave　洞穴

(B) At the beach　海灘

(C) At the restaurant　餐廳

(D) In the parking lot　停車場

6. What are the listeners asked to do?　聽者被要求做什麼？

▶ 聽者被要求的事項會以You should~、You'd better~、You could~等等的形態在後半段出現。

(A) Enjoy doing water sports　享受水上運動

(B) Take part in the activities　參加活動

(C) Throw their garbage in trash cans　將垃圾丟到垃圾桶裡

(D) Look around the beach　看看海灘

聆聽對話時

Welcome to Rich National Seashore. My name is Melissa. ⁴ I'll be your tour guide today, and I'll take you all around beautiful Rich Bay.

▶ 關於說話者、聽者、地點的答題線索會在前半段出現。說話者說會提供導覽，所以(A)為正確答案。

歡迎來到利奇國立海岸公園。我叫做梅麗莎。我是各位今天的導遊，會帶各位到美麗的利奇海灣走走。

We will do several activities, including water sports, and ⁵ we will also visit famous Carmond Cave. We will arrive there before 10 a.m. Then, we'll take a short break.

▶ 關於說話者、聽者、地點的答題線索會在前半段出現。說話者表示會拜訪洞穴並稍作休息，(A)為正確答案。

我們會進行幾樣活動，其中包含水上運動，我們還會拜訪有名的卡孟德洞穴。我們會在早上十點之前抵達那裡，然後稍作休息。

To help preserve the environment, please do not throw any trash in the sea. ⁶ You should carry your trash with you and put it into the trash cans which are located at the entrance when we return. ▶ 關於要求、叮嚀的答題線索會在後半段出現。You should後面提到要把垃圾丟到垃圾桶裡。(C)為正確答案。　為了幫忙保護環境，請勿丟任何垃圾到海裡。各位應隨身帶著垃圾，在回來的時候，丟到位於入口的垃圾桶裡。

詞彙整理 **National Seashore** 國立海岸公園 **guide** 導遊 **bay** 海灣 **several** 幾個的 **activity** 活動 **water sports** 水上運動 **cave** 洞穴 **preserve** 保護 **trash** 垃圾 **trash can** 垃圾桶 **entrance** 入口

攻略POINT ❶ 關於說話者、聽者、地點的答題線索會在前半段出現。
　　　　　❷ 關於要求、叮嚀的答題線索會在後半段出現。

導覽的結構

導覽的鋪陳	導覽相關句型
問候、主題	• Welcome to the audio tour.　歡迎使用語音導覽。 • We'd like to remind ~.　我們想提醒～
特徵、優點等細節	• I'll be showing ~.　我會帶各位看～ • This program is ~.　本活動是～
叮嚀、要求事項	• And remember to ~.　請記得～

Voca Check - up! **導覽相關詞彙**

conference 會議 **job fair** 就業博覽會 **convention** 大會 **function** 盛大集會 **activity** 活動 **organization** 組織 **group** 團體，集體 **sign up** 申請，註冊 **schedule** 行程 **itinerary** 日程 **enroll** 報名 **go over** 檢閱 **hold** 舉辦 **take place** 發生 **fill out a form** 填寫表格

4. What is said about the cathedral?

(A) It's now a museum.

(B) It was built about 100 years ago.

(C) It's the most historic building in the world.

(D) It's located in Southeast Asia.

5. How long will the tourists stay at the cathedral?

(A) Thirty minutes

(B) One hour

(C) Two hours

(D) Three hours

6. Where are the people asked to return?

(A) To the cathedral

(B) To the train

(C) To the airport

(D) To the hotel

▶ 答案與解析請參考解析本第94頁

REVIEW TEST

1. Where is the introduction taking place?

   (A) At a conference
   (B) At an awards ceremony
   (C) At an employee training session
   (D) At a local broadcasting station

2. What is the purpose of the talk?

   (A) To notify the staff about a meeting
   (B) To advertise a new book
   (C) To introduce a guest speaker
   (D) To select a new manager

3. Who is Michael Rupin?

   (A) A salesperson
   (B) A conference planner
   (C) The general manager of a hotel
   (D) An accountant

4. Who most likely is the speaker?

   (A) A photographer
   (B) A technician
   (C) An architect
   (D) A tour guide

5. According to the talk, how does the B.P. Mosque differ from other mosques?

   (A) It has a different color than other mosques.
   (B) It looks older than other mosques.
   (C) It is larger than other mosques.
   (D) Its design is different than those of the other mosques.

6. What will the listeners do next?

   (A) Go to see some other mosques
   (B) Look at another one of Mr. Peter's structures
   (C) Take a short break at the mosque
   (D) Return to their hotel on their tour bus

7. What is the purpose of the talk?

   (A) To welcome a new employee
   (B) To launch a new product
   (C) To advertise a new laptop
   (D) To announce an award winner

8. What type of business do they work at?

   (A) An electronics company
   (B) An architectural firm
   (C) A delivery company
   (D) An office supply store

9. What is the audience going to do next?

   (A) They will wait for the next guest.
   (B) They will listen to a speech by Ms. Johns.
   (C) They will attend a staff meeting.
   (D) They will have lunch with Ms. Johns.

Event	Time
Award distribution	6:00 P.M.
Special performance	7:00 P.M.
Chairman's speech	7:30 P.M.
Plans for next year	8:00 P.M.

10. Look at the graphic. What time will dinner be served?

    (A) At 6:00 P.M.
    (B) At 7:00 P.M.
    (C) At 7:30 P.M.
    (D) At 8:00 P.M.

11. What did Mary-Kate Thomas win an award for?

    (A) Volunteering at a community center
    (B) Writing a newspaper article
    (C) Raising funds for homeless shelters
    (D) Promoting local publishing houses

12. What will Mary-Kate Thomas receive?

    (A) Money
    (B) Theater tickets
    (C) A painting
    (D) A trophy

▶ 答案與解析請參考解析本第94頁

聽寫訓練

　　　　　　　　🎧 dictation-49.mp3

Questions 4-6 refer to the following introduction.

Thank you for coming to _____. I'm pleased to announce _____
_____ is Jinny. She joined the Sales Department _____
_____. She has _____, and they were all very successful. Our
sales _____. And now I _____
Jinny to come onto the stage _____. Let's _____
_____ for Jinny, who has worked _____ our company.

　　　　　　　　🎧 dictation-50.mp3

Questions 4-6 refer to the following introduction.

_____, everyone, now we are at the _____ and _____
_____ in Europe. This cathedral was built _____.
_____, this place _____ for being the most beautiful
cathedral in the world. You have _____ and
to enjoy looking around the cathedral. _____ our tour bus will be _____
_____ right here, and you must _____
_____ this bus. You must be _____.

　　　　　　　　🎧 dictation-51.mp3

Questions 1-3 refer to the following introduction.

Ladies and gentlemen, welcome to the _____. I'd like to introduce our
_____, the _____,
Michael Rupin. I'm sure all of you know his _____
_____, which has sold _____. Many people
are eager to hear about _____
because of his good reputation. Now, everyone, _____ Mr. Michael Rupin.

Questions 4-6 refer to the following introduction.

Good morning. I'll be your guide today. First, we will start our tour _____

_____. Please _____. You can see a

mosque that _____. It is

called the B.P. Mosque. It was built by the _____. He always

sought to _____ for each of his structures. _____

_____ about this mosque, we will _____

_____ and look around _____. After that, _____

on the tour will be _____.

Questions 7-9 refer to the following introduction.

Welcome to our _____. I'm very pleased to

announce _____ of the year, Ms. Stephanie Johns. Thanks to her efforts,

_____ this

year compared to last year. Ms. Johns, would you _____

_____? We'd also like you to _____

_____ with us. Would all of you join me _____?

Questions 10-12 refer to the following speech and schedule.

Good afternoon and welcome to the _____

_____. Before the events get underway, I would like to _____

_____. Due to a catering problem,

_____, which was scheduled to be served with the distribution of awards, is

now scheduled for _____. You will be able

to _____

_____. We are very sorry for those of you who are hungry right now. Um... Now,

_____ of the day which

goes to Mary-Kate Thomas, whose _____ on

our city streets has won a number of awards.

I would now like to award Mary-Kate with _____, which she has very

kindly agreed to _____. Let's _____

_____ for Mary-Kate Thomas.

Voca Preview

請勾選不認識的單字，學習完類型分析後再重新確認勾選的單字。

- end 結束
- inexpensive 低廉的
- at half price 以半價
- function 功能
- adorable 可愛的
- set up 設定
- medical journal 醫學刊物
- subscribe to 訂閱
- nationally 全國性地
- plenty of 充足的
- waste 浪費
- precious 寶貴的
- conveniently 便利地
- affordable price 可負擔的價格
- reputation 聲譽
- feature 特徵
- excellent 優秀的，傑出的
- durable 耐用的
- ingredient 材料
- a variety of 各式各樣的

- houseware 家庭用品
- free gift 贈品
- wireless 無線的
- miss 錯過
- complimentary gift 免費禮物
- limited time 限定時間
- expired 過期的
- effective 有效的
- mark down 減價
- underwear 內衣
- fitness facility 運動設施
- grocery store 食品雜貨店
- electronics store 電子產品店
- gift certificate 禮券
- extremely 極度地，非常
- off-season 淡季
- furthermore 而且，此外
- eco-friendly 環保的
- property 財產，房地產
- discount rate 折扣率

類型分析 **15**

各大主題攻略－廣告

WARMING UP
REVIEW TEST
聽寫訓練

WARMING UP

診斷評估　閱讀題目後，在兩秒內掌握題目重點。

1. What kind of business is being advertised? ....
2. When does the promotion end? ....
3. How can the listeners get more information? ....

尋找線索　觀察獨白，找出上述題目的線索後，掌握內容。

Did you know that this is the perfect time to get your winter clothes at inexpensive prices? At Big & Big, we offer the best prices on all kinds of winter clothes that you are looking for. Coats, boots, jackets, and all other winter apparel are available at half price now. You should hurry up because this offer is only available from Wednesday to Sunday. For more information, please visit our website at www.bignbig.com.

確認解答＆要點　確認正確答案，了解跟廣告有關的特徵。

診斷評估：掌握題目的重點

1. What kind of business is being advertised?　廣告的是何種類型的行業？
　　▶ 詢問廣告對象

2. When does the promotion end?　活動何時結束？　▶ 詢問活動結束的時間點

3. How can the listeners get more information?　聽者該如何獲得更多資訊？
　　▶ 詢問獲得更多資訊的方法

尋找線索：分析測驗內容

[1] Did you know that this is the perfect time to get your winter clothes at inexpensive prices?　▶ 可以知道廣告的行業類別是服飾業的依據
你知道現在是以低廉價格購入冬季服飾的絕佳時間點嗎？

> 廣告前半段會介紹廣告對象、廣告的物品或服務、廣告業者等等。

At Big & Big, we offer the best prices on all kinds of winter clothes that you are looking for. Coats, boots, jackets, and all other winter apparel are available at half price now.　我們Big & Big以最棒的價格提供您正在尋找的各式各樣的冬季服飾。大衣、靴子、夾克，以及其他所有冬季服飾皆以半價販售中。

[2] You should hurry up because this offer is only available from Wednesday to Sunday.　▶ 可以知道活動進行期間的依據
此優惠只從星期三進行到星期日，所以行動要快。

> 廣告中間會出現關於公司的說明、產品特徵和優點、購買優惠、折扣資訊等。

[3] For more information, please visit our website at www.bignbig.com.
　▶ 可以獲得更多資訊的依據
欲了解更多資訊，請拜訪我們的網站www.bignbig.com。

> 廣告後半段會出現購買地點和聯絡方式等更多資訊。

詞彙整理　**inexpensive** 低廉的　**at half price** 以半價　**hurry up** 快點　**offer**（商店提供的）優惠，提供

產品廣告

聆聽廣告獨白時，要仔細聆聽說明產品特徵的different、special等詞彙。尤其是在後半段出現的命令句「If＋主詞＋動詞, please~.」，會跟題目有直接的關係。

 代表題型 先在十秒內讀完三道題目，聆聽獨白後選出正確答案。 95.mp3

---

4. What is being advertised?

   (A) Office supplies
   (B) A medical journal
   (C) A fashion magazine
   (D) A newspaper

5. What advantage does the company offer?

   (A) Discounts on magazines
   (B) Discounts on newspapers
   (C) Free magazines
   (D) Free newspapers

6. How can customers subscribe?

   (A) By visiting the website
   (B) By sending an email
   (C) By going to the Milan Times office
   (D) By calling a phone number

攻略解題法 了解該如何作答與產品廣告有關的題目。

4. What is being advertised? 廣告的東西是什麼？

▶ 這題詢問的是廣告產品，所以要仔細聆聽前半段。

(A) Office supplies 辦公用品

(B) A medical journal 醫學刊物

(C) A fashion magazine 時尚雜誌

(D) A newspaper 報紙

5. What advantage does the company offer? 公司提供什麼好處？

▶ 關於購買優惠的答題線索，通常會在中間出現。

(A) Discounts on magazines 雜誌折扣

(B) Discounts on newspapers 報紙折扣

(C) Free magazines 免費雜誌

(D) Free newspapers 免費報紙

6. How can customers subscribe? 顧客該怎麼訂閱？

▶ 關於訂閱／購買方法和聯絡方式的答題線索會在後半段出現，通常是please~的句型。

(A) By visiting the website 拜訪網站

(B) By sending an email 寄電子郵件

(C) By going to the Milan Times office 前往《米蘭時報》辦公室

(D) By calling a phone number 打電話

聆聽對話時

[4] Why don't you subscribe to the Milan Times newspaper?

▶ 廣告產品或服務的種類會在前半段出現。(D)為正確答案。

您何不訂閱《米蘭時報》？

We are a nationally popular newspaper that provides our readers with plenty of information. You don't have to waste your precious time buying the paper anymore. Now, you can conveniently receive the paper at your home and get it at an affordable price. 我們是提供讀者豐富資訊，廣受全國歡迎的報紙。您不用再浪費您的寶貴時間購買報紙了。現在您可以用便宜的價格，在家方便地收報紙。

[5] If you subscribe to the Milan Times, you'll get a free copy of our weekend fashion magazine. ▶ 像購買優惠這樣的詳細資訊會在中間或後半段出現。這裡提到會贈送免費的雜誌，所以(C)為正確答案。 如果您訂閱《米蘭時報》的話，可免費獲得一本我們的時尚週刊雜誌。

[6] For more information or to subscribe now, please call 2451-2359.

▶ 購買方法、購買地點、聯絡方式等會在後半段的命令句中出現。(D)為正確答案。

欲知更多資訊或立刻訂閱，請撥打 2451-2359。

詞彙整理 **subscribe** 訂閱 **nationally** 全國性地 **waste** 浪費 **precious** 寶貴的 **at an affordable price** 以可負擔的價格

攻略POINT ❶ 關於廣告產品或服務的種類，要仔細聆聽前半段。

❷ 購買優惠的答題線索，通常會在中間或後半段出現。如果出題順序是第二題，那會在中間出現；如果是第三題，則會在後半段出現。

❸ 購買方法、購買地點、聯絡方法等，要仔細聆聽後半段的命令句（please~）。

產品廣告的結構

產品廣告的鋪陳	產品廣告相關句型
廣告的物品或服務、廣告對象、關於產品的問題	• We have a good reputation for having the latest fashions. 我們擁有提供最新時裝的優良聲譽。 • Are you looking for ~? 您正在找~嗎？ • Are you having trouble ~? 您有~的問題嗎？
產品特徵與優點、介紹公司	• One of the features 其中一個特徵 • Our firm has ~. 我們公司擁有~。
購買優惠	• We offer the best prices. 我們提供最棒的價格。 • You'll also receive ~ free. 您還可以免費獲得~。 • You'll get a free gift ~ 您會收到一份免費的禮物~。
營業時間	• We open for business at 9:00 A.M. 我們的開門時間是早上九點。 • We open at 5:00 A.M. in the morning every day. 我們每天早上五點開門。
購買地點與聯絡方式	• Give us a call at ~. 撥打~給我們。 • Please call ~. 請撥打~。 • Visit www.milantimes.com. 請拜訪www.milantimes.com。

Voca Check - up! 廣告相關詞彙

reliable 可信賴的 **excellent service** 優質服務 **helpful employee** 有幫助的員工 **durable / strong** 耐用的 **good quality** 好品質 **best deal** 最棒的交易 **material** 材料 **ingredient** 材料 **reasonable price** 合理的價格 **affordable / low price** 便宜的價格

4. What is the advertisement for?

(A) A network system

(B) Furniture

(C) Electronic devices

(D) Kitchen supplies

5. What advantage of the new digital camera is mentioned?

(A) It is very easy to use.

(B) It is cheaper than last year's model.

(C) It is the smallest camera in the world.

(D) It comes in a variety of colors.

6. How can the listeners get more information?

(A) By visiting a store

(B) By sending an email

(C) By calling a special number

(D) By visiting a website

Unit 39　折扣廣告

Step 1　實戰重點

聆聽折扣廣告時，要仔細聽在後半段出現的折扣期間、折扣優惠。尤其是要專心聆聽表示期間和價格的數字。

 代表題型 先在十秒內讀完三道題目，聆聽獨白後選出正確答案。 97.mp3

4. What does the advertised business sell?

   (A) Housewares

   (B) Furniture

   (C) Electronic equipment

   (D) Books

5. What will the customers receive?

   (A) A discount

   (B) Free delivery

   (C) A membership card

   (D) A free gift

6. When does the sale end?

   (A) On Friday

   (B) On Saturday

   (C) On Sunday

   (D) On Monday

攻略解題法 了解該如何作答與折扣廣告有關的題目。

> 聆聽對話前閱讀題目時

4. What does the advertised business sell? 此則被廣告的業者販賣的是什麼？

　　▶ 這題詢問的是廣告的物品／公司種類，所以要仔細聆聽前半段。

(A) Housewares　家庭用品

(B) Furniture　家具

(C) Electronic equipment　電子設備

(D) Books　書

5. What will the customers receive? 顧客會獲得什麼？

　　▶ 詳細的購買優惠的答題線索會在中間出現。

(A) A discount　折扣

(B) Free delivery　免費運送

(C) A membership card　會員卡

(D) A free gift　免費禮物

6. When does the sale end? 折扣何時結束？

　　▶ 與日期相關的線索，例如折扣截止日期，會在前半段或後半段出現。

(A) On Friday　星期五

(B) On Saturday　星期六

(C) On Sunday　星期日

(D) On Monday　星期一

 聆聽對話時

4 Are you tired of looking for a new computer? We have everything related to computers, including monitors, wireless keyboards and mouses, and printers.

　　▶ 要仔細聆聽在前半段出現的「interested in、look for」後面的內容。廣告會以「您對～感興趣嗎？」、「您在找～嗎？」開場來引人注目。這種句子可以讓我們確認廣告的業者、產品、服務等種類，還有對象是誰。(C)為正確答案。

您找新電腦找得很累嗎？我們擁有一切跟電腦相關的產品，包含螢幕、無線鍵盤和滑鼠，以及印表機。

Starting this Friday, Kiara Electronics is having our annual sale. **5** We are also offering free delivery during the event. ▶跟購買優惠有關的詳細資訊，會在中間或後半段出現。廣告說會提供免費運送，所以(B)為正確答案。

從星期五開始，齊雅拉電子將進行年度特賣。活動期間我們還會提供免費運送。

6 The sale only lasts from Friday to Sunday this week. So don't miss this great chance

　　▶ 尋找折扣／促銷期間等資訊時，要仔細聆聽前半段或後半段。這則獨白是在後半段提到相關內容。(C)為正確答案。

此特賣只在本週的星期五至星期日進行。所以千萬別錯過這個大好機會。

詞彙整理 **wireless** 無線的 **annual** 每年的，年度的 **offer** 提供 **deliver** 寄送 **miss** 錯過

攻略POINT ❶ 此類詢問廣告的業者、產品、服務等種類和廣告對象的題目，要仔細聆聽在前半段出現的「interested in、look for」後面的內容。
　　　　　 ❷ 此類詢問購買優惠細節的題目，要仔細聆聽中間和後半段。
　　　　　 ❸ 折扣／促銷期間會在前半段或後半段提及。

折扣廣告的結構

折扣廣告的鋪陳	折扣廣告相關句型
廣告的物品或服務、廣告對象、關於產品的問題	• Update your mobile phone.　請更新您的手機。 • Are you looking for ~?　您正在找～嗎？ • If you have a problem ~.　若有問題～。
折扣優惠	• Winter clothing is half price.　冬季服飾現在半價。 • Members will receive a complimentary gift.　會員將會收到免費禮物。 • Apparel is fifty percent off.　服飾五折。 • ~ is only available until the end of the month.　～只提供到本月底為止。
購買地點與聯絡方式	• Order~ on your mobile phone today.　請在今天用手機訂購～。

Voca Check - up! 廣告相關詞彙

clearance sale 清倉拍賣　**opening sale** 開幕特賣　**anniversary sale** 週年特賣　**holiday sale** 節慶特賣　**today only** 只有今天　**limited time only** 限定期間內　**expired** 過期的　**effective / valid** 有效的　**special offer** 特價商品　**discount** 折扣　**off** 折扣　**mark down** 減價，打折

4. What items are on sale?

(A) New arrivals

(B) Winter clothes

(C) Summer clothes

(D) Summer shoes

5. According to the advertisement, what items are discounted?

(A) Underwear

(B) Skiwear

(C) Sweaters

(D) Swimming suits

6. How can customers get a free beach bag?

(A) By purchasing at least five items

(B) By spending more than $200

(C) By paying with cash

(D) By bringing a coupon

▶ 答案與解析請參考解析本第98頁

1. What is being advertised?

   (A) Real estate
   (B) A sporting goods store
   (C) A furniture factory
   (D) A paint store

2. When will the apartments be available to rent?

   (A) The following month
   (B) Next year
   (C) Next Friday
   (D) At the end of the year

3. What is free for all residents of Luxury Apartments?

   (A) The supermarket
   (B) The fitness facilities
   (C) The playground
   (D) The parking lot

4. What kind of store is this?

   (A) A grocery store
   (B) A bookstore
   (C) An electronics store
   (D) A furniture store

5. According to the advertisement, why should customers visit the store?

   (A) To get free products
   (B) To get discounts
   (C) To talk with the staff
   (D) To get their furniture repaired

6. When will the sale be held?

   (A) On Monday
   (B) On Sunday
   (C) On Saturday
   (D) On Friday

7. What type of store is being advertised?

   (A) A stationery store
   (B) An electronics shop
   (C) A bookshop
   (D) An office supply store

8. What will a customer receive by purchasing a bestseller?

   (A) Stationery
   (B) A gift certificate
   (C) A free book
   (D) A discount

9. According to the advertisement, how can customers find a list of bestsellers?

   (A) By visiting a website
   (B) By calling a special number
   (C) By visiting the store
   (D) By sending an email

Room Type	Rate
Superior Room	190 Euro
Executive Standard	215 Euro
Executive Suite	245 Euro
Luxury Suite	270 Euro

10. Who most likely is this advertisement intended for?

    (A) Company executives
    (B) Renovation workers
    (C) Travelers
    (D) Hotel staff

11. Why is the business offering a special deal?

    (A) To celebrate their anniversary
    (B) To promote the opening of a business
    (C) To raise money for renovation
    (D) To commemorate their remodeling

12. Look at the graphic. For what price will the Luxury Suite room be available this month?

    (A) 190 Euro
    (B) 215 Euro
    (C) 245 Euro
    (D) 270 Euro

▶ 答案與解析請參考解析本第98頁

聽寫訓練

Unit 38　產品廣告　｜ Step 3 實戰演練

🎧 dictation-52.mp3

Questions 1-3 refer to the following conversation.

The UCA Company's new digital camera _____, and it has _____. First, it's _____. It has an auto-system, so you _____ the camera _____ once. It uses Wi-Fi as well, and it can _____ a personal computer _____. _____ is easy for anyone to use. For more information, visit our website at www.ucaelectronics.com.

Unit 39　折扣廣告　｜ Step 3 實戰演練

🎧 dictation-53.mp3

Questions 4-6 refer to the following advertisement.

Winter is _____. The summer season _____, so we are having _____ for the winter season. We have everything from swimming suits to _____-_____. We are offering _____ summer items. Furthermore, if you _____ $200, we'll give you _____. _____. This offer will _____. Start saving now!

Review Test

🎧 dictation-54.mp3

Questions 1-3 refer to the following advertisement.

Luxury Apartments will _____. This is _____-_____ complex. The property is located _____, and there are _____. All residents of Luxury Apartments will be able to enjoy _____, _____, and a tennis court 24 hours a day. To look around Luxury Apartments, please call 3451-1156.

Questions 4-6 refer to the following advertisement.

Are you planning to _____
_____? Then TNT Furniture is offering a great chance for you. We will be having _____
_____. The newest styles of furniture will be arriving at our
store soon, and we will also provide _____. But
you should come to our store _____
_____. _____ since the discounted
furniture is _____. This sale will _____
_____.

Questions 7-9 refer to the following advertisement.

Olive Bookstore is pleased to announce that we are having _____. This
event is being held to _____ - _____ and also to thank
our customers. _____, you will _____
_____ on it. _____
_____ we have in our store, please _____
at www.olivebooks.com. We hope to see you at Olive Bookstore.

Questions 10-12 refer to the following advertisement and price table.

It's the most _____ here at _____ !
To celebrate _____, we are providing our guests with _____ - _____
_____. Spend your holidays in our newly _____
_____. This month only, our _____
_____
_____, and the Luxury Suite room will be available for the price of our
Executive Suite. Hurry up and make your booking, _____
_____ !

PART 4

Directions: You will hear some short talks given by a single speaker. You will be asked to answer three questions about what the speaker says in each short talk. Select the best response to each question and mark the letter (A), (B), (C), or (D) on your answer sheet. The talks will not be printed in your test book and will be spoken only one time.

71. What is the purpose of the speech?

   (A) To introduce a new employee
   (B) To introduce a guest speaker
   (C) To give an award
   (D) To name a professor

72. Who is Melissa Rin?

   (A) A designer
   (B) An accountant
   (C) An electrician
   (D) A general manager

73. How long has Ms. Rin worked in the fashion industry?

   (A) Thirty years
   (B) Fewer than thirty years
   (C) More than thirty years
   (D) Thirty-five years

74. What is the purpose of the announcement?

   (A) To give information about staff training
   (B) To introduce a new employee
   (C) To announce a new policy
   (D) To ask for donations

75. Where can employees get a form?

   (A) On the company website
   (B) At the Human Resources Department
   (C) At the library
   (D) At the information desk

76. When does an employee have to get approval from a supervisor?

   (A) 7 days before a business trip
   (B) 6 days before a business trip
   (C) 5 days before a business trip
   (D) 4 days before a business trip

77. What is the company trying to do?

(A) Attend an environmental seminar
(B) Save electricity
(C) Implement an eco-friendly program
(D) Relocate to another state

78. What does the speaker mean when he says, "I know what you guys are probably thinking"?

(A) He understands the listeners' doubts.
(B) He agrees with the listeners.
(C) He talked with the listeners before the meeting.
(D) He predicts that the company will face some difficulties.

79. What will the listeners most likely receive if the plan is successful?

(A) A celebratory dinner
(B) A special incentive
(C) Some additional days off
(D) A motivational speech

80. What kind of business is being advertised?

(A) A restaurant
(B) A bookstore
(C) An electronics store
(D) A grocery store

81. Where is Green House located?

(A) Near city hall
(B) Near the shopping center
(C) Near the post office
(D) Near the cathedral

82. According to the advertisement, how can customers get more information?

(A) By visiting a website
(B) By sending an email
(C) By visiting a restaurant
(D) By making a phone call

83. What is the report about?

(A) Business
(B) Health
(C) Weather
(D) Sports

84. What is predicted for the weekend?

(A) Snow
(B) Rain
(C) Brightness
(D) Fog

85. What will the listeners hear next?

(A) Music
(B) The weather forecast
(C) Business news
(D) Sports news

86. Who most likely is the speaker?

(A) A museum guide
(B) A singer
(C) An artist
(D) A filmmaker

87. What does the speaker imply when he says, "Seating is limited"?

(A) People have to present their photo ID cards.
(B) It will take more than a week to prepare for an event.
(C) The expansion project at the museum is underway.
(D) People should arrive at the event venue beforehand.

88. What does the speaker mention about the tour?

(A) Groups of 10 or more receive a discount.
(B) Photography is not permitted.
(C) Children are not allowed to join.
(D) Large bags are not allowed.

89. What is the main purpose of this message?

    (A) To confirm a reservation
    (B) To advertise a resort
    (C) To arrange transportation
    (D) To cancel a reservation

90. How much should Mr. Victor pay for the deposit?

    (A) $400
    (B) More than $200
    (C) Less than $200
    (D) $200

91. According to the message, what will the speaker provide for the listener?

    (A) A discount
    (B) A drink
    (C) A free meal
    (D) Transportation

92. What is the report mainly about?

    (A) A shopping center
    (B) A city park
    (C) A public museum
    (D) A public library

93. What caused the delay in construction?

    (A) Heavy snow
    (B) Heavy rain
    (C) A lack of money
    (D) A lack of workers

94. According to the report, what will happen on Friday?

    (A) A special sale
    (B) An opening ceremony
    (C) A festival
    (D) Repair work

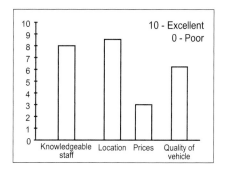

95. What is the radio broadcast mainly about?

    (A) A public hearing
    (B) An annual event
    (C) Local traffic conditions
    (D) A financial report

96. Look at the graphic. Which building will be most likely affected by the accident?

    (A) The community center
    (B) The bank
    (C) The city hall
    (D) The library

97. What does the speaker recommend?

    (A) Taking a detour
    (B) Using public transportation
    (C) Visiting a website
    (D) Participating in an event

98. What kind of business does the speaker work for?

    (A) A hotel
    (B) A travel agency
    (C) A car rental company
    (D) An airline

99. What does the speaker say the business recently did?

    (A) Placed an order
    (B) Moved into a new office
    (C) Opened a new location
    (D) Did a survey

100. Look at the graphic. Which area does the speaker want the listeners to talk about?

    (A) Knowledgeable staff
    (B) Location
    (C) Prices
    (D) Quality of vehicle

▶ 答案與解析請參考解析本第101頁

PART 4

Directions: You will hear some short talks given by a single speaker. You will be asked to answer three questions about what the speaker says in each short talk. Select the best response to each question and mark the letter (A), (B), (C), or (D) on your answer sheet. The talks will not be printed in your test book and will be spoken only one time.

71. Where most likely are the listeners?

    (A) At an airport
    (B) At a train station
    (C) At a bus stop
    (D) At a port

72. What has caused the delay?

    (A) Aircraft maintenance
    (B) Repair work on the runway
    (C) An accident
    (D) Bad weather

73. What will the listeners do next?

    (A) Present their boarding passes
    (B) Board the plane
    (C) Go to Gate 13
    (D) Fasten their seatbelts

74. What is the purpose of the advertisement?

    (A) To mention an annual sale
    (B) To introduce a company
    (C) To invite a customer to an event
    (D) To announce the opening of a new business

75. What is the company known for?

    (A) Its experienced staff
    (B) The high quality of its products
    (C) Its inexpensive prices
    (D) Being the oldest design company in the city

76. According to the advertisement, why should the listeners call the company?

    (A) To make an appointment
    (B) To receive a brochure
    (C) To make a reservation
    (D) To talk with a staff member

77. Who is the speaker?

    (A) An office worker
    (B) A salesperson
    (C) A lawyer
    (D) A foreign tourist

78. Where is this talk most likely being made?

    (A) At a restaurant
    (B) At an airport
    (C) At a company
    (D) At a shopping mall

79. What should the listeners do if they have a question?

    (A) Send an email
    (B) Visit the information desk
    (C) Speak with a staff member
    (D) Wait until the tour is finished

80. Where is the announcement being made?

    (A) At a gift shop
    (B) At a bookstore
    (C) At a shopping mall
    (D) At a supermarket

81. What time will the store close during the sale?

    (A) 8:30 P.M.
    (B) 9:00 P.M.
    (C) 9:30 P.M.
    (D) 10:00 P.M.

82. What does the speaker mean when he says, "This could be the best chance you've ever had"?

    (A) People will receive discounts on bulk purchases.
    (B) Discounts will be applicable to furniture.
    (C) People will enjoy a free performance.
    (D) There will be the biggest sale soon.

83. According to the speaker, why should listeners choose this business?

    (A) It has many locations.
    (B) It has expert staff members.
    (C) It is open around the clock.
    (D) It offers the lowest prices in the region.

84. What special offer is being made this month?

    (A) A free checkup service
    (B) A next-day delivery service
    (C) A generous discount
    (D) Complimentary installation

85. Why does the woman say, "Are you still hesitating"?

    (A) To ask for technical help from the listeners
    (B) To offer more discounts and benefits
    (C) To encourage listeners to contact the business
    (D) To thank the audience for their patronage

86. Where does the speaker work?

    (A) On a technical support team
    (B) In the Human Resources Department
    (C) In the Sales Department
    (D) In the Marketing Department

87. What happened?

    (A) A new employee started working.
    (B) A document was stolen.
    (C) Some old furniture was moved.
    (D) An error occurred in a program.

88. What is Ms. Rilly asked to do?

    (A) Talk to other staff members
    (B) Sign a contract
    (C) Copy a document
    (D) Restart her computer

89. What is the purpose of the talk?

    (A) To give an award

    (B) To promote a restaurant

    (C) To introduce a new staff member

    (D) To discuss a new policy

90. Who is Mr. James?

    (A) A student

    (B) A chef

    (C) An architect

    (D) A technician

91. What will be held on Friday?

    (A) A welcome party

    (B) A retirement party

    (C) A party celebrating the company's founding

    (D) An opening ceremony

Ratings

Customer Service ★★★★★★
Cleanliness ★★★★★★
Location ★
Atmosphere ★★

---

92. Where does the speaker work?

    (A) At a museum

    (B) At a beauty salon

    (C) At a restaurant

    (D) At a dental office

93. Look at the graphic. What area does the speaker want to invest more in?

    (A) Customer Service

    (B) Cleanliness

    (C) Location

    (D) Atmosphere

94. What does the speaker ask the listeners to do?

    (A) Make some suggestions

    (B) Complete some paperwork

    (C) Watch a presentation

    (D) Review some documents

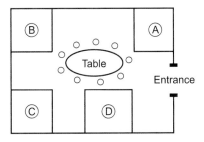

Organization Chart	
Department	Floor
Research and Development	Second
Engineering	Third
Accounting	Fourth
Marketing	Fifth

95. What is the speaker calling about?

    (A) A change in a schedule
    (B) A venue for an event
    (C) A new company policy
    (D) A seating arrangement

96. What does the hotel offer to do?

    (A) Give a refund without a penalty
    (B) Offer free valet service
    (C) Provide a discount on room rates
    (D) Upgrade a room reservation

97. Look at the graphic. Where will the refreshments table be placed?

    (A) Location A
    (B) Location B
    (C) Location C
    (D) Location D

98. Why did the speaker call?

    (A) To request a document
    (B) To plan a conference
    (C) To arrange an interview
    (D) To reschedule an appointment

99. What event does the speaker mention?

    (A) An upcoming election
    (B) A controversial newspaper article
    (C) An annual conference
    (D) A construction project

100. Look at the graphic. Where most likely does Ms. Lee work?

    (A) Second floor
    (B) Third floor
    (C) Fourth floor
    (D) Fifth floor

▶ 答案與解析請參考解析本第107頁

PSV 0030

一次戰勝新制多益 TOEIC 必考聽力攻略＋解析＋模擬試題

作　　者 — SINAGONG 多益專門小組、趙康壽、金廷垠（Julia Kim）
譯　　者 — 林芳如
主　　編 — 林菁菁、林潔欣
編　　輯 — 黃凱怡
校　　對 — 曾慶宇、劉兆婷
企劃主任 — 葉蘭芳
封面設計 — 江儀玲
內頁排版 — 王信中

董 事 長 — 趙政岷
出 版 者 — 時報文化出版企業股份有限公司
　　　　　 10803 臺北市和平西路三段 240 號 3 樓
　　　　　 發行專線 — (02) 2306-6842
　　　　　 讀者服務專線 — 0800-231-705‧(02) 2304-7103
　　　　　 讀者服務傳真 — (02) 2304-6858
　　　　　 郵撥 — 19344724 時報文化出版公司
　　　　　 信箱 — 臺北郵政 79~99 信箱
　　　　　 時報悅讀網 — http://www.readingtimes.com.tw

法律顧問 — 理律法律事務所　陳長文律師、李念祖律師
印　　刷 — 和楹印刷有限公司
初版一刷 — 2019 年 8 月 23 日
定　　價 — 新臺幣 599 元

時報文化出版公司成立於 1975 年，
並於 1999 年股票上櫃公開發行，於 2008 年脫離中時集團非屬旺中，
以「尊重智慧與創意的文化事業」為信念。

一次戰勝新制多益 TOEIC 必考聽力攻略＋解析＋模擬試題／
SINAGONG 多益專門小組, 趙康壽, 金廷垠（Julia Kim）作 . -- 初版 .
-- 臺北市：時報文化, 2019.08
　面；　公分
ISBN 978-957-13-7896-1(平裝)

1. 多益測驗

805.1895　　　　　　　　　　　　　　　　　108011687

Original Title: 시나공토익 BASIC LISTENING
SINAGONG TOEIC Basic Listening by SINAGONG TOEIC Institute & Jo gang-soo & Julia Kim
Copyright © 2018 SINAGONG TOEIC Institute
All rights reserved.
Original Korean edition published by Gilbut Eztok, Seoul, Korea
Traditional Chinese Translation Copyright © 2019 by China Times Publishing Company
This Traditional Chinese edition published by arranged with Gilbut Eztok through Shinwon Agency Co.

ISBN 978-957-13-7896-1
Printed in Taiwan